He'd never been a coward.

Men he'd served with in the Corps would be willing to swear that there wasn't a damn thing in the universe that scared Jericho King. But here he was, avoiding one small, curvy woman as if she were Typhoid Mary and he was the last healthy man on the planet.

After years of military living, he liked his privacy. Liked the fact that his clients came and went, hardly making an impact on his world at all. His employees knew when to back the hell off and leave him alone, and when he needed a woman, he went out and found one.

Nothing permanent. Nothing lasting. Just a few good nights with great sex and some laughs. That's the way he wanted it. The way he needed it.

Yet now, everything had changed. In the space of a few hours, Daisy Saxon was turning his world on its head.

And he only had himself to blame.

THE LAST
LONE WOLF

BY
MAUREEN CHILD

All the characters in this book have no existence outside the imagination of
the author, and have no relation whatsoever to anyone bearing the same name
or names. They are not even distantly inspired by any individual known or
unknown to the author, and all the incidents are pure invention.

Published in Great Britain 2011
by Mills & Boon, an imprint of Harlequin (UK) Limited,
Eton House, 18-24 Paradise Road, Richmond, Surrey TW9 1SR

© Maureen Child 2010

ISBN: 978 0 263 88213 1

51-0511

Harlequin (UK) policy is to use papers that are natural, renewable and
recyclable products and made from wood grown in sustainable forests. The
logging and manufacturing processes conform to the legal environmental
regulations of the country of origin.

Printed and bound in Spain
by Blackprint CPI, Barcelona

To Rosemary Estrada—

A great neighbor, a good friend and the mother of the
four nicest girls I know.

This one's for you, Rose.

Maureen Child is a California native who loves to travel. Every chance they get, she and her husband are taking off on another research trip. The author of more than sixty books, Maureen loves a happy ending and still swears that she has the best job in the world. She lives in Southern California with her husband, two children and a golden retriever with delusions of grandeur. Visit Maureen's website at www.maureenchild.com.

Dear Reader,

Writing about the Kings of California is always fun for me. I love these guys. I love the interaction between the brothers and the cousins and I have such a good time finding that one special woman for each of the guys.

Jericho King was especially fun for me. He's so crabby. A former Marine, he now lives in what he considers near-perfect isolation on top of a mountain. He runs a leadership camp, so at times he has to put up with clients. But otherwise, his life is quiet, orderly, unsurprising.

Until, of course, Daisy Saxon shows up. Daisy's brother, Brant, was a Marine killed in the line of duty and Jericho is her last link to the brother she loved. So she's determined to make a place for herself in Jericho's life—whether he approves or not!

I hope you enjoy this book, set on a fictional mountain in Southern California.

Please write to me at maureenchildbooks@gmail.com or at PO Box 1883, Westminster, CA 92684-1883, USA.

Until next time, happy reading!

Maureen

One

"**N**ow *that* looks like trouble." If there was one thing Jericho King could recognize, it was trouble. Fifteen years in the Marine Corps had given him almost a sixth sense—a sort of internal radar. He could spot potential problems coming at him from a mile off.

This particular problem was a hell of a lot closer.

Jericho squinted into the late afternoon sunlight and watched as a short, curvy woman with long brown hair bent over and reached into a neon-green compact car parked on the gravel drive.

"Still, not a bad view," the older man beside him muttered.

Jericho chuckled. Sam had a point. Whoever the brunette was, she had a great butt. His gaze moved over that behind and then down and along a pair of truly sensational legs. She was wearing a pair of bright-

red, three-inch heels that, even as she stood there, were
sinking into the gravel and dirt drive.

"Why do women wear those idiotic shoes, anyway?"
Jericho asked, not really expecting an answer.

"Generally," Sam Taylor mused, "I think it's to get
men to look at their legs."

"They ought to know they don't have to work that
hard," Jericho told him with a slow shake of his head.
"Well, we don't have time to deal with her today. So
whoever she is, I'll take care of it fast. Bet she's looking
for that day spa on the other side of the mountain. I'll
get her straightened out and on her way."

He took a single step forward before Sam's voice
stopped him.

"Y'know," he said, "I don't think she's lost. I think
she's the one I talked to about the cook job. You
remember, you put me in charge of hiring Kevin's
replacement?"

"Yeah but, a *cook?*" Jericho narrowed his gaze on
the woman, still bent over, rummaging around in her
car as if looking to find a stray gold nugget. "Her?"

"If that's Daisy Saxon," Sam told him, "then yeah."

"Saxon. Saxon…" Knowledge slammed into Jericho
hard and fast. Shifting a glance at his foreman, he asked,
"Did you say Saxon?"

"Yeah, your hearing's still okay," his friend said, then
added, "Why? What's the problem?"

What's the problem?

"Where would I start?" Jericho muttered as the
woman straightened up, turned and spotted him and
Sam standing on the wide, front lawn.

She clutched an oversize purse to her chest as she

stepped onto the lawn and headed toward them. Her long brown hair lifted in the wind, her dark brown eyes were locked on him and her full mouth was set in a firm line of determination.

Jericho watched her as something inside him stirred. He squelched the feeling fast. This woman wouldn't be staying, he told himself. If she was really Daisy Saxon, then there was no place for her here. Hell, he thought, just look at her. Was there ever a more *female* woman? When women arrived at his camp, they were dressed for it. Jeans. Hiking boots. This one looked as though she'd just left an upscale mall. She was soft and pretty and delicate. And delicate wouldn't last here on the mountain.

Not in Jericho's world anyway.

He'd hear her out, apologize about the job confusion, then send her on her way. It would be best for everyone— especially her. She didn't belong here. He could tell that much just by looking at her. It only took seconds for these thoughts and more to rush through his quickly overheating mind.

"Pretty thing," Sam mused.

Jericho didn't want to notice, but damned if he could seem to help it.

The woman took maybe four uneven strides in those stupid heels before she tripped on a sprinkler head and went sprawling, sending her purse flying.

"Damn it." Jericho started for her.

But in the next instant, a tiny, furry creature jolted out of her purse and charged him with all the enthusiasm of a rabid pit bull. The grass was high enough that all

Jericho could see of the miniature dog was its reddish-brown ears flapping in the wind.

Yips and barks in a pitch high enough to peel paint shot through Jericho's head as the improbably small dog, teeth bared, did its best to intimidate.

It wasn't much.

Sam's laughter erupted from beside him and Jericho muttered, "Oh, for God's sake."

Then he gently eased the mutt out of his way with one foot. The dog stayed on him though, even as Jericho neared the fallen brunette, who was already pushing herself up off the lawn.

Her hair fell in a tangle around her face. There were grass stains on the front of her shirt and disgust written on her face.

"Are you okay?" he asked, bending down to help her up.

"Fine," she murmured, taking his hand and staggering to her feet. "Nothing like a little humiliation to bring color to a woman's cheeks." Bending down again, she scooped up the little yapper. "Oh, Nikki, honey, you're such a brave little peanut. What a good girl, protecting Mommy."

"Yeah, she's a real killer."

"Mommy" now flashed him a look no friendlier than the one her tiny dog was shooting him. "She's very loyal. I appreciate loyalty."

"Me, too," he said, staring down into brown eyes that shone like fine whisky held up to a light. "But if you're looking for protection, you might want to upgrade to a real dog."

"Nikki is a real dog," she told him and cuddled the

little creature close. "Now, I realize I haven't made the best impression in the world, but I'm here to see you."

"Do I know you?"

"Not yet," she told him. "But I know you're Jericho King, right?"

"I am," he said flatly and watched as her gaze slid back to his.

"Nothing like making a fabulous first impression," she whispered, more to herself than to him. A moment later, she lifted her chin and said, "I'm Daisy Saxon. We haven't spoken, but you wrote to me a year ago after…"

"After your brother died," he finished for her, remembering that moment when Brant Saxon had died following a dangerous mission into hostile territory.

Jericho had seen men die before. Too many over the years he'd served in the Corps. But Brant had been different. Young. Idealistic. And dead way before his time. The kid's death had hit Jericho hard, precipitating his retirement and leading him here, to this mountain.

The fact that he blamed himself for Brant's death only added to the misery he felt now, facing the man's sister.

Pain whipped through her eyes like a lightning flash. There and gone again in a moment. "Yes."

In an instant, Jericho saw Brant Saxon, remembered the fear on his face that had faded into resignation, acceptance, as he lay dying. And Jericho remembered the kid wresting a promise from him. A promise to look after Brant's sister if she ever asked for help.

Well, he'd done his best to keep the promise, hadn't he? He'd written the more "official" sorry-for-your-loss

letter, then he'd called her later, offered to do whatever he
could. But she'd turned him down. Politely. Completely.
She had thanked him for his call, told him she would
be fine, then she'd hung up—ending, as far as Jericho
was concerned, any responsibility he'd had to her.

Until now.

So why in the hell was she on his mountain a year
after telling him thanks but no thanks?

"I know a good bit of time has passed since we
spoke," she was saying and Jericho tuned back in. "But
when you called me, after Brant died, you offered to
help me if you ever could."

"Yeah," he said, folding his arms over his chest.
"About that. I never heard from you, so…"

"It's taken me a while to come to terms with Brant's
death," she admitted, then sent a quick glance around
her, checking out the property and Sam, still standing
on the lawn watching them. "Could we talk about this
inside maybe?"

Irritation spiked inside him and was instantly
squashed. He didn't want to owe her but he knew he
did. He'd given his word, not just to her brother, but to
her. And one thing Jericho King never did was break his
word. So he was going to have to deal with her whether
he was happy about that or not.

He looked at her as she stood there, shivering a little
in the cold wind blowing through the pines. Didn't even
know enough to wear a jacket in the mountains. Even
in California, fall could be a tricky time of year in the
higher altitudes. But, he told himself, she was clearly
not an outdoors kind of woman.

Of course she wanted to be inside. It was where

she belonged. She was the kind who liked the great outdoors…from the other side of a window while sitting beside a fire and sipping a glass of wine. He knew her kind of woman all too well. And as he realized that, Jericho acknowledged that maybe he wasn't going to have to chase her off at all. Maybe she'd come to her senses on her own and admit that she wasn't suited to working here.

Besides, he could give her a cup of coffee at least before sending her off. Let her get a good look at the place she wanted to be a part of. See that she wouldn't like it. Wouldn't fit in. Wouldn't last.

"Sure. Let's go inside."

"Thanks," she said. "It's really cold here. When I left L.A. this morning it was seventy-five degrees."

"We're higher up," he pointed out dryly. Then he picked up on what she said. "You left this morning? And you're just getting here? At most, it's a three- or four-hour drive with traffic."

She rolled her eyes, planted a kiss on top of her silly dog's head and shrugged. "There was lots of traffic, but the truth is, I got lost."

Jericho just stared at her. "Didn't you have a GPS?"

"Yes," she said with a small sniff. "But—"

"Never mind." He turned, waved Sam off and led the way toward the house. When she didn't fall into line beside him, he turned back to look at her. "What's the problem?"

Scowling, she jerked her leg and said, "My heels sank into the lawn."

"Of course they did." He walked back to her and said, "Step out of them."

When she did, he snatched the shoes up, handed them to her and said, "This kind of shoe won't work here."

She followed him, hurrying barefoot across the grass. She caught up to him, balancing the dog-filled purse in one hand and her shoes in the other. "But they look good," she told him.

"How'd that work out?"

"Well," she said on a half laugh, "it's a first impression you won't forget."

Jericho felt a short dart of admiration course through him. She wasn't easily shot down. Then he stopped and looked down at her. Her cheeks were pink, her eyes were flashing with humor and there was a smudge of dirt on the tip of her nose.

She was way too beautiful.

"What?" she asked. "Do I have dirt on my face?"

"As a matter of fact…" He bent, scooped her up into his arms and heard her "whoosh" of surprise.

"Hey, you don't have to carry me."

"Those heels wouldn't work on the gravel either, and you're barefoot, Ms. Saxon."

She packed a lot of curves into her small body. As she wiggled in his arms, he felt a reaction that surely would have happened to any red-blooded, breathing male. The problem was, he didn't want to react to her. All he wanted from Daisy Saxon was her absence.

"Right. Got it. Heels, bad. I'll remember. And call me Daisy," she told him. "After all, since I'm snuggled in against your chest, no point in being formal."

"I suppose not," he said tightly, as a small, low-pitched growl erupted from the dog she held close. "That's a ridiculous dog," he muttered.

She looked up at him. "Brant gave her to me just before he shipped out."

"Oh." Well, hell.

He ignored the dog's warning growls and Daisy's stream of chatter about the house, the grounds, the weather, the fact that her car was almost out of gas and the nice people she'd met at the spa when she was lost.

His ears were ringing by the time he reached the front door of the main house. For a man used to the gypsylike life of career military, even owning a home was different. This place, though, was special.

This place had been in his family for almost a hundred years. One of his long-ago grandfathers had built the original cabin, then later it had been expanded into the King family getaway. Jericho and his brothers had spent nearly every summer of their childhoods here at the lodge.

It sat high on the mountain, square in the middle of several hundred acres of forest, streams and rivers. The cottage had grown into a veritable castle constructed of logs and glass, blending in so well with its surroundings, it practically disappeared into the surrounding woods. It was a sort of camouflage, he supposed, which was something he was all too familiar with.

He'd bought out his brothers' shares of the place years ago and, knowing even then what he would eventually do with the place, had hired an architect to make some changes. The building had been expanded yet again, becoming at last a sort of fantasy mansion, with sharp angles, a steep roofline and enough rooms that Jericho never needed to run into a soul if he didn't want to. He'd had the work done before he left the Corps so it would be ready for him. When he left the Corps, Jericho had headed straight here.

This place was both a touchstone to the past and a foothold on his future. He opened the arched, dark wood door, stepped inside and set Daisy on her feet quickly. Best to get that curvy body away from his as fast as possible.

She slipped her heels on and did a slow turn, taking in what she could of the house from the foyer.

"Wow," she whispered. "This is really..."

Cathedral ceilings arched high overhead, with pale, varnished logs crisscrossing in geometric patterns. The last of the afternoon sunlight slanted through the glass and lay dazzling golden patterns on the gleaming wood floors.

"Yeah, I like it." He led the way into the main room, right off the hallway, and she followed as he'd expected her to, those heels of hers clicking musically against the uncarpeted floors.

"It echoes in here," she said.

Jericho frowned as he looked back at her. "It's a big room."

"And practically empty." She shook her head as she glanced around. He followed her gaze. The furnishings were utilitarian but comfortable. There were sofas, chairs, a few tables and lamps and a long wet bar against one wall. There was a river-stone hearth tall enough for him to stand up in, and the view of the mountains was breathtaking.

"It looks like a barracks."

He shot her a look. "Clearly you've never seen barracks."

"No," she admitted, walking in, holding her dog and petting it as she moved, "but you've got this gorgeous place and it's decorated like…" She stopped and smiled apologetically. "Sorry. None of my business, is it?"

Jericho frowned again. What the hell was wrong with the room? No one else had ever complained. Then he told himself, city girl, and dismissed her observation entirely.

"So. Sam tells me you want to cook for us."

"Yes." She gave him a blindingly brilliant smile and Jericho felt that hard jolting punch of desire slam into him again. The woman was carrying concealed weapons.

"About that…"

Daisy saw the hesitation in Jericho King's ice-blue eyes. There was regret there, too, and she knew that he was about to turn her down. Destroy the plan she'd come there to set into motion. Well, she couldn't let that happen, so before he could say anything else, Daisy started talking.

"I spoke to Sam, your foreman. Was that him out front?" She carried Nikki with her as she crossed the room to stare out the wide front windows. She kept talking as she walked. "I should have said hello, oh, he probably thinks I'm a crazy person, showing up and falling flat on my face."

She didn't look back at Jericho. Couldn't afford to. Not yet.

He'd unsettled her. He looked so big and gorgeous

and, well, grim. Probably didn't smile much, she thought, which might be a good thing because he'd affected her so much glowering at her, one smile might have done her in completely.

Funny, she hadn't expected this. Hadn't thought that one look at him would start her insides burning and her heart galloping madly in her chest. He was so tall. So strong. When he'd swept her up into his arms, it had been all she could not to sigh at him.

She'd chosen Jericho because of the bond he'd had with her brother. She hadn't expected to feel such an immediate attraction to the man. But that was good, wasn't it? At least, for what she had in mind it was a good thing. All she had to do was find a way to keep him from sending her packing before she did what she'd come here to do.

After all, she couldn't get pregnant with Jericho King's child if she wasn't here, now could she?

TWO

"So," Daisy asked, plastering a confident smile on her face, "When do I start?"

She watched him watching her and yet, whatever he was thinking at the moment didn't show in his eyes. Those pale blue depths were shuttered, effectively closing her out. But that would change, she thought. Given a little time, she'd bring him around, win him over. Judging by the look on his face, though, that wouldn't be easy.

"Ms. Saxon—Daisy," he corrected before she could say anything. "I've been out of town for the past few days. Sam told me only a few minutes ago about you applying for this job."

"I wasn't trying to keep it a secret," she said, meeting his gaze directly. "I mean, you offered to help me after Brant, but I didn't want to use that offer to get this job. I wanted to earn it on my own merits, you know? I didn't want you to feel obligated or anything, so I went through Sam when I heard about the job opening." Which was true, she thought, though she had counted on the fact that Jericho would feel obligated enough to keep her on once she was here. "I'm a very good cook, by the way. Sam saw my references and my résumé. When we spoke, he said he thought I'd do fine here."

"I disagree," he said tightly, and Daisy geared up for battle. "The fact is, I don't think you working here is a good idea at all."

Daisy swallowed hard. She really hadn't counted on this. Frankly, she'd expected Jericho to sort of go along with the idea. The whole obligation thing. He had once promised to help if he could. And her late brother had idolized the man. Somehow, she'd expected the "great Jericho King" to be just a bit more understanding. Well, he might not want her to stay, but she wasn't gone yet.

"Why not?" She threaded her fingers through Nikki's dark red hair so he wouldn't be able to see her hand shaking. But even as nerves rattled around in the pit of her stomach, Daisy told herself to get a grip. She wasn't going to let him see she was nervous. Wasn't going to acknowledge that even to herself. Not again. From here on out, it was affirmations. Focus on the positive. See the goal and get it.

With those thoughts and a dozen others just like them rushing through her mind, Daisy lifted her chin and waited for him to speak. Whatever excuse or reason he gave her, she was going to counter it. She would fight to be here. To stay here. To accomplish her goal.

To do that, she was going to show him just how much

he needed her here. How much she could bring to him and to his camp. And she was going to start right now. She had the element of surprise on her side.

"This place isn't like the spa you saw today in your travels across the mountain."

"You can say that again," she noted, turning a glance to the beige sofas and chairs. "Honestly, do you have something against color?"

"What?"

"Beige," she said, waving one hand to indicate the furniture in the room. "Beige isn't a color. It's the absence of color."

"Actually," he said, "that would be black."

"Well, beige is close," she insisted. "When you're running a place like this, you shouldn't go for industrial chic. You should have warmth in this room. And a few throw rugs would cut down on the echo."

"I don't mind the echo."

"I'm guessing the meals you serve your guests are as imaginative as the décor."

"I don't have décor," he pointed out.

"That's what I said."

"I meant," he said through gritted teeth, "I'm not interested in making this place into a fashionable inn."

"Oh, I agree. That would be all wrong. After all, you're going for the whole manly Survivorman thing, right? It doesn't have to be fussy," Daisy countered, already seeing in her mind's eye how it could look. A few pillows, some colorful braided rugs, maybe some splashy paintings on a few of the bare walls. "You want your clients to be comfortable, don't you?"

"This isn't a vacation camp. People come here to learn skills. Leadership. They come here to pit themselves against the mountain and Mother Nature."

"And when they come back to the inn victorious you want them to still be roughing it?"

He inhaled sharply and Daisy thought maybe she'd gone a little far. So she backed up fast. "I'm not saying you should put up lace curtains or use chintz slipcovers. I'm just saying that making this room a little more... comfortable would go a long way toward making your guests feel at ease. Couldn't hurt to think about it, right?"

"How did we get onto this track?" he wondered aloud.

"We were talking about how good I'd be for your business," Daisy told him and shushed Nikki when she growled.

He spared a dark look for her dog before he met her gaze again and said, "No, I was telling you I don't think this is a good idea."

"But you're wrong," she argued.

"I don't think so."

"You haven't given me a chance at all," she said, fighting both the glint in Jericho's eyes and the flutter of nerves in her belly. "You don't even know me. Plus, you haven't tasted my cooking. You haven't tried my fried chicken or home-style scalloped potatoes or my fudge mountain cake—"

"This isn't about... Fudge mountain?"

Daisy grinned as his eyes narrowed thoughtfully. "It's amazing. I'll make it for you."

Jericho took another deep breath, and she was frankly

astonished that his broad, muscular chest could expand even farther. The man really was huge. And yet, he didn't give off the kind of "danger" vibe she associated with very big men. There was something…quiet about him. And that something was very attractive.

"It's not that easy," he said.

"Oh, making the cake isn't easy, but I promise you it's worth the effort." She deliberately misunderstood him. Keep him off balance, she told herself. *He's not sure what to do about you, so keep him that way,* she told herself.

"The job, Daisy," he said, and waved her over onto one of the couches. "Offering you this job isn't that easy."

"Sure it is. You offer, I accept. Easy."

He took a seat on the chair opposite her and braced his elbows on his knees. "When Sam was telling you about the job, did he bother to mention the survival test?"

She blinked. "Survival test?"

"I didn't think so." He scrubbed one hand across his face. "You see, there's a policy here at King Adventure. All new hires have to spend the weekend on the mountain with me. They have to prove they can make it here. Prove they have some survival skills."

Daisy set Nikki down onto her lap and stroked the little dog's back. Her mind was racing and her stomach was churning. Survival? All she knew about surviving on a mountain was finding a good hotel with a nice fireplace and room service. Why in heaven should a cook have to prove herself in the wild?

Anxiety pumped through her system and her positive

thoughts began to crumble like broken cookies. But even while doubts slapped at her, she knew she couldn't give up on her idea before she even really got started.

"No," she said, "I didn't know about that."

"See?" His voice was kind, his eyes shone with relief and the patient smile on his face only irritated her immensely. "It just wouldn't work out, Daisy."

"Well," she shot back, "it's not like you're going to drop me off in the middle of nowhere with a knife and a piece of string. Are you?"

One corner of his mouth lifted briefly. "No."

"Then I can do it," she said, covering her own doubts with a veil of confidence.

Now he simply shook his head. "No, you can't. Hell, you couldn't take a few steps across the lawn without falling on your face."

She flushed and felt the heat of it stain her cheeks. "That was an accident."

"And out in the forest, an accident like that one could kill you."

"Then I won't let it happen again," she argued.

"Damn it, why won't you listen to reason on this?"

"Because I need this job," she told him flatly, fingers curled protectively around Nikki. "My roommate got married and I couldn't keep the apartment on my own. My old job was downsized when the owner hired his cousin's nephew as head cook and—" She broke off quickly because she wasn't about to beg. And she wasn't the kind of woman to go all weepy, either, using tears to get her way.

"It's been a rough couple of months," she said simply. "So when I heard about this job opening, it seemed perfect. It *is* perfect. And I think I should get the same chance to prove myself as any other employee here has had."

He pushed himself out of his chair and stalked a few paces off. Glancing at her over his shoulder, he said, "It wouldn't be easy."

"No," she agreed, already dreading being out in the great outdoors. "Probably not."

"Why are you so determined to do this?"

"I told you why," Daisy hedged. "I need the job."

"If you're that good a cook, you could work anywhere."

"I want to work here."

"Which brings me," he said tightly, "back to the original question. Why are you so determined to work *here?*"

She lifted her chin, squared her shoulders and said softly, "Because you knew Brant."

He rubbed his face again in irritation. "I know it's not easy, losing family."

"My only family," she corrected and hated that her voice broke on the words. "Brant and I only had each other. When he died, I was alone. And I don't like alone."

Which was the absolute truth as far as it went.

She couldn't give him the whole of it, now could she?

She'd already admitted that she really did have nowhere else to go. She had no one. Her brother, Brant, had been her only family. Daisy was completely on her own now. And she hated it. She watched other families and felt her heart ache. She watched mothers with their children and something inside her wept. Daisy really wanted love in her life again. But she didn't want another man.

No, thank you. She had both been there and done that and hadn't even gotten the T-shirt. She'd convinced herself a couple of times that she was in love and it had ended badly. She wasn't interested in risking another broken heart. She wouldn't set herself up for that kind of disappointment again. But she did want to love and be loved. She wanted to have a family again. To be part of something again.

She wanted a child.

That thought settled everything inside her. Nerves drained away, anxiety faded and a cool, calm feeling swept through her. Whatever she had to prove to Jericho, she'd do it—for the chance at family. She'd made a decision and now she was going to go through with it. But he couldn't know what was driving her. Daisy couldn't very well tell him that she'd chosen him to be the father of her child.

If she felt a quick sting of guilt over the idea of tricking a man into being a parent, she smothered it a moment later. It wasn't as if she was asking him to marry her. Or to even take an active role in the raising of their child. All she really needed from him was his sperm.

Which just sounds awful, she thought with an inward groan. But it wasn't as callous as all that. She'd chosen Jericho because of his relationship with her late brother. Because he had been close to the only family Daisy had had.

And because Jericho King and the Marine Corps had stolen her family.

They owed her one.

"I don't baby prospective employees."

"Baby?" Daisy flushed, as if he were reading the thoughts racing through her mind.

Scowling, Jericho clarified. "I meant, I won't make it easy on you."

"Oh." She laughed to herself, then shook her head. "I didn't ask you to." Oh, boy, she thought wryly, she'd probably regret saying that. He looked tough and she could only imagine that whatever he put her through to "earn" her way in wouldn't be pleasant. But she'd made up her mind to come here. To make her dream come true. And nothing he could do or say would stop her.

"You're as stubborn as your brother was."

Daisy smiled fondly. "Where do you think he learned it?"

Damn it.

"I'm not asking for a favor," she said quickly, wanting to speak up for herself before he summarily dismissed her. "I'm applying for a job I happen to be perfect for. I'm a terrific cook, you'll see. All I'm asking for is a chance."

In his letters home to her, Brant had often mentioned that Jericho King had the best poker expression he'd ever seen. Brant had insisted that no one ever knew what Jericho was thinking. Apparently, leaving the Marine Corps hadn't changed that about him.

She didn't have a clue what his thoughts were. Hers were very clear, though.

She needed to stay here. She fixed a confident smile on her face, while Jericho King's blue eyes were locked on her. She wouldn't let him see that the thought of a survival test terrified her. Wouldn't let him know that she felt on edge. But everything she'd told him had been absolutely true.

His jaw went so tight she could actually see the muscles in his cheeks twitch. He wasn't happy with the situation, but he wasn't telling her to leave, so Daisy took that as a good sign. She pressed her case. "I can promise you that you won't be disappointed by my performance as cook. I'm not asking for a handout, Mr. King."

"Jericho."

A good sign and she'd take it as such. Her smile brightened. "Jericho, then. All I'm asking for is a job. I can do it. You won't be sorry."

"No," he mused as he walked back toward her. "But you might be."

She huffed out a relieved breath. "Does that mean I'm hired?"

"Provisionally," he told her. "There's still the mountain test. I can't let you off the hook for that one. Every employee here has taken the weekend in the wilderness. You'll have to make it through, too. For now, I'll show you where you can stay. Let you get settled, then we'll head into the mountains in a couple of days."

Daisy held on to Nikki and pushed up off the sofa. Her first goal had been met. She was still here. And Jericho had no idea that once she had a foothold, she'd never let go. She knew exactly what she looked like—a helpless female. Well, looks could be deceiving, she told herself. She'd been on her own for years. She'd practically raised Brant on her own and she'd done a damn fine job of it, too. She could handle whatever Jericho dished out and when it was all over and done, she'd still be standing. Plus, she'd have the right to be here, with the man she needed to help her rebuild her family.

She tipped her head back to look up at him and graced him with what she knew was a brilliant smile. "Thanks. Thanks for this."

"Don't thank me yet," he muttered and led the way out of the main room toward the staircase. "Before too long, I suspect you'll be cursing the day you ever drove up here."

Only, she thought, if she didn't get pregnant.

It was a hell of a thing, Jericho told himself, when a man was reduced to sneaking around his own damn house.

He'd never been a coward. Men he'd served with in the Corps would be willing to swear that there wasn't a damn thing in the universe that scared Jericho King. But here he was, avoiding one small, curvy woman as if she were Typhoid Mary and he was the last healthy man on the planet.

She'd already settled herself in as if she'd been on the mountain for years. Her idiot dog was scrambling up and down the stairs, those tiny claws tapping against the wood floor until it sounded like a swarm of crickets had been set loose in the house.

Even the air was different, he thought. The faint trace of her flowery scent seemed to hang on the air, flavoring every breath he drew.

Jericho was on edge and he didn't like it. Hell, he'd arranged his life so that he dealt only with the people he wanted around him. After years of military living, he liked his privacy. Liked the fact that his clients came and went, hardly making an impact on his world at all. His employees knew when to back off and leave him alone, and when he needed a woman, he went out and found one.

Nothing permanent. Nothing lasting. Just a few good nights with great sex and some laughs. That was the way he wanted it. The way he needed it.

Yet now, everything had changed. In the space of a few hours, Daisy Saxon was turning his world on its head. And he only had himself to blame. He could have turned her out on her pretty little ass. Hell, should have.

But truthfully, he hadn't been able to. The weight of what he owed her and her brother was still too heavy around his neck. Whispers of guilt, regret, slipped through his mind. If she knew the truth, she'd never have come here. So the only option for him was to agree to let her take the survival test on the mountain. Then she'd fail and leave and it wouldn't be his doing.

He went down the back stairs figuring to grab something to eat so he could avoid the whole sitting-down-to-dinner situation. There was plenty of work for him to do. Paperwork piled up because he tended to avoid it whenever possible. So he'd lock himself into his study with a sandwich and avoid talking to Daisy until tomorrow.

He slapped one hand to the door, pushed it open and stopped dead. Damn it.

"Hi," she called out from her spot by the stove.

She was wearing a pair of tight jeans, a yellow, long-sleeved shirt and an apron that was so large for her the strings were tied three times around her narrow waist. Not only was she here and cooking, whatever she had going smelled great.

"What are you doing here?" He stepped into the room and glanced around. "Where's Kevin?"

"Oh, I told him I'd fix dinner tonight. He's going into town to see his girlfriend."

Jericho scowled at that. Not only did she take over his damn house, she started giving his employees the night off.

"You know, I didn't even realize you had a town close by. Imagine that, I got lost for what felt like hours and never saw the town?" She shook her head and laughed a little. "Must make it easier than driving all the way down the mountain when you need supplies."

He just stared at her. The woman talked more than anyone he'd ever known.

"It's not a problem that Kevin left for the night, is it?" she asked, watching him warily. "I only thought that since I'm going to be taking over his job soon—"

He narrowed his eyes on her. "That hasn't been decided yet."

"Oh, I know, but I believe in positive thinking."

"Uh-huh."

She smiled again. "Yes, I can imagine what you think of it, but affirmations can really make a difference in your life. Think it, be it, you know."

"What?"

She laughed again and the rich, throaty sound rolled through the room and settled over him like a blessing.

"I just mean, you put out into the universe what you want to happen and it generally will."

"The universe."

"Sure. If all you do is think negative thoughts, then it's hardly surprising when you only experience negativity, right? So, same goes with the good stuff. Imagine you're happy doing exactly what you want to do and the universe will find a way to provide you with that dream."

He shook his head. "So the universe is going to help you through the mountain tests?"

"You bet!" She stirred the contents of a stainless steel pot on the stove. Instantly, even more unbelievably tantalizing aromas drifted into the air. "I'm envisioning myself succeeding and gracefully accepting your congratulations."

He smiled in spite of everything. She seemed so damn sure of herself. How were you supposed to argue with a woman who thought she could arrange her life simply by thinking?

The scent of whatever she was cooking reached him again and Jericho's stomach rumbled in appreciation, but he wasn't about to be seduced by a pot of soup. "You go ahead and keep imagining. I've got actual work to do. I'm just going to make a sandwich, then I'll be gone."

"Sandwich?" she said, and looked horrified at the notion. "That's not a meal for a man like you. I think we can do way better than that. Why don't you sit down and I'll fix you a snack that will hold you over until dinner."

He thought about refusing. He really didn't want to spend any more time around her than he absolutely had to. Especially if she was going to be spouting all of her New Age bull. But if he walked out now, she'd know he was avoiding her and he wasn't about to let that happen.

Instead, he walked to the high bar table at the back side of the cooking island and took one of the tall seats. He watched her as she pulled an oven door open and reached in with a hot pad to pull out a cookie sheet dotted with what looked like golden-brown half pies.

"This is an amazing kitchen," she was saying. "This warming drawer for instance. Keeps food hot but doesn't continue to cook them. And oh, my. The refrigerator shelf under the island—" She shook her head, patted her heart and sighed. "Keeps all of your vegetables right next to the sink and the cutting boards." She laughed a little and did a more dramatic sigh. "And I'm not sure, but I think I had an orgasm when I saw the Sub-Zero fridge." She caught herself, winced a little and gave him a sheepish smile. "Did I just say that out loud?"

"You did," he told her and wished he hadn't heard her. She said the word *orgasm* and his body went on red alert, instantly prepared to show her just what an orgasm should really feel like. At the very least, she wouldn't have had to wonder if she'd had one or not.

"Sorry," she said and walked to a cupboard for a plate. "I get a little emotional about great kitchens, and let me tell you, this one's a beauty!"

"Uh-huh." He didn't care. Until he'd hired Kevin to cook for them, the most the kitchen had seen was a lot of microwave action from him and Sam and the others who lived here. As long as the kitchen held a fridge for food and beer and provided a sink and ready fire, that was all he needed to know. Jericho remembered the kitchen remodel he'd done to the place years ago, but he'd simply turned the designer loose and hadn't asked any questions.

Their clients were served simple food and plenty of it. No one had ever complained. Now though, he gave it a quick look, following her pleased gaze. He took in whitewashed plank walls, dark cedar cabinets, dark green granite counters and a gleaming wood floor. There was an industrial-size cooking range, double ovens, a couple of microwaves and a refrigerator big enough to hold supplies for a battalion. That wasn't even counting the two big freezers situated in the butler's pantry.

Overhead lights banished shadows, and through the wide windows on every wall, night was creeping its way across the mountain. Inside, though, the oversize room was feeling a little cramped at the moment.

She was standing just opposite him on the other side of the island. In front of her was more granite and a snaking stainless sink that served, as he recalled Kevin telling him once, as an "entertaining sink." Apparently, you could stock drinks in ice at one end of the sink, then as the ice melted, it simply drained away.

Didn't impress Jericho any. A cooler was just as good.

"You seem to have found your way around," he said finally, when he noticed she was simply staring at him waiting for him to say something.

"I have. It's like exploring an amazing new country." She slid open the refrigerated drawer, plucked something from inside and dropped it onto a plate beside a pie she'd already taken from the cooking tray. "Now, I want you to try this and I think you'll be glad I talked you out of having a sandwich," she said, sliding the plate across the counter toward him.

Jericho shifted his gaze from her to the plate and back again. "What is it?"

"It's *good*," she said, giving him a teasing smile. "Honestly, don't you have any adventure in your soul?"

"I've had plenty of adventures," he countered. "I just don't usually include food in them."

Still, he thought, it did smell good, not that he was going to admit it anytime soon. The half-a-pie was still steaming and alongside it sat a small bowl with a couple of radish roses, curls of carrot and celery beside a small dish of what looked like ranch dip. He lifted his gaze to hers. "Raw vegetables? Not a favorite."

"I'll make a note," she said with a shrug. "But for now, you could eat them anyway. They're good for you." Then she waved at the plate. "Try the pasty."

"Pasty?" One eyebrow lifted. "Not the definition of pasty that I'm familiar with."

It took a second to register, then she blushed—actually blushed, for God's sake—chuckled and that soft sound rippled through the room. "I can imagine. But *this* is a meat pasty. They're from Cornwall, originally, I think. Some say it pah-stee," she said. "Wives made them for miners' lunches. They were easy to carry and hold and satisfying enough to take care of a hardworking man's hunger."

Jericho nodded absently as she talked. Picking up the half pie, he sniffed it again, almost suspiciously, then took a bite. The piecrust simply dissolved in his mouth and the filling was... He groaned.

Daisy gave him a bright smile. "You like it!"

"You could say that," he muttered around another mouthful. He really hated to admit it, but she was a hell of a cook. "It's great."

"I'm so glad. I made them to go along with the home-made soup. I know soup isn't a very substantial meal, but with the fresh bread and the pasties…"

He held up one hand. Clearly extreme measures were needed if a man was going to get a word in edgewise. "You made fresh bread?"

"It's just a couple of loaves of quick bread." She sounded almost apologetic. "That way I didn't have to wait for the yeast to rise."

"Right." She'd only been here a few hours and she'd made soup, bread and this incredible pie he couldn't stop eating. Kevin was a good enough cook, but he didn't have half the drive this one small woman did. Plus, he wasn't exactly adventurous with his cooking, which was, frankly, one thing Jericho had liked about him. But, if this pasty of hers was any indication, he had a feeling "adventures in food" was going to be a good thing.

And, he had to admit, she might look like a flighty little thing, but she sure as hell wasn't afraid to work. She'd done more in a couple of hours than Kevin managed to do in a day. To be fair, Kevin probably would have enjoyed doing more, but cooking for a bunch of men probably sucked the creativity out of him. Daisy was still fresh enough that she was excited about her work.

While she talked, Jericho nibbled on the raw vegetables, surprising even himself. He'd always been more of a meat-and-potatoes man by choice. And frankly, being in the military had pretty much flattened his taste buds long ago. Food there was fast and plentiful. Cooked to keep a man on his feet, not to have him lounging around a table tempting his palate. But whatever kind of dip this was she'd concocted for the vegetables was damn tasty and the pie was good enough it could bring a grown man to his knees.

As if she could read his mind, she wagged her index finger at him and said, "You'll like my soup, too. Soups are actually one of my specialties, which will work out really well up here during the winter."

"What kind of soup?" he grudgingly asked, since he was being tempted by the satisfaction filling his stomach at the moment.

She turned around, went back to the stove and lifted the lid on the pot again. Steam rushed up, carrying an amazing scent. "It's beef and barley. I found all of the supplies in the fridge and the pantry and it's so brisk and cold out right now, I thought soup would be good for tonight."

"It'll be fine," he said, already looking forward to sampling it as he finished off the pasty and wished he could get another one.

"I have got great recipes for tomato soup and chicken and leek—"

"Leek?"

She glanced at him. "You'll like it, I swear."

He probably would, he thought and warned his stomach not to get used to the good life.

"Anyway, when it snows up here, there'll be lots of good, hearty soups and breads and stews. Then in summer, you'll love my barbecued chicken wraps and—"

He cut her off before she could get too wound up. "Don't be making long-term plans just yet."

"Affirmations, remember?" she countered with a grin. "As for dinner, I'll do even better tomorrow night. What would you like? Pot roast? Pasta? Chicken enchiladas? Do you have any favorites?"

God, his mouth was watering just listening to her. Between her looks and her abilities with a stove, she was definitely double trouble.

Then she stopped and whirled around to look at him. "Better—what do you *hate?*"

A reluctant smile curved his mouth. Hell, he had to give her points for tenacity. He'd given her an inch and she was quickly scrambling to take the whole damn mile. He admired that in anybody. And for a woman alone, fighting to make a place for herself, it took even more guts to stride right in, settle herself and immediately go to work carving out her own niche.

But as much as she wanted this job, heck, as much as he'd like to get accustomed to eating this well, he couldn't let that happen. For her own sake.

And he almost regretted that fact.

Almost.

There's not much I won't eat," he finally admitted. "But we're not interested in anything fancy up here. I've gotten used to eating simple, plain food. Plus, it's better for the clients when they're here. Roast beef is going to give a man more energy on the mountain than a plate of snails."

"Ew. Snails." She smiled and shuddered. "No worries in that department, I promise."

"Okay, good." He finished off the pasty and thought about grabbing another as he watched her move around the kitchen. She sure as hell looked as if she knew what she was doing. Of course, he'd read her references, but tasting what she could do with food was different than reading about it.

He nibbled at the carrot and celery curls, dipping them in the accompanying sauce. She was a good cook, but that didn't mean she would make it here. Hell, he told himself, look at her.

His gaze locked on her, he noted her delicate but curvy build. Her hair was in a ponytail that swung back and forth across her back like a pendulum with her movements. She was humming something just under her breath and when she opened a cupboard and reached for something, Jericho was treated to a glimpse of very pale, very smooth skin displayed when her blouse hitched up.

His mouth went dry and his blood stirred. Damn, it had been too long since he'd indulged in a long weekend of sweaty sex. And now that *that* thought had taken root in his mind, he was picturing Daisy Saxon in his bed, that thick, soft hair of hers spread across his pillow. Her smile aimed at him as he moved in for a long, languorous kiss. Her breath sliding from her lungs as he entered her.

Instantly, he shut down that train of thought and squirmed uncomfortably on the bar stool. He didn't need her here. Didn't want her here. Couldn't have her here.

So he was just going to have to get rid of her—fast.

Three

"It's amazing," Daisy whispered, almost as if she were in church. She'd awakened early—too many years of getting up and moving in the restaurant business—and after getting dressed, she'd taken Nikki outside to enjoy the mountain quiet. Her little dog was off exploring the yard and all of the shrubbery, leaving Daisy alone in the shadows.

Now, she was standing on the lawn, staring back at the house and realizing that in the pearly morning light, Jericho King's log and glass mansion looked almost like a fairy-tale castle.

She'd been too busy yesterday finding her way there and then falling on her face to notice much about the place. Her gaze swept over the façade and another murmur of appreciation slipped from between her lips. Wide balconies stretched along the second floor, with arched, twig-style railings. Behind those balconies, glass panels soared, allowing views of the tree-studded mountain and the lake in the distance.

The lodge itself was surrounded by tall pines, and the wind whispering through the branches sounded like sighs.

"It's a good place, all right." Jericho's voice rumbled from right behind her and Daisy jumped.

"I didn't hear you come up."

"I walk quietly. Tend to in the woods." He stared up at the house as dawn painted the honey-colored logs with rosy hues.

She nodded but silently guessed that his stealthiness also came from so many years spent in the military. "Well, it's so quiet here anyway, it's as if you're afraid to make too much noise. I feel almost as if I'm in church or something. In the city," she said on a sigh, "there's always noise. Cars, trucks, sirens. Here...stillness."

"One of the things I like best about it," he said.

"I can see why," she agreed. "I get tired of the crowds and the hustle and bustle myself. Somehow everything always seems to be rushed down in the city. Being here is almost like being on vacation!"

"Except for the working aspect," he said dryly.

"Right." She nodded and then continued talking. "Anyway, I woke up early and decided to look around a little. I didn't actually get to see much yesterday and—" She broke off, looked up at him and added, "But I didn't see anyone else so I thought I was the only one up."

He laughed shortly, shoved his hands into the pockets of a battered, brown leather bomber jacket and said, "Trust me, everyone's up." He turned and pointed across the wide compound at a smaller log version of the main house. "Sam and the guys live there and they've got a small kitchen outfitted so they can make coffee or whatever. You won't see them much in the mornings, but come lunchtime and at dinner, they'll be crowding around the table like they're starving."

"Good," she said, looking up at him with a determined smile. "I like cooking for people who like to eat."

"They do," he told her. "As for right now, they're all just busy doing the daily chores."

"Right. Of course." Foolish, she supposed, to have assumed she'd had the place to herself. But yesterday, all she'd seen was the main house and the barn. She'd never noticed the other building set back against the trees. Now she at least knew why the house had been so empty when she and Nikki had gotten up.

As if the thought of her had conjured the dog from thin air, Nikki barreled across the lawn, charging Jericho with a ferocity belying her size. Her low growl erupted from her tiny chest and when she reached them, she stood in front of Daisy as if daring the big man to hurt her.

Shaking his head at the dog, Jericho said, "You know that's just coyote bait."

She gasped, bent down and snatched up her dog. Cradling her close, Daisy stroked a hand down Nikki's back and shot a nervous glance around her at the surrounding trees. "Don't say that."

"Dogs like that don't belong here," he told her and his blue eyes were cold and remote. "Hell, it's small enough it could get carried away by a hawk."

"Great," she muttered, looking up. "Now I have to check the skies, too?"

"Wouldn't be a bad idea," he said, shooting the still growling dog a look of mutual dislike. Then he shifted his glance to Daisy. "Why are you really here?"

"I told you."

"Yeah, but you could work anywhere. You're a good cook."

"Thanks!" She smiled at him and accepted the casually delivered compliment as if he'd delivered it with a speech and a glass of celebratory champagne.

"So why here?"

Daisy thought about that for a long minute. Wasn't as if she could tell him why…not exactly, anyway. So she did the best she could and walked a wide circle around the absolute truth. Setting Nikki down on the grass, she stood up and said, "I told you that I wanted a change…"

"Yeah, but this seems like a radical jump to make."

"Maybe," she admitted, taking another look at the fantasy lodge draped in sunlight, "but what's the point in making a change if it's a safe one? If I just move from one apartment in the city to another? From one restaurant to another? That's not change. That's just… *ch*."

"What?"

"You know," she explained, "not a whole change, just a partial one, so a *ch*."

He shook his head again and rolled his eyes. "Why here, though?"

"Because you knew my brother," she blurted, giving him at least that much of the absolute truth. "And because Brant wrote to me about you. He admired you. A lot."

His features froze up and his eyes went glacial. Daisy had to wonder why.

"He was a good kid," Jericho said after a long moment or two of silence.

"Yeah," she agreed, "he was."

She'd come a long way in the past year. Used to be that thoughts of Brant would have tears filling her eyes and her throat closing up on a knot of emotion. Now, though, she could remember him and smile. She drew on all of the happy memories she had of him to comfort her and the tears were coming fewer and further between these days.

Still, when she spoke about him, her voice went a little wistful. "He was several years younger than me, you know. Our parents died when he was very small, so I practically raised him. Always felt more like his mom than his sister."

"He told me about you."

"He did?" An eager smile curved her mouth. Oh, this was what she'd wanted. What she'd hungered for. Someone else who had known Brant. Who could remember him with her and keep his memory fresh and meaningful. Plus, Jericho King had known him at the end of Brant's life and those were pieces that Daisy needed. She wanted to know everything. "What did he say about me? No, wait." She stopped and held up one hand. "If he was complaining about me, maybe I don't want to know."

His features relaxed enough that one corner of his mouth lifted. "Don't worry," he told her. "Brant only had good things to say about you. Used to tell his buddies all about your secret sauce for hamburgers. Talked about it so much he had the other guys begging him to shut up because he was torturing them."

"Oh, I'm so glad." Her eyes welled with unexpected tears and a too-familiar ache settled around her heart. "Thank you for telling me. It's hard for me, you know, not knowing what his life was like before he died. I mean, some of his friends wrote to me after…but it's really good to hear you talk about him. To know you knew him. And liked him. I— Damn it."

"Hey, don't cry." His eyes flashed and his voice was sharp. "Seriously. Don't."

She sniffed and huffed out a laugh. "I'm not going to. Oh, trust me, when I got word that Brant had died, I cried for days. Weeks."

Turning, she started walking because she just couldn't stand still a moment longer. Nikki was right on her heels as she moved across the lawn and Jericho was just a step behind the dog.

"It felt sometimes that I'd never stop crying. The slightest thing set me off. His favorite song playing on the radio. Finding his old first baseman's glove on the floor of his closet. Even Nikki made me cry."

"That I understand," he muttered.

Daisy laughed and was grateful for it. He was such a guy. "I meant, Brant gave her to me for my birthday just before he shipped out. So she was my last link to him and when he was gone—" Shaking her head a little, she sighed, looked down at the tiny dog and smiled. "But I realized after a while that Nikki was a blessing. With her, I wasn't completely alone, you know? I still had something from Brant with me."

"Yeah, I get that," he said softly.

She looked up at him, her gaze locking with his. "I appreciated the letter you wrote me."

His jaw worked as if he were chewing on words to taste them before allowing them to escape. "And I'm sorry I had to write it."

"Oh," she said, giving him a tremulous smile as she reached out to lay one hand on his arm, "so am I. I wish with all my heart that Brant was still here. But he isn't. And I wanted you to know that it helped hearing from you. That reading about his friends and how much he meant to all of you gave me some comfort. You know, in case you were wondering."

He looked mortally uncomfortable and Daisy asked herself again, *Why?* Surely it would be a good thing for him to know that what he'd done had helped her get through a truly hideous slice of life.

"He was a good Marine," he said after a long moment of silence.

"High praise indeed, coming from you," she said, remembering all the letters Brant had written to her. "My brother talked about you all the time in his letters to me. About how he admired you. How he tried to emulate you. Learn from you."

Clearly unhappy with the conversation, Jericho bent down, snatched up a fallen twig from the grass and sent it sailing toward the tree line. "He did fine. Would have made a hell of a career Marine."

She knew that was exactly what Brant had wanted. Knew that her little brother had wanted to serve his

country and test himself alongside other Marines. It had
been important to him. So important that he'd given his
life for his beliefs. And though her heart hurt still at his
absence, being around Jericho—a man that had known
and served with Brant—made it almost seem as if she
hadn't lost him completely.

That was only one of the reasons she'd come here to
get pregnant, she reminded herself. Jericho had known
and liked Brant. But he was also a part of the very
military that had taken the last of her family from her.
Wasn't it only right that he now give her a family?

She winced at the direction of her own thoughts. She
wasn't a woman used to lying or manipulating. And a
part of her wasn't happy with what she was doing. After
all, she was planning on tricking a man into making a
child with her. Things didn't get much more devious
than that.

But what choice did she have, really? She wanted a
family again. Wanted to love again. And if she came
right out and asked, she was sure Jericho wouldn't say,
Sure, let's get right on that!

No, this was the only way. The only way to fill the
hole in her heart left by Brant's death.

"You know," she said thoughtfully, "I almost met you
before."

"When?"

"At Camp Pendleton. I went to see Brant before he
shipped out and while he was showing me around the
base, he spotted you." She smiled at the memory. Her
brother had been so excited, so proud. He'd introduced
Daisy to most of his friends and taken her to his favorite
spots on base. "You were coming out of some building

and Brant was dragging me over to meet you when a colonel walked up to join you. When the two of you left together, Brant was disappointed."

She also recalled clearly just how good Jericho King had looked in uniform. Tall and built and, even from a distance, clearly gorgeous. She'd been a little disappointed at not meeting him herself. Yet, here she stood now, more than a year later, at his home. *Life took you on some pretty strange journeys,* she thought.

"He was a good Marine," Jericho said again, as if struggling to give her whatever it was she needed to hear. "He had a lot of friends in the unit."

"He was always like that," Daisy answered with a wisp of sorrow in her voice for days gone past. "People liked being around him."

He nodded but didn't say anything. As they came to the edge of the lawn, the rising sun began to clear the treetops, spilling what looked like gold dust across the tips of the pines. "I liked your brother," he finally said, staring off down the mountain as if searching for signs of an invading army. "Because of that, I'm going to tell you something you need to hear whether you want to or not."

"Sounds ominous."

He tore his gaze from the distance and looked down at her. "You don't belong here, Daisy."

"What?"

She hadn't expected that, but looking at him now she couldn't imagine why not. Harsh shadows cast by sunlight sliding through the trees lay across his face, darkening his eyes and making him look even more formidable than usual. His mouth was a grim, straight line as he said, "You don't belong here, on the mountain. This is not your kind of place, Daisy."

Worry gnawed at her insides for a few uncomfortable moments, then that sensation gave way to aggravation. Was he going to change his mind? Toss her out before he'd even given her a chance to prove herself? He didn't know her. Didn't know what she might be capable of or not. How dare he think he could decide what she could and couldn't do.

"It's my kind of place if I say it is," she told him.

He blew out a breath and his mouth tightened even further until she could see that muscle in his jaw twitch again. "It's not that easy. Besides, I don't think your brother would want you here."

She blinked at him. Using her brother to get rid of her? "Excuse me?"

"You think Brant would be crazy about the idea of you living on a remote mountain top with a bunch of ex-Marines? Living with a bunch of guys isn't easy."

Former Marines? All of them? She shook that thought away and stayed focused on the conversation.

"Brant was a Marine. He'd probably love the fact that I'm here. He'd consider me to be perfectly safe surrounded by the kind of men he trusted."

"You're making this harder than it has to be," he muttered.

"No," she told him flatly. "You're the one doing that. All I did was apply for a job. Which I got. You've already tasted my cooking and loved it. So the only complaint you've got against me is that I don't *belong* here? Not good enough."

She stared up into pale blue eyes that seemed to be

boring directly into hers as if he were trying to read her thoughts before she could say them. "Now, I'll remind you that Brant was my *younger* brother. He didn't make decisions for me, and it would be really difficult for him to start doing it now."

Jericho King's scowl was an impressive thing. She imagined it had once frightened young recruits into jumping to attention and springing into whatever action Jericho had expected from them. She refused to be intimidated by it.

"I knew him," he pointed out. "I think I can figure out you being here wouldn't thrill your brother."

"Yes," she agreed, "you did know Brant and I'm glad to have that connection. Somehow," she added, "it makes his memory come more alive when I'm around other people who remember him. *But* I knew him better, I think, than you did. And even if he were here to cast a vote on all of this, it wouldn't be up to him. This is my decision."

"And mine," he reminded her.

His face looked hard and his eyes were as cold as twin blocks of ice. The rising sun spilled more light and created darker shadows all at the same time. She watched Jericho's face, hoping to spot a chink in his armor. But she found nothing. There was no give on his features, no soft understanding or kind consideration. This was the face of a warrior. A man tested in battle and honed down to a fine edge. If she expected to hold her own with him, she'd need every ounce of her own strength and self-confidence. If she let him know she was worried in the slightest, that would give him far too much of an advantage in this little test of wills.

She took a breath, blew it out again and said, "Okay, yeah. It's your decision, too. But you promised me a chance. And I'm holding you to it."

He blew out an impatient breath. "You've got to be the most stubborn woman I've ever met."

"If you think I'm insulted by that, you're wrong." Daisy bent down, scooped up Nikki and held her close. "Maybe I've never been on a battlefield, but I've had to work hard for everything I've ever had."

"That's not—"

"I know what it's like to push yourself." She cut him off neatly and poked him in the chest with the tip of her index finger. "I've been on my own a long time. I raised my brother by myself with no one to help. I know what it is to be so tired all you want to do is lie down and not get up for a year. And I know what it's like to ignore that urge because you've just got way too many things to do." She lifted her chin and fixed her gaze on his. "I'm not afraid. I'll do whatever's necessary to get what I want."

He nodded abruptly. "You know what? Fine. You don't want to listen to reason, that's your choice. You want to do this, we'll do it. Be ready at dawn tomorrow. We'll head up the mountain and then we'll see just how badly you want this stupid job."

He had to be out of his mind. That was the only explanation for any of this. In the soft, hazy light just before dawn, Jericho checked the sky, hitched his backpack higher and glared at the house. As if firing dirty looks at the place would make Daisy Saxon appear.

"It ain't dawn yet," Sam said as he walked up quietly.

No, it wasn't. So she wasn't late yet. "Close enough."

"Uh-huh." The older man shoved one hand through thinning gray hair. "So what's the plan, JK? You taking her out on the mountain just to submarine her?"

He shot one wary glance at his friend. Was he that easy to read? Would Daisy figure out that he was going to see to it that she failed her survival test? Besides, it wasn't as if he were going to deliberately sabotage her. He just wouldn't be offering her any extra help. And left to her own pitiful devices, he had no doubt she'd be finished before the day was out.

"What do you care?" he asked, neither confirming nor denying the man's suspicions.

Sam gave him a look Jericho hadn't seen since the older man had been his drill instructor when he first joined the Corps. When he was through with boot camp, Jericho and Sam had become friends and had kept in touch through all of their separate postings over the years. Sam had been a Marine for twenty years when he mustered out and coming here to King Mountain had seemed the logical choice.

The older man had been restless—too young to retire and too old to stay in the Corps—so he'd come here and become a part of King Adventure. He'd had as much a part in making the camp successful as Jericho had and they got along fine usually, two men with like minds, though they were separated by nearly two decades in age.

They were family, Jericho realized. But then, so were all of the guys who worked for him. Misfits mostly—men with no families, nowhere to go. Some had seen combat and didn't feel comfortable around lots of people. Some had simply yearned for wide-open spaces and a job with fewer restrictions than the nine-to-five route. Whatever their reasons, they'd all come here looking for work and wound up finding a place to call home.

And until this very moment, he and Sam hadn't butted heads over anything important in years.

"She seems like a nice kid, is all," he was saying. "And I don't want to think you're taking her on the mountain just to break her spirit."

Jericho felt a rush of irritation swamp him as he looked at one of his oldest friends. The fact that guilt was riding right under that irritation was only more frustrating. Did the man have to read him so well? "Damn it, Sam, I would have thought you'd not only understand but agree with me on this. Did you get a good look at her? You can see for yourself she doesn't belong here."

He snorted and shoved his hands into his jeans pockets. "I see nothing of the kind. I see you trying to get rid of a pretty woman because she makes you twitchy."

Twitchy didn't even begin to cover what Daisy did to him, Jericho thought, but damned if he'd admit to it. "Bull. I'm doing this *for* her, not *to* her."

"Yeah, you can say that all you want, but I've known you too long to buy into it." Sam shook his head and smiled knowingly. "That girl in there gets to you and you don't like it, so you figure to haul her ass out before she settles in."

Another shot too damn close to home, Jericho told himself and wondered if he'd somehow lost his poker face over the past couple of years of civilian life. Or maybe he was only transparent to people who'd known him so damn long. "It's not just that—"

Sam snorted again.

"Fine, you want me to admit it? She's hot. Hot enough that I've been on edge since she fell onto the lawn practically at my feet." He scowled into the distance, where the rising sun was just kissing the treetops. "Hell, she's a walking forest fire. But it's more than that. I served with her brother. Her *dead* brother. Now she's looking to me to provide a kind of link to him or something."

"That so bad?" Sam countered. "Everybody needs connections, JK. She lost her brother. Isn't she entitled to whatever it is she can get from us? From you? Don't we at least owe her the straight-up chance at getting what she wants?"

Jericho really hated to be lectured. Especially when the lecturer had a point.

"I saw you at dinner last night," Sam went on, his voice a little lower, filled with what almost sounded like understanding. "And off the subject, the girl cooks a mean pot roast—but I saw the way you looked at her."

That's just great, Jericho told himself. He'd gone so far as to be fantasizing over a woman at his dinner table—and doing it obviously enough for others to notice. Just one more reason to get Daisy gone. His legendary control was clearly dissolving, which was something he would not put up with.

"Drop it, Sam."

"I'm not saying I blame you any. She's a pretty one. But if you're thinking she's one of your weekend types, you can think again." The older man narrowed his eyes. "That's a good girl. A nice one. And she deserves better than a quick roll in the hay and a one-way ticket off the mountain."

He knew that. Knew that Daisy Saxon had "complications" written all over her. It was just part of why he wanted her the hell away from him. He wasn't looking for complicated. He preferred simple.

"Sergeant Major," Jericho grumbled, "when the hell did you turn into a nanny?"

"I'm sayin' what I'm sayin'. And part of what I'm sayin' is that you owe that girl's brother better than to treat her badly." Sam glared at him. "You give her a real shot on the mountain, JK. See if she's got what it takes to make it here. And be honest with yourself about why you want her gone."

While Sam stalked off toward the two-storied barn several hundred yards away, Jericho was left to fume in silence. Been a long time since anyone had dressed him down like that and damned if he cared for it.

He made his own rules now. He hadn't answered to anyone since he left the Corps and he wasn't about to start now. Yes, he thought, he owed Daisy Saxon something because of her brother.

But was what he owed her a job? Or was it getting her back to the world she belonged in? Off the mountain. Back in the city. He was torn now. Undecided when before it had all seemed so clear. Maybe he *was* being too hard on her. Maybe he should give her a chance and just learn to live with his body's discomfort when he was around her. Maybe...

"We're ready!"

He turned to look at the back door of the house as Daisy stepped off the porch. He sighed. She looked great. And completely inappropriate for the hike they had stretching out in front of them. If he'd had any doubts a minute or so ago, they were gone now. She was very clearly not the outdoorsy type of woman.

Her hair was pulled into a long tail at the back of her neck. Her face was bright as a new penny and wreathed in smiles. She was wearing designer jeans with a red sweater and shiny black boots with a two-inch heel, and she had a duffel bag slung over one shoulder while she cradled her fake dog with her other arm.

Jericho sighed. Nope, he thought. He was doing the right thing.

She just didn't belong.

Four

Daisy was willing to put up with the backpack Jericho had forced her to wear. She had even thanked him for the heavy jacket he borrowed for her from Kevin, the cook. She had dutifully changed into sneakers when he threatened to break off the sweet heels on her favorite boots. But she absolutely refused to leave Nikki behind.

"Everything's new to her, and she'll be afraid without me." She continued the argument even though he'd surrendered ten minutes ago. She glared at his broad back as he hiked five feet ahead of her through the trees.

He didn't even turn around to look at her when he said, "That dog has no business on the trail. She'll get eaten or lost or God knows what."

"No, she won't," Daisy insisted, snuggling Nikki's

cheek to her own. The tiny dog's rapid heartbeat felt like the brush of butterfly wings against her palm. "I'll take good care of her."

"Unbelievable."

At least she thought that was what he muttered but she couldn't be sure. He was certainly grumpy on a hike. He didn't even seem to be charmed by the beauty all around them. Daisy was, though. Barely gone from the lodge, they'd been swallowed up in the thick woods and one look back over her shoulder assured her that she couldn't even see Jericho's home anymore. If he hadn't been with her, she'd wander through the forest for days without finding her way, which made her a little anxious. But a moment later, she dismissed the worry—since she *did* have Jericho—and gave in to her surroundings.

Her head swung back and forth as she tried to take in everything at once. The floor of the forest was spongy and soft, making her feel almost as if she were on springs when she walked. Layers of pine needles cushioned the ground and sent up a fresh scent every time she took a step. The trees all around her seemed to scrape the sky.

As they walked on, there was the occasional clearing where late-blooming wildflowers struggled to survive in the cooling weather. And then there was the sky. She didn't think she'd ever seen anything that shade of blue. Down in the city, there was so much smog and so many buildings, the tiny scraps of sky you could see were never that beautiful. It made even the relentless walking more enjoyable. When she fell, landing face-first on the cushiony ground, she could only blame it on not watching her step.

"Ow!"

Nikki jumped from her grasp instantly and darted into the undergrowth before Daisy could call the dog back. Then Jericho was at her side in an instant, grabbing hold of the shoulder of her red sweater and pulling her to her feet in one smooth motion.

"Are you all right?"

"I'm fine," she muttered, more embarrassed than hurt. She brushed pine needles, dirt and who knew what else off the front of her sweater and the knees of her jeans. "I was watching the sky, and— Nikki honey, come back here!"

"Keep your eyes on where you're going, all right?"

"I will, it was just pretty and— Nikki!"

The dog barked from somewhere nearby and Jericho muttered a curse.

"I scared her when I fell," Daisy said in defense of her dog. "I think I tripped on a rock or something."

"You sure you're all right?"

"I'm fine. Just humiliated." The little dog raced toward her then and hopped on its hind legs as if doing a celebrational dance. "There you are, sweet girl! You scared Mommy running off like that."

"Mommy?"

"She's all mine," Daisy said with a grin as she bent down to attach a bright-red leash to the chest halter the little dog wore.

"Right." Jericho shook his head. "Can we go now?"

"Sure." She was determined to be upbeat and positive through this entire experience. She'd earn her place on this mountain if it killed her. "I'm sure I can walk another ten miles no problem. We've already come about that far, right?"

He raised one eyebrow. "We've gone about two miles so far."

"Really? Well, that's disappointing," she said, silently acknowledging the aching burn in her thighs and calves. "It really seemed longer."

"You're telling me," Jericho muttered, then started walking again. Daisy fell into step behind him, keeping one eye on the trail and the other eye on Nikki.

Though being at that altitude made talking, climbing and breathing all at the same time a little difficult, Daisy struggled on.

"I looked you up, you know, before I came here," she called out.

"Is that right?"

She frowned when he kept walking without so much as a glance at her. He couldn't have let her know any more clearly that he wasn't interested in what she was saying. But that didn't silence her.

"Well, not just you, but this place. The mountain itself. Did you know that grizzly bears used to live here?" Just saying that aloud had her checking the tree line warily even though she knew the animal was mostly extinct in California now.

"Yep," he said, "I knew."

"And," she added, "did you know that King Mountain is the largest piece of acreage bordered on wilderness area that's still in private hands?"

"Knew that, too."

She frowned and chewed at her bottom lip. Of course he knew, it was his land after all, but he could at least pretend to be polite about listening. "I saw a waterfall, too, on one of the maps I looked at. Are we going to see that on this trip?"

"Might."

Aggravating man, she thought as her temper began to simmer. He was deliberately not talking to her. Probably trying to make her be quiet by his lack of response. Clearly, he didn't know her very well. Her mother used to say that Daisy could talk to a stump. Which, she mused, she actually was doing.

"I still can't believe you own your own mountain," she said, shaking her head, as if trying to wrap her mind around it. "I mean, did you know your name is on actual maps? King Mountain."

"Yeah," he muttered, "I know. Did you know that you shouldn't talk so much on the trail?"

"Really? Why?"

He turned and glared at her over his shoulder. "There are wild animals out here. You might want to pay attention to your surroundings."

"But you're here."

"Yeah, I am…"

"What kind of wild animals?" she asked after a moment's pause in which she thoroughly scanned the surrounding tree line for any sign of slavering beasts hidden in the shrubbery. "There aren't grizzlies, I know, but…"

"There are still black bears. And brown bears," he said. "Not to mention coyotes, the occasional wolf and oh, yeah, mountain lions."

"Seriously?"

"Thought you researched the mountain."

"I did but—" Nowhere had she read about mountain lions. How had she not considered that?

"Still glad you brought that dog?" he asked.

Visions of Nikki being carried off by God knew what flew through Daisy's mind and she reined in the dog's leash as she hurried her steps to close the distance between her and Jericho. He might be surly, but he knew what he was doing out here and she was pretty sure he wouldn't let her or Nikki get eaten.

"More glad now than before," she told him when she was no more than an arm's reach from him. "She's better off with me. Where I can make sure she stays safe."

"And who's making sure *you're* safe?" he asked, shooting her a sidelong glance.

"That would be you," she told him, giving him a bright smile.

"I'm not here to help, you know," he said. "It's my job to be with you on this trail. But I'm here to see how you handle yourself out here. I'm the observer. The taskmaster."

"I know that, but—" They came around a sharp bend in the trail and Daisy stopped dead, conversation forgotten. "That's just gorgeous," she whispered, the words sliding from her on a breathy sigh.

She felt him come up right beside her. Felt the heat of him reaching out for her, felt the sizzle of awareness that ricocheted through her in response. But she didn't take her gaze off the picture in front of her.

A clearing. Knee-high grasses, spotted with deep-red wildflowers. And moving through it with a sort of balletic grace was a deer. As if it weren't quite real, the animal stepped through splotches of sunshine and dipped its great head to nibble at the grass. Caught in the moment, Daisy reached out, took Jericho's hand in hers and squeezed it, almost reassuring herself that she was really there. Really seeing something so beautiful and wild and perfect.

His long fingers wrapped around hers and he held on for a breathless moment and the two of them were linked—suspended in time.

Then Nikki barked and the deer lifted its massive head, looked directly at them, then bolted in the opposite direction.

As if the dog had spooked more than just the deer, Jericho dropped Daisy's hand and said brusquely, "We should get moving."

Her heart was pounding, thundering in her chest until she felt as if every breath was a battle. Her skin was still humming, as though his skin was still pressed to hers. The heat of his touch slipped inside her and Daisy folded her fingers into a fist, futilely trying to hold on to the sensation. When she could trust her voice, she asked, "Are we really going ten more miles?"

"No. Just a couple more before we make camp."

Though she was grateful, the thought of even two more miles made Daisy really want to whimper, but she controlled herself. She couldn't afford to look weak. Couldn't let him see that her legs were already aching and her shoulders hurt from the weight of the stupid backpack. She was going to prove to him that she could fit into his world, then she would be that much closer to what she wanted.

"Only a couple?" she forced herself to say. "What're we waiting for?"

One of his black eyebrows lifted into a high arch and he gave her a speculative look that hid as much as it said. But after another moment or two, he simply said, "Keep the dog quiet. Some animals won't be startled by it barking. They'll be curious. Maybe hungry."

She gasped. "You're doing that on purpose, aren't you? Trying to scare me."

"You should be scared, Daisy. This isn't a city park. This is the wilderness and the animals you'll meet out here aren't the kind you're used to seeing on TV or in the movies. They don't laugh and dance and they don't like people."

"I'm not an idiot," she told him. "I know that wild animals are just that. Wild. I also know I'm a little out of my element—"

He choked out a laugh at that one.

"*But,*" she continued doggedly, "I'm going to do this."

He shrugged and walked off with long, lazy strides. "If you're bound and determined, then get a move on."

She tamped down the exasperation bubbling inside her and swallowed back a sea of retorts she wanted to hurl at his back. Then she realized that he was getting way too far ahead of her. So Daisy held Nikki a little closer and hurried to catch up to the man who was, at the moment, the very center of her world.

Why wasn't she making him crazy? Jericho asked himself for at least the tenth time in the past couple of hours. When he was out on the mountain, he liked silence. Sure, some of his clients were incapable of being quiet for very long at a stretch, but Daisy Saxon was in a class all by herself. The woman hadn't stopped her rambling conversations since they'd left the house.

She talked about the forest, about her former job, her late brother and the boyfriend who had not only left her for her friend, but also had stolen her credit card on the way out the door. That story had just amazed him, though he hadn't commented. The man had to have been an idiot to walk out on Daisy, in Jericho's opinion, and she was better off without him.

And when she wasn't talking about her own life, she was pestering him with questions about his. She talked about the sky, what kind of music she liked best and how she planned to make him that fudge mountain cake of hers as soon as they got back to the lodge.

His ears had been ringing for hours and damned if he hadn't half enjoyed listening to her. She was interested in everything. Had an opinion on everything as well and wasn't afraid to voice it.

But in all the ranting, he acknowledged silently, she hadn't complained *once*. And that surprised him. It wasn't often Jericho was surprised by anything. So the fact that Daisy could make him rethink his original opinion of her was astonishing.

The last bunch of clients he'd had out on the mountain included a bank manager, who had prided himself on his rugged individuality, had wept like a baby after a few hours on the trail. He'd bagged the wilderness trip and called it quits as quickly as he could.

Yet Daisy, not a peep.

He knew she was tired. Her steps were less brisk and even her attempts at conversation were beginning to slow to a trickle. But she hadn't stopped. Hadn't asked to rest. Hadn't whined about a damn thing, and Jericho had to admit he admired her for it. She was more than he'd thought. But in the long run, did that mean anything?

She stumbled and, instinctively, he reached out and grabbed her elbow to steady her. Just touching her sent another zing of heat shooting through him, so he let go of her fast and when he spoke he was harsher than he should have been.

"Watch your damn step or you're going to break a leg or something and I'll have to hump you out."

"Hump?"

"Carry," he explained curtly.

She nodded. "Right. Sorry. I was watching Nikki."

"Let me watch the damn dog," he told her in little more than a growl. "You watch where you put your feet."

"Wow, King Crabby." She didn't wait for his response. "You really don't want me out here, do you?"

"I just think it's a mistake."

"Yes, so you've told me, but it's not." She turned her face up to him and a brilliant smile curved her luscious mouth. "And admit it, I'm doing better than you thought I would. Go ahead," she urged, "say I'm doing well."

He blew out a breath. "The fall notwithstanding, yeah, you've done all right so far."

"Thank you! What a nice thing to say."

He chuckled in spite of himself. She was still smiling and her eyes shone with humor and pleasure in the moment. She had to be exhausted and irritated with his behavior, but damned if she didn't keep her own spirits up.

"You're an odd one, aren't you?"

"Not odd," she corrected, "just different. For example, when someone else is crabby, I don't get crabby back. I try not to let their mood affect mine."

"Uh-huh," he said, picking up on her not-so-subtle jab. "That was a nice shot. You've got good aim."

"I know," she said, glancing at her dog to make sure the tiny thing was still in sight. "So how much farther?"

One dark eyebrow winged up. "Tired?"

"Nope." She lifted her chin and met his gaze. "I could go for hours yet. Just curious."

"Sure," he said with a shake of his head. "All right. Listen."

"To what?"

He sighed. "You have to be quiet to listen."

"Right." She snapped her mouth closed and frowned in concentration. After a moment or two her eyes slowly widened. "What is that? It sounds like hundreds of people talking in whispers."

"It's the river," he told her. "Just around that bend there, by the crooked pine. We'll set up camp there tonight."

She sighed heavily and he heard the unspoken relief in the sound.

Still, he had to give her points, if only internally. As close to the edge of collapse as she might feel, she wasn't letting him know it. The woman was running on sheer grit and determination. And that was something Jericho approved of. He even thought that maybe he'd dismissed her too easily, judging her by her looks and her clothes and telling himself that no one that pretty, that dainty, was made of stern enough stuff to make it in his world.

The problem was, he didn't want to be wrong about her. His life would be much easier if she just failed this little test and took herself back to where she came from.

By the time they made camp, Daisy was clearly exhausted, but worked right through it. She helped him lay out sleeping bags, then watched as Jericho set up a campfire ring. He set large rocks in a small circle, while clearing away any nearby brush that might catch with a stray spark.

When he was finished, he laid a couple more flat-sided rocks inside the ring and built a campfire. Once the flames were going, Daisy took over, surprising him again. She carried the battered tin coffeepot down to the nearby stream, filled it with water and set it on one of the rocks to boil.

"You almost seem to know what you're doing," he commented.

"Well, I was a Girl Scout like a hundred years ago," she said quietly. "I went on a couple of overnight trips and I can still remember watching our troop leader setting up camp." She flashed him a smile and in the firelight, her features were soft, ethereal and downright beautiful.

Darkness surrounded their campsite and stars were glittering like jewels flung carelessly across the sky. Nikki was curled up on a sleeping bag and he and Daisy sat across the fire from each other.

While she waited for the water to boil, she reached

into her backpack and drew out a couple of large, covered plastic dishes.

"What's that?"

"Dinner!" She grinned at him. "I made more beef pasties late last night to bring along. And I've got some great corn chowder here, too. All we need to do is heat it up."

Surprised again, he shook his head. "You realize this isn't supposed to be a picnic."

"We have to eat and I just thought it would be easier this way. Don't worry," she told him with a tender touch of sarcasm. "Tomorrow we can chew on bark if you insist. But tonight, dinner's on me."

A short laugh shot from his throat. "Chew on bark?"

She tipped her head to one side and looked at him with a bemused expression on her face. "You should do that more often."

"Eat bark?"

"No," she said. *"Smile."*

Jericho watched her then as she expertly scooped coffee into the pot, then sat back to let it boil on the edge of the fire. "You keep surprising me," he said after another moment of shared silence. "I expected you to fold early today."

"I know."

"That why you hung in?"

"Partially, I suppose," she admitted, drawing her knees up and wrapping both arms around them. "And partially to prove to myself I could do it." She gave him a rueful smile. "I'm not saying my legs aren't screaming at me, or that I'm not so tired I couldn't flop backward over a boulder and fall right asleep, but I did it."

He nodded, willing to give her that much at least. "You did."

"So, does that mean I've proved myself?"

"Not yet," he said, reluctantly thinking about what she had to face on the coming day. She'd be a lot more exhausted tomorrow night than she was at this moment, he thought and realized that he didn't like thinking about that. "You've got to make it through the full two days and nights."

"I will, you know."

Her voice was steel covered in velvet. Soft but strong, and the purpose in her eyes flashed at him in the firelight. "I'm convinced you'll give it a good shot," Jericho said.

"That's something, anyway," she mused.

Just beyond their campsite, the river rushed through the darkness, swiftly moving water sounding like hundreds of sighs rising together. A cold wind swept through the trees and had Daisy tugging the edges of her borrowed coat closer together.

"I can't believe it's so cold up here. In L.A., it's still warm at night."

"We'll probably have first snow by the end of the month."

"Can't wait to see it," she said, her eyes still glittering at him.

"We'll see." Jericho reached out, tapped the coffeepot carefully with his fingertips and, satisfied, picked up a cloth to grab the pot by its curved handle. He poured each of them a cup of the steaming black brew, then watched as Daisy pulled a cook pan closer and dumped her corn chowder into it to heat.

"It'll be ready in a few minutes," she said, picking up her coffee cup for a sip. "So while we wait, tell me about Brant."

That caught him off guard and Jericho's gaze snapped to hers. "What do you mean?"

"I mean, what was it like over there? Was Brant happy where he was—before he died?"

Five

Frowning, Jericho said, "Happy? Nobody's happy on a battlefield."

"You know what I mean," she persisted.

He stared into his coffee as if looking for answers. Finally, he said, "Yeah, I do. The thing is, people always ask that question, but they don't really want to know what a war zone is like."

"I do. I want to know what my brother's life was like before it ended."

Lifting his gaze to hers, he kept his face deliberately blank. "Brant did his job. He was good at it. He was well-liked."

When she opened her mouth to ask another question, he cut her off. "Daisy, let it go."

"I can't," she told him, regret shining in her whiskey-brown eyes. "I have to know."

Jericho sighed a little, took a drink of his coffee and told her what he could, with some judicious editing. Civilians would never understand what it was like in a combat zone. Would never know the moments of pure adrenaline rush, followed by the searing hours of boredom. They wouldn't understand what it was to put your life in someone else's hands and to trust them with yours, or the fierce loyalty that the military experienced on a daily basis.

And how could they?

So he kept it simple and as vague as he could possibly get away with. "The days were blistering hot and the nights were so cold," he said, "you half expected to wake up with icicles on your nose."

"Brant complained about the cold in an e-mail once. I sent blankets," she told him. "To everyone in his unit."

"I know," he said, giving her a real smile now as his memory raced back in time. "There was a lot of celebrating that day. After that, every mail call, Brant's friends huddled close, wanting to get in on one of your packages from home."

"I'm glad," she said, though her features were wreathed in sadness.

He could give her this much. To let her know that her efforts had been appreciated by more than just her brother. "Touches of home are really cherished when they're hard to come by. I can tell you all of the hot chocolate and instant coffees and dry foods you sent made him real popular. MREs get pretty tasteless after a while."

She nodded. "Meals Ready to Eat. Brant told me

about them. He actually had me taste one once. It was tuna casserole." She grimaced.

Jericho laughed. "It's an acquired taste. Actually, I brought some with me on this trip, just in case. So if you want to—"

"No, thanks," she said, reaching out to give her chowder a stir.

The scent of the soup filled the air and Jericho could admit at least to himself that he was relieved she'd brought along provisions for tonight. What she'd packed looked a hell of a lot better than the MREs.

"You were with him when he died, weren't you?"

The question was so softly asked, posed with such hesitation, the sound of the river nearly drowned it out. But Jericho heard her and also caught the worried expression on her face, as if she were half afraid to hear his answer.

He was stepping onto dangerous ground here. Might as well have been a minefield. Not enough information and she'd still be thirsty for more. Too much information and her dreams would be haunted. No information at all and she'd rag on him until he gave her something.

Again, he kept it simple. "Yeah, I was."

"He wasn't...in pain, was he?"

If he had been, Jericho wouldn't have told her, but as it stood, he could be honest about this at least. "No, he wasn't. He talked about you. Asked me to help you out if you ever needed it."

"My little brother trying to protect me," she mused and looked at him. The trail of a single tear coursed down her cheek like a drop of silver sliding over porcelain.

"That's what brothers do," he said, thinking of his own brothers. Jefferson, Justice and Jesse. He hadn't seen much of them since he'd come home.

By choice, really. He'd wanted, needed, the solitude of the mountain and his brothers had respected that. Of course, he thought with an inward smile, his sisters-in-law were less understanding and had managed to drag him off the mountain for a few family things.

And on those rare occasions, he had been struck by a surprising jolt of envy that had shamed him some. Hell, he was glad for his brothers. They were all happy, doing what they loved doing—raising families. Jericho had decided as a kid he wasn't interested in living his life in the traditional manner. But seeing his brothers with their families always left him feeling a little like the outsider.

"You have three brothers, don't you?"

"Yeah," he said, jolting from his thoughts.

"Are you close?"

"Used to be," he admitted. "Still are, really, but we grew up, we each chose a different path and we all got busy building lives. Jefferson lives in Ireland now, so no, we don't see much of each other anymore."

"That's a shame," she said, spooning chowder into two bowls and handing him one. "Family is important. It's the *only* important thing."

Which made him remember that now that she'd lost her brother, Daisy had no family. Though he didn't see much of his, he couldn't really imagine life without them, either.

In the firelight, Daisy looked lovely, delicate, with her soft hair falling over her shoulders, reflections of the flames dancing in her wide, brown eyes. She ate her soup and thought her thoughts and couldn't possibly have known that just looking at her was making him... *want*.

Which just naturally brought to mind Sam's warnings before they'd left the lodge that morning. Maybe the older man was right. Maybe Jericho was just being twitchy and not being fair to her.

But, hell, it was *his* mountain.

Who said he had to be fair?

Jericho watched Daisy maneuver her way carefully across a rope bridge in the early morning light and found himself silently rooting for her. She was a surprise in many ways. Not only did she have spine, she seemed inherently incapable of quitting. She wasn't afraid to try something—take a risk—if it meant getting herself closer to her goal.

Plus her incessant good humor was starting to rub off on him. Hard to maintain a stern demeanor when you were faced down by a brilliant smile every time you turned around. Yeah, she wasn't what he'd expected at all. And though his original opinion that she didn't belong on the mountain still held, he had to give her credit for a hell of a lot more than he would have guessed.

Frowning, he watched her take small steps and then slide her hands along the top rope of the bridge. He'd had several obstacle-course projects made and installed before he'd opened the camp. This was one of his personal favorites.

A single, heavy rope was the base of the bridge with

more ropes angling up from the base in a *V*. Stretched between two tall pines, the bridge was only four feet off the ground, so anyone falling wasn't going to die. Though the bruises gathered would be a painful reminder of failure. He'd seen plenty of men topple off that bridge, cursing their own clumsiness and ineptitude, but Daisy was making it. Sure, she was taking twice as long as most people to complete the course, but careful didn't mean failure.

The wind lifted her long ponytail and snapped it like a flag. Her jeans were dirty and her hands were curled so tightly around the guide rail ropes that her knuckles were white. But she was doing it.

He stood below her, watching every step and wanting her to succeed.

"Why does it have to sway so much?" she demanded, not risking a look at him but keeping her gaze fixed, just as he'd told her to, on her final goal.

"It's a *rope,*" he reminded her, "bound to sway."

"I don't understand how this is a survival thing," she muttered, scooting her clenched fists farther along the guide ropes. Her feet slid forward another inch or two.

"If you have to get to the other side of a river fast, you'd understand."

"Be faster to swim," she pointed out and gave him a fleeting grin.

"You're doing fine. Pay attention to where you're putting your feet. One in front of the other."

"I know," she said, swallowing hard. "Good thing you made me change out of my boots before we left the lodge. Never would have done this in them."

He smiled to himself and kept pace with her. The

dog at the end of the leash he held barked and pranced and in general made a racket as it tried, futilely, to reach Daisy. "How can you concentrate with this dog shooting off its mouth?"

"I'm used to it. Nikki's very chatty," she admitted and one of her feet slipped off the rope. She gasped but caught herself before she could fall. "Whoa, boy. That was close."

"It was." And he didn't want to think about the feeling that had jolted through him with her misstep. He'd watched dozens, hundreds of people walk this rope bridge and never once before had he had a vested interest in how they managed it.

Lots of them had taken tumbles, too, and it hadn't bothered him a bit. Yet damned if he wanted Daisy falling.

Shaking his head, Jericho acknowledged that he was having a problem. He was supposed to be discouraging her from passing these little tests. Instead, he'd helped her as much as he could. Maybe it was because of her brother, Jericho told himself. Maybe he felt as if he owed her something. But then again, maybe it was just because he wanted her.

He could admit that much to himself. And whatever he was feeling for her had only intensified since that morning. He and Daisy had gone to sleep the night before, lying on opposite sides of the fire.

But the nights were cold at this altitude and when Jericho woke up this morning, it was to find a curvy, beautiful, warm woman snuggled up close to him, spooning herself along the front of his body. Which completely explained the dream he'd been having, filled with images of hot, sweaty sex. He woke up to an aching groin and his blood pumping fast and thick through his veins. Ever since that moment of wakefulness, his body had been strung taut as a violin string.

"Jericho?"

He snapped out of his thoughts and focused anew. "No more talking. Just concentrate."

"Okay," she countered, keeping her gaze fixed on the end of the rope bridge, "if I can't talk, then you talk to me."

He shook his head. "You're unbelievable."

"That's not talking," she said.

"Fine," he said, tugging on the leash to pull the dog back into line, "I'll talk. Let's see…we've got a batch of clients arriving end of next week. Only be here for a long weekend."

"Who are they?" she asked as her foot slipped. "Whoops!"

"Concentrate."

"Right. I'm good. Fine. Keep talking."

"They're part of a law firm from Indiana," he said. Remembering how the last bunch of lawyers had performed, Jericho wasn't looking forward to it. Lawyers seemed incapable of unwinding. Even in the wilderness, they were wired, tense. Without their PDAs and cell phones, they acted like spoiled children missing a favorite toy. They didn't like being in the outdoors and usually resented being sent here by their companies.

"Not looking forward to it," he said. "Lawyers complain too much."

"True enough. I'm almost across."

She was. Close enough to the end that she was liable

to start speeding up to get it over with. "Slow down. Careful steps."

"I am, I am," she told him in an undertone. "So if you don't like lawyers why have them here?"

"They're paying customers, like anyone else."

"Uh-huh. Did you ever think of opening up the camp to kids?"

"Kids?"

She laughed loud and long, and the joyful sound of it rose up through the trees like smoke. He narrowed his gaze on her and scowled when she set herself swaying wildly with her laughter. "You sound so horrified!"

"Knock it off and pay attention to what you're doing."

"Oh, relax! I'm good. In fact," she added, her voice rising, "I'm *done!*" She stepped onto the platform at the end of the rope bridge and threw both hands into the air in a victory pose. "I did it! By myself!"

Sure, he thought, not counting his shouted instructions and constant watchfulness. But damned if he could deny her the victory dance. "Yeah, you did. Enough celebrating. Now we go hit the climbing wall."

"Wow, way to pop my balloon."

"You want to be congratulated?" he asked. "Do it all, then we'll talk. Now climb down, take this silly excuse for a dog and let's hike to the wall."

"Climbing a wall?" Her features fell like a kid faced with a pop quiz. That only lasted a second or two, though. She lifted that stubborn chin of hers and said, "Fine. Let's do it."

"Damned if I'm not starting to like you," he said and

had the satisfaction of seeing surprise flicker across her face.

"Thanks."

He watched her climb down from the platform and walk toward him with a spring in her step. The little dog on the end of the red leash jumped and pulled, trying to get to her, so Jericho dropped the leash and the poodle raced to Daisy. The tiny dog was scooped up and cuddled while it wiggled in ecstasy.

Jericho thought briefly that he couldn't blame the animal for the reaction. In fact, he almost envied the ridiculous little dog.

"Jericho?"

Her voice sounded confused. "What?"

She smiled at him. "Just wondering where you were. I was talking to you and you just zoned out."

Well, that was humiliating. "I was thinking about the wall," he lied.

"Oh. Okay." She sounded disappointed now, but added, "Let's go and get it over with then."

Get it over with. Hmm. That had been his plan in bringing her up here. Walk her through, watch her fail and get her off the mountain. What the plan was now, he wasn't sure.

"So," she asked as Nikki trotted ahead of them, "why'd you freak when I suggested you bring kids up here?"

"I didn't freak," he said, and assured himself that was true. A man who'd spent as many years in the military as he had wouldn't be "freaked" by the idea of having kids run amok at his camp. "I was just…surprised by the suggestion."

She pushed a low-hanging bough out of her way, ducked her head to pass under and said, "I don't know why. In my old neighborhood, there were dozens of kids who would have loved to be here for a week or two." She took a moment to glance around and he followed her gaze.

Early morning light tipped the edges of the pine branches. A soft wind sighed through the trees and a bright blue jay shot through the air like a colorful bullet. The woods never failed to center him. To give him the sense of peace that was as elusive as it was sought after. Just the thought of having dozens of teenagers rampaging through the forest he considered a sanctuary was enough to make him grit his teeth. But Daisy clearly liked the idea.

"Kids in the city have no idea really. What a world with no sidewalks or freeways looks like," she said wistfully. "They've never seen the stars the way you can up here and I'm sure they've never heard silence so deep."

"I'm not set up to have kids here," he said, guiding her around a stack of boulders. "This is a leadership camp. We train CEOs and other corporate types how to use teamwork. How to count on each other and learn from each other. How to overcome negatives and turn them into positives."

"All of which kids would benefit from learning," she pointed out.

"Not my job," he insisted. What the hell would he do with a dozen or more kids running wild on the mountain? Hell, just the liability issues alone would be staggering.

"You talk tough, but you're not such a hard guy, Jericho King."

One dark eyebrow lifted when he glanced back at her. "Don't kid yourself."

"Oh, I'm not," she said, smiling into his scowling face. "See, I've talked with Kevin, your cook—who is, I hesitate to point out, barely more than a kid himself—"

"He's twenty."

"My point exactly," she said smugly. "Anyway, he told me that not only did you hire him here with no references, but that you're also loaning him the money to go to the Culinary Institute of America. So he can be the chef he dreams of being."

"That's different." And real damn irritating to find out that Kevin was shooting his mouth off. Jericho was going to have to have a talk with the kid.

"How is it different?"

He wasn't sure. Kevin had wandered up to the mountain a little more than a year ago looking for work. He'd been scrawny and exhausted from carrying around a chip on his shoulder for so long. He'd had a rough life but he'd stood up to it and made himself into a good kid despite the odds. He'd proven himself in the kitchen so quickly that Jericho had kept him on. Now, he was helping the kid get a start. No big deal.

Gritting his teeth, he said, "The difference is, I didn't go hunting down a bunch of kids to sponsor. Kevin found us. He just showed up and wouldn't leave. Besides, he stopped being a kid a long time ago. He's been on his own since he was fifteen and—"

"And you gave him a chance to be what he wanted to

be," Daisy said, laying one hand on his forearm. "I'm just saying it would be nice if other kids had the same opportunity."

Reluctantly, Jericho pulled free of her touch and said abruptly, "Maybe you should stop worrying about other people and give a thought or two to passing your own test."

That kept her quiet for a while, but in the silence, Jericho's mind raced with the thoughts and ideas she'd planted there.

Damn it.

Six

Daisy was exhausted and every bone and muscle in her body ached like a bad tooth, but beneath the misery was a sense of accomplishment. She'd done it. So far she'd passed his silly tests and was well on her way to earning herself a place at his lodge. He wouldn't be able to send her away now and she was that much closer to having the time to seduce him, make a child and have a family.

Over the past couple of days, she'd gotten to know Jericho King better than she would have by dating him for a month. Even though he resisted conversation, she'd been able to pry words out of him. And she'd had the opportunity to watch him. To study him. There was a sense of quiet confidence about him that was very attractive, and she had to admit that his stoic standoffishness only added to it.

There was a closeness between them now that under normal circumstances would never have happened so quickly. They'd worked together to make camp, to eat, to live. They'd slept curled up together...well, she thought, they had as soon as she'd moved over to him for warmth and stayed to snuggle. They'd talked more than most couples did in a week and they'd each learned something about the other, she told herself. He had learned that she wasn't going to quit and go away.

And she had learned that he was unlike any other man she'd ever known. He seemed so solitary. So comfortable with his aloneness that Daisy was drawn closer and closer in an attempt to breach the walls he'd erected around himself so completely.

"These plants are edible," he was saying, "if you dig them up and pound the root. Won't be tasty, but it would keep you alive."

She nodded as if she were making mental notes, but she didn't care about edible roots. After all, she wouldn't be wandering the forest foraging for food. Once her test was finished, she'd be at the lodge and wouldn't step into the woods again without an experienced guide.

So instead, she watched the man. Jericho moved through the trees with a confidence born of self-reliance. He was a complex man. He hadn't wanted her here and hadn't made that a secret. But earlier, when he could have stood back and watched her struggle to climb the stupid wall—watched her fail—he hadn't. Instead, he'd planted one big hand under her behind and boosted her up enough that Daisy was able to scramble to the top and then drop over the other side, victorious.

She knew she never would have been able to make

that climb under her own steam. Hard to admit, but she simply didn't have the upper-body strength to accomplish the task.

"Your best bet, if you're lost in the woods, is to stay put," Jericho told her, glancing over his shoulder at her to make sure she was paying attention.

"Hug a tree. Right."

He shook his head and sighed. "But you wouldn't stay in one place, would you?"

"Probably not," she agreed cheerfully.

"Fine, so at least figure a way to mark your trail, so those looking for you can find you."

"Good idea." She gave him a wide smile and nodded as he showed her how to snap the ends of branches, or lay out rocks in an arrow pattern or— *Oh,* she thought, *let's face it.* If she was lost up here, she'd probably die. So she just wouldn't get lost.

"Wouldn't it be easier if I never left the lodge?" she asked.

"Yeah," he said, straightening up to look down at her. "But you will. It's in your nature. At least tell someone where you're going when you do."

"I can do that." She smiled again. "You realize that you just admitted that I'm staying on?"

"I'm considering it. You passed that test," he grudgingly admitted. "Though you still have to make the campfire yourself tonight and cook dinner you didn't bring with you, not to mention making it back to the lodge alive."

"I will."

He ignored that. "We'll find dinner, then the responsibility's on you."

"I can do it," she said firmly. "You'll see."

He shook his head and sighed a little.

"So," she asked, "what's next, *boss?*"

"We're headed home. We'll camp by the river again tonight on our way back."

"Let's go, Nikki," she called out and the little dog raced back to her, ears flapping, tiny feet flying across the pine needle–littered forest floor. Nikki paused in passing Jericho long enough to snarl at him, then leaped into Daisy's waiting arms.

He muttered something she thought it was just as well she hadn't quite heard. Then she asked, "So why did you help me? You could have let me fail, but you didn't."

He shrugged. "You would have made it. Eventually."

"No, I wouldn't," she admitted, though it cost her. "I was beat and just hanging by my fingertips when you gave me that boost. So why?"

He stopped, looked back at her and with his features set in an unreadable mask, said simply, "I respect guts. And you've got 'em."

When he turned around to continue leading the way to the river, Daisy inhaled sharply and felt a swell of pride rise up and burst inside her. It was a compliment casually given from a man who wasn't used to giving them at all. She couldn't have felt more proud and satisfied if he'd handed her a medal.

"You're going to kill the bunny?"

Jericho heard the outraged tremor in Daisy's voice and knew that he wouldn't be eating rabbit stew for supper. He'd set the snare early that morning when they broke camp, knowing they'd be camping here again tonight. And he'd been pleased to find a nice fat rabbit waiting to be dinner. He should have known it wouldn't be that easy.

He looked up into her wide, distressed eyes. "It was going to be dinner," he said.

"Oh, my God." She looked at him as if he were some mad dog serial killer. "I can't eat a bunny."

"Yeah. I'm getting that." The trapped rabbit scampered in place, desperately trying to get free of the rope that had tightened around one of its hind feet. Jericho looked at it and sighed. Then he bent down, loosened the rope and straightened up as the rabbit scooted off into the underbrush. Dry pine straw rustled under the animal's running feet and then there was silence, the only sound the rushing of the nearby river.

"I can't believe you did that," Daisy said as Jericho turned to face her.

He shrugged off her gratitude. "You weren't going to eat it so…"

"Thank you." She said it simply and honestly and Jericho nodded.

"You're welcome. Now, I'm going to go catch some trout for dinner—" He took a step, stopped and looked at her again. "Unless you've got a soft spot for fish, too."

"Nope. Pan-fried, baked, grilled, barbecued, even smooshed in a blender to make a mousse," she assured him. "I like it all."

"Good to know," he told her, shaking his head, "though here's something to keep in mind if you do end up with this job…"

"Yes?"

"I don't eat fish mousse."

"I'll make a note," she said, one corner of her mouth lifting into a half smile.

"Good." He turned around again, headed for the river, when Daisy stopped him by calling his name. "Yeah?"

She came to him in three long strides, wrapped her arms around his waist and gave him a hard hug. "Thank you. For the rabbit."

She was so close, so warm, pressed so intimately against him that all of Jericho's carefully designed reticence and resistance melted away. He'd been on edge for the past two days. Damn hard to maintain a tough shell around a woman so determinedly positive. But he'd cautioned himself to keep that safe distance between them. To not get drawn in by big amber eyes and a wide, welcoming smile.

But she was the kind of woman who got under a man's skin whether he wanted her there or not. Hell, he'd been fighting the urge to kiss her for hours. No, that urge had been with him since the moment she'd first stepped out of her car to sprawl across his lawn.

Now, with her lush curves leaning into him and her full, delectable mouth curved into a smile directed at him, how was he supposed to resist temptation? He doubted any red-blooded male would have been able to.

So he did what his body demanded and silently told his mind to butt out. Cupping her face in his palms, he held her still and watched as her eyes widened, softened, then slowly slid closed. A soft sigh of anticipation slipped from between her lips and Jericho kissed her.

The first taste of her was electric—incredible—and only fueled his hunger for more. He deepened the kiss and felt her surrender. Felt his own body begin a slow burn that enveloped him from head to toe. He held her face and moved his mouth over hers, parting her lips with his tongue, sliding into her mouth to capture the essence of her and draw it into himself.

His body tightened until he thought he might just explode from the agony of want. She moaned softly and he echoed that small sound and felt it build within him. Seconds ticked past, became minutes and might have spun into hours and he wouldn't have known. Wouldn't have sensed anything beyond the sensations roaring through him.

And that random thought was enough to bring him up and out of those feelings like a drowning man breaching the surface of a lake. He came up gasping, his heartbeat thundering in his chest, his blood pounding in his ears. He'd lost himself in her. Completely lost control in a way that hadn't happened to him in years. He didn't like it.

She opened her eyes and looked directly into his. Her mouth was soft and lush and he wanted nothing more than to taste her again. To lay her down on the forest floor and bury himself deep inside her. And because that craving was so strong, he took a single, deliberate step back. What the hell was he doing?

If he had any sense left at all, he'd get her off his mountain so damn fast, she'd be nothing but a blur of motion. But could he *not* give her the job because he didn't trust himself around her?

If he hired her, she'd be a constant source of temptation. If he didn't, wouldn't it be as if he'd sent her away for his own peace of mind? And wouldn't that make him a damn coward? He'd promised Brant Saxon to help his sister if she needed it.

He owed that kid, too, Jericho told himself and briefly recalled the eager young man who'd died too soon. The guilt still haunted him. Regret a constant companion. Was Jericho really going to turn his back on a promise made to a dying comrade? Daisy Saxon was here. Now. She needed the help he'd once promised to give.

And if he turned her away, it would be not because she'd failed, not because she didn't belong, but because Jericho King had encountered a woman who worried him.

Pushing those and other even more disturbing thoughts out of his mind, Jericho said, "Okay, that didn't just happen."

"It didn't?" She blinked at him and her eyes looked dazed.

He knew the feeling, but damned if he'd admit it. "No, it didn't. I'm the boss, you're the cook and that's where it all ends." He backed up again and half turned toward the river. He took a step, stopped and said over his shoulder, "Start the campfire. I'll go catch some fish for dinner."

As he walked away, Daisy lifted her fingers to her lips, enjoying the buzz of sensation lingering there and whispered, "Shouldn't be a problem starting the fire. I'm already going up in flames."

As they finished eating two hours later, stars swept across an indigo sky. He hadn't said much, Daisy mused. But then, he hadn't had to. She'd known exactly what he was thinking without him saying a word. Mostly because she was thinking the same thing. That kiss they'd shared had set off a chain reaction inside her that was still fizzing like a lit sparkler.

She'd come to him wanting a child. Now, she also wanted *him*. Which complicated the situation, but didn't really change anything. And oddly enough, the more he withdrew, the more she was drawn to him. What did that say about her?

When she gathered up the dishes and the pan she'd used to cook in and stacked them to carry to the river to wash, Jericho beat her to it. "I'm supposed to be doing all of this, remember?" she said. "Part of the whole survival-prove-you're-worthy test?"

He smirked at her, shook his head and carried the small load to the river. She fell into step behind him, determined to earn her way. She'd cooked a good dinner. At least, she was taking the fact that Jericho had eaten two of the fish himself as a good sign. But part of being outdoors, camping, was the cleanup and she wouldn't walk away from a job half done.

"Seriously, I'm cleaning up." She caught him at the river, took the plates and pan from him and dropped to her knees in the sand beside the rushing water. He crouched, too, and waited until she met his gaze to speak again.

"Accepting help doesn't mean you can't do it yourself."

"I know, but you're the one who said it was all up to me and I want to do this. I want to prove to you that I can do this job."

"You already have."

That stopped her. "Really?"

He shrugged, glanced away, then looked back at her and gave her a reluctant smile. "You're a good campfire cook."

"Yeah?" Ridiculously pleased, Daisy grinned. "Thanks, I did notice you ate a lot."

He laughed shortly. "Yeah, well, I've never had pan-fried trout with an herb sauce on the trail."

"Well, I brought along a few things from the lodge kitchen. With the right spices, you can make any meal a banquet…"

"So I'm learning."

It only took a few minutes to clean up the dishes and then they were walking back to the campfire, a companionable silence stretching out between them. Once the supplies had been put away, she sat down across from him. And the quiet lingered, becoming a tension that felt almost brittle. Daisy spoke up finally, because she never had been able to be quiet for long anyway.

Besides, it was time to find out exactly where she stood. She took a breath and faced the hard truth. She wanted to bring up the subject before he did, so that she could put her own spin on her less-than-stellar performance on his series of "tests."

He'd admitted that he was considering giving her the job, and if his decision was going to be based on her skills at his tests, then she wanted to defend herself before he made his final decision.

"About the rope bridge," she began. "I know I didn't go very fast, but I did eventually make it."

"You did."

"And I think if I'd had a little more time—" *like a million years,* she added silently "—I probably could have made it over the climbing wall on my own steam."

"You did better than some I've seen."

That was a bit lowering, she thought. Not good, she told herself, but better than some. Remembering just how poorly she'd done at the climbing, she could only feel sorry for whoever was actually worse than her.

"All in all, you did a good job," Jericho said and Daisy's thoughtful gaze narrowed on him. He shrugged. "Frankly, I didn't expect you to hold up as well as you have."

"Oooh. Big surprise." She smiled though, giving him silent encouragement to keep talking. If he was feeling generous toward her, she wanted to hear it.

"Right. Well." Firelight danced across his features, tossing shadow and light over the sharp planes of his face, making his guarded eyes even more difficult to read than they normally were. "Like I said, you've got spine. And that's important. Maybe more important than being able to climb a wall on your own."

"So I didn't lose points because you had to give me a boost?"

"No," he said. "You didn't ask for help, after all."

"True," she said eagerly. "And I wouldn't have."

"I know."

"So you said earlier, you were considering giving me the job." Daisy took another deep breath and blurted out her question. "Have you decided? Because if your mind still isn't made up, we can go back to the wall. I can try it again. I'm pretty sure I could do it with enough time…"

He chuckled briefly. "You really don't know the meaning of quit, do you?"

"Not when I really want something," she admitted.

"Yeah, I get that. So we don't have to go back to the wall."

"You've made your decision, then."

"I have." He nodded. "If you still want the job, you have it."

"Really?" Bubbles of excitement burst into life inside her. Funny, but she hadn't realized just how stressed she'd been about this. If he hadn't offered her the job, she'd had no backup plan. No way to convince him to let her stay. No strategy for getting him into bed and making her pregnant. Now, thankfully, one wouldn't be needed. She'd be here, on the mountain with him, every day.

Every night.

And soon, she'd have the baby, the family she wanted so badly. All she had to do was say yes.

"Of course I want the job," she told him.

"All right then, it's settled."

But he didn't look happy about it. "Can I ask you something?"

"Why not?"

"Why are you being nice to me?" Maybe she shouldn't push her luck. Maybe she should just accept his job offer at face value and count her blessings. But Daisy had to know why he'd decided in her favor. "We both know I never would have passed your tests if you hadn't helped me. So why did you?"

He scrubbed one hand across his face and blew out a breath. Then he shifted his gaze to the flames dancing in the fire ring to avoid looking directly at her. "I came out here expecting you to fail, like I said."

To be honest, so had she. "And..."

"And you didn't." He looked directly into her eyes. "You didn't quit. Didn't whine. Didn't give in. You kept pushing yourself no matter what."

Daisy smiled. "So blind stubbornness earns points with you?"

One corner of his mouth lifted briefly. "You could say that."

"Well, yay me."

"We'll see."

"About what?"

"How you'll work out around here. Yes, you're hired, but that's not saying you're going to want to stay."

"I won't quit." Not until she had what she'd come here for. Not until she was pregnant. Her gaze drifted to his mouth, his firm, soft lips and everything inside her tingled, as if her whole body had been asleep and was suddenly waking up. Then he started talking again and those tingles subsided just a bit.

"Like I said, I like your attitude. But know this. Stubborn might not be enough to keep you here when the snow starts flying and you're cut off from the main road for days at a time." He laid his forearm across one updrawn knee and looked at her across the fire. "It's not easy living up here. You're a woman not used to the quiet—"

"I like the quiet," she argued.

He laughed shortly. "You can't be quiet yourself for more than ten minutes at a stretch."

She frowned, but could hardly disagree.

"I'm just saying, if you figure out this isn't what you want after all, there's no shame in walking away."

Daisy tipped her head to one side and watched him. "And you expect me to, is that it?"

"I didn't say that."

"You didn't have to," she told him. "Still, I guess the only way to convince you that I'm right for this job is to prove it to you. Yet again."

He nodded. "You're getting your chance."

"That's all I ever asked for." Daisy knew he still didn't believe that she could make it there, but she'd show him. She'd convince him. And then, she thought, remembering that simmering kiss, she would seduce him.

She had to admit that she was looking forward to the coming seduction with a lot more eagerness now than she had when she first arrived. There were dark fires simmering inside Jericho King. She'd felt the heat of them all too briefly and couldn't wait for the chance to experience it again. And when they did, he wouldn't be telling her that it hadn't happened. Smiling to herself, she gasped when the first, eerie howl lifted into the air.

"What was that?"

"Coyote."

"Oh, God." She blew out a breath and pretended to not be shaken by the wild, eerie sound still reverberating through the mountains. "I didn't hear them last night."

"Probably farther away then. They move around a lot, but they always come back to their home ground."

"Which is here," she mused, staring off into the darkened forest surrounding them.

"They were here first," he told her with a shrug.

"Well, that makes me feel so much better." She'd get used to it, she told herself firmly. After all, it wasn't as if she had to *live* outside with wild animals. She and Nikki would have their own room at the main lodge and they'd be careful to not stray too far from the... *Nikki*.

Daisy turned her head, looking for her dog and felt her heart chill when she didn't see the tiny poodle. Now that she thought of it, she hadn't seen Nikki since dinner. As if to deliberately terrify her, another howl from what was probably a very hungry coyote lifted into the air.

Seven

"Jericho," she cried, "Nikki's gone. Nikki! Nikki baby, come to Mommy."

She jumped to her feet as yet one more howl sounded out, sending shivers down her spine. That one seemed closer than the one before, she thought frantically. How many of the blasted things were out there?

"Damn dog," Jericho muttered, scrambling to his feet as Daisy began to walk a fast, frenetic circle around the fire. She peered into the woods, struggling to see past the encroaching dark, straining to hear the slightest sound, the faintest yip. But there was nothing. It was as if the forest had swallowed up her dog.

"Where is she?" Daisy sent a quick, panicked look at Jericho. "She must have wandered off when I wasn't looking. Oh, God, how could I have been so careless? Nikki!"

Before he could say anything, Daisy rushed off blindly into the tree line, pushed by a driving sense of urgency. If there were coyotes close by, Nikki would be helpless. Nothing more than a snack to an animal three times her size.

With her heart in her throat, Daisy shoved through low-hanging pine branches, hardly noticing when the limbs and needles poked at her. "Nikki! Come here, girl!"

"Daisy, damn it!" His shout followed her into the brush but didn't stop her.

Her gaze swept the darkness, checking every shadow. Beside herself with worry now, she called the dog to her again and then listened for an answering bark that never came. The farther she got from the river, the more terrified she became. Nikki wouldn't have strayed this far. But she might have gone another way. How would Daisy find her? They should go to the lodge. Get a search party. Flashlights. Something. But she couldn't leave without Nikki, so Jericho would have to go for help alone.

She'd wait here. She'd keep looking. She had to find the little dog that was her last remaining link to the brother she'd lost. Visions of Nikki hurt, or worse, filled her mind and strangled the breath in her lungs. Her imagination was running at full steam so she screamed when a hand came down on her arm and spun her around.

"Stop," he ground out, holding onto her upper arms. "You're not going to find the damn dog running through the woods like a crazy woman. Hell, you don't even know where you are. How can you find her if you're lost, too?"

"I'll find her. I'll just keep looking until I do. I can't lose her," she said, her voice hardly more than a whisper. "She's all I have. She's my family. She's…"

He gave her a hard shake to get her attention, then released her and stepped back. "You go running off like that in the dark and you're going to end up at the bottom of a ravine. You don't know these woods."

"No, but you do," Daisy said, grabbing hold of his shirt with both hands. "Find her, Jericho. Please find her."

Clearly disgusted, he said, "I'm going to. But you're going back to camp." He turned her around, pointed her at their campsite and gave her a gentle shove. "Go back now and wait by the fire or I'll be looking for you *and* the stupid dog."

She wanted to argue. Wanted to tell him that she wouldn't be sent off to wait for the big strong man to come to her rescue. But even as she started to speak, Daisy realized he was right. She'd only slow him down. He knew these woods. This was his territory and she'd only make his search that much more difficult if she insisted on going along.

So for Nikki's sake, she'd do what he said. She'd sit down and she'd wait. "Okay. Okay, I will. But find her, Jericho. She must be so scared…"

Muttering darkly under his breath, he jerked his head at her, silently telling her to go back. Then he moved off without so much as a whisper of sound and disappeared into the deep shadows of the forest.

Daisy shivered and walked back to the campsite.

She waited, but she couldn't sit. How could she? She was alone by a campfire, and Jericho was off moving through the darkness in silence and Nikki... If anything happened to her dog...

Daisy continued to pace in tight, worried circles around the perimeter of the campfire, her mind racing, her heart pounding. The coyotes howled again and she wondered if they were hungry. If they'd already spotted a tiny poodle snack. If Jericho would never find the little dog because she'd already been...

"She's fine." Jericho's voice broke into Daisy's thoughts and she whirled around to face him.

He stepped into the firelight and held a trembling Nikki against his chest in one huge hand.

"You found her!" Daisy raced to him, scooped up her dog, murmuring soothing sounds and sighs as Jericho watched her with a bemused expression on his face. "Where was she?"

Nikki's tiny pink tongue swiped Daisy's face in gratitude just before the little dog sent Jericho a look of complete canine adoration.

"Cowering under a rock," he said, with a shake of his head. "She was shaking so hard, the leaves on the bush beside her were trembling. Quite the ferocious little watchdog you've got there."

"You're making fun of her, but you saved her. Poor baby, alone in the woods." She looked at him, her heart in her eyes and felt something inside her tremble as violently as Nikki was. "Thank you for finding her. I was so scared."

"It's fine. She's fine."

"I don't know what I would have done if anything had happened to her."

"Nothing did."

"Because of you. My hero."

He stopped, frowned and told her succinctly, "I'm nobody's hero."

But he was, Daisy thought as she watched him walk down to the river, effectively closing himself off. Jericho King might be a reluctant hero, Daisy told herself, but that didn't change the facts. He was a man to count on. A man to admire.

The perfect man to be the father of her child.

He woke up with both Daisy and the dog curled up into him again and this time, it was even more difficult to ignore the warmth of her curvy body pressed up against his. Now he knew what she tasted like. Now he knew what it was like to hold her, to feel her surrender herself. And now he was being haunted by those memories. Which only made him more determined to ignore the feelings, the temptations racing through him.

She was now officially his employee and he wouldn't take advantage of the situation. A man had to have rules of conduct for himself, or he was nothing. Besides, he wasn't the kind of man to allow a woman into his life and Daisy was in no way the one-night-stand kind of female. She had "commitment" stamped all over her. All he had to do was look into her eyes and he could practically see a white picket fence and 2.5 kids—not to mention her idiot dog.

Jericho eased away from her, despite the reluctance nagging at him. He wasn't going to step into a bear trap and he wasn't going to indulge himself and hurt her. So he'd just keep his distance whatever it took and hope that she got over this whim of hers to live on the mountain.

"Daisy!" His voice was sharper than it should have been, but even as he thought that, he figured it was just as well. He didn't want her getting attached to him because nothing good would come of it.

"Huh? What?" She rolled over, the dog yipped and shot up to all four feet while Daisy was still blinking sleep out of her eyes. "What's going on? It's *dark*."

"Almost dawn," he corrected, giving one quick look at the already-lightening sky. "Time to get moving."

"Right," she said, nodding as she pushed herself into a sitting position. "I'll fix breakfast and then we can—"

"We're going now," he told her. No more cozy meals, just the two of them over a dancing fire. "There's trail mix in my pack. You can eat on the way."

"Ooh, yummy," she murmured dryly, scrubbing both hands over her face. "Why the hurry?"

He looked down at her. Eyes slumberous, hair tangled and falling about her face, lips full and all too tempting. *She* was the damn hurry, he thought angrily. Being alone with her was turning into a lesson in torture. One he, thankfully, didn't have to put up with. He'd just get her back to the lodge, let her settle in and from now on, he'd make sure he was never alone with her. Safer all the way around.

His body didn't agree, but it would just have to find a way to deal with disappointment.

"Test is over," he said shortly, going down on one

knee to stuff supplies into his pack. "Time to get back to work."

"Okay…" She pushed to her feet and Nikki trotted to Jericho's side, sat beside him and leaned against his thigh. "I'll just…"

He paused in his packing, shot her a look and nodded. "Fine. Go take care of things, but hurry it up."

While Daisy stepped into the forest for some privacy, Jericho looked down at the little dog snuggling in close to him. "You and your mistress are turning out to be a real pain in the ass." When the dog only huffed out a contented sigh, Jericho scowled at it. "You're not going to get to me though, either of you."

"Anyone want seconds?" Daisy asked, lifting the cast-iron skillet temptingly.

Firelight danced across her features, highlighting her grin and making her look more beautiful than Jericho had ever seen her.

"Count me in," Max Stuben, CEO of a furniture dynasty, spoke up, holding his plate out. "Daisy, after seeing what you can do over a campfire, I have half a mind to go home and shoot my chef."

She laughed, delighted, then said, "A little extreme, Max, but I appreciate the compliment. Jericho and I like to keep our clients happy, don't we?"

When she looked up at him, Jericho couldn't help smiling back. Damned if the woman hadn't charmed every one of his clients.

Harry Morrison, bank president, added, "I'm impressed with how well you handle yourself out on the trail, Daisy. Why, if my wife were here, she'd be complaining about everything. You seem to love it."

Jericho slid a glance to watch her reaction. She was the least likely woman ever to enjoy being on the mountain, yet she seemed to be doing just that.

"Well, at King Adventure, we really go out of our way to make sure all of our employees are capable of doing everything we ask of our clients. Isn't that right, Jericho?" She looked over at him, a wide smile still on her face.

"That's right," he said, remembering her own tests and how determined she had been to win.

"And maybe," Daisy said to Harry, "your wife wouldn't complain as much if she felt more support."

Chagrined, Harry just shrugged off the comment and Jericho had to hand it to her. She'd very nicely defended a woman she'd never met.

"When you're finished there, we'll clean up and sack out," Jericho said. "We'll be getting an early start in the morning."

"Slave driver," Max muttered good-naturedly.

"You have no idea," Daisy said with a laugh. Then she picked up a few things and carried them down to the water's edge.

Jericho followed after her and when he stopped by her side, she said, "I think it's going well, don't you?"

"Yeah, it is. How are you doing?"

"Great!" When he just looked at her, though, she shrugged and said, "Okay, I admit, I don't love the trail as much as you do, but I can do this."

"You don't have to, you know. You can work at the lodge without making these trips."

She scrubbed at one of the plates and when it was clean to her satisfaction, she set it on a towel and picked up the next one. "I want to show you that I can do this."

"You don't have anything left to prove, Daisy."

"Maybe," she said, "but it's important to me to carry my own weight."

"You treat these guys any better and they're going to be trying to hire you away."

She laughed a little. "Max already offered to back me in opening my own restaurant. But I think he was kidding."

Frowning, Jericho glanced back at the men sitting beside the fire. "I'm not so sure."

Daisy stood up and laid one hand on his forearm. "No worries, Jericho. I'm exactly where I want to be."

She picked up the clean dishes and walked toward camp, leaving Jericho staring after her. The problem here was, Daisy was exactly where he wanted to be, too.

Only two weeks had passed, and Jericho was a man possessed. He spent most days doing everything he could to avoid being around Daisy. But it seemed that no matter what, she found a way to be near him. Her scent clung to the air of the main house. Every breath he drew reminded him of her.

Her laughter rang out and his ears were attuned for the sound, even from rooms away. The meals she prepared were raved about and even their clients, the fussy lawyers and busy bureaucrats, were charmed by her.

He couldn't even escape her at night. His dreams were

full of her. And the knowledge that her room was only three doors down the hall from his plagued his mind constantly.

Her dog wasn't helping the situation any, either. Ever since he'd found the little thing that last night in the forest, the poodle had officially adopted him. He could hardly take a step without watching first where he set his boot, afraid he'd crush the damn thing. He'd taken plenty of ribbing about his newfound friend from the other guys, too. Hell, he'd often thought about getting a dog himself, but his plans hadn't included a dog so small it could sit on the palm of his hand.

"Is there a reason you look like you want to bite through a brick?"

Jericho came up out of his dark thoughts with a fierce scowl on his face. He turned on his old friend and said, "This is all your fault, you know."

"What'd I do?" Sam argued, his own features twisting up into a frown.

"You brought Daisy here. You're the one who offered her the damn job." Of course *Jericho* was the one who had hired her, but that was beside the point. "She doesn't belong and she never will and pretending otherwise is just making a bad situation worse."

Sam's features cleared up and a smile tugged at his mouth. "She's getting to you, isn't she?"

"Hell, no, she's not," he lied. Damned if he'd admit to Sam what he couldn't admit to himself. "She's just a distraction is all."

"She is that," Sam agreed and opened a stall door to pour feed for one of the horses. When he was finished, he stepped back, closed the stall again and walked to the next one. "A pretty woman's always a distraction. And one that can cook, too?" He whistled, low and long, shaking his head for emphasis. "Well, that woman's a treasure to a man who isn't too stupid to see what's right in front of him."

Jericho stared at his friend's back hard enough to bore holes right through his body. "Now I'm stupid?"

"Didn't say that, but won't argue the point, you being the boss and all."

"Thanks very much," Jericho muttered and shot a look toward the main house. The barn doors were open, watery winter sunlight slanting across the neatly swept stone floor. Inside the house, Daisy would be bustling around the kitchen preparing lunch for the employees. She was probably singing, he told himself, in that slightly off-key voice of hers. His insides stirred at the thought, and he told himself he was in bad shape.

"You're the one making yourself miserable, you know," Sam told him casually as he continued making his rounds down the row of horse stalls. "Nobody else here has a problem with her. She's doing a good job and she's nice on top of it."

"Nice."

Sam shot him a look. "Yeah, nice. You might want to try it."

Oh, that was the problem, Jericho thought, shoving both hands into his jeans pockets. He wanted to be *more* than nice to her. He wanted her under him, over him. He wanted to slide his hands over those luscious curves, look down into her whiskey eyes and see his own desire-ravaged face reflected back at him. And he wanted it now.

"You don't know what you're talking about," he muttered and stalked out of the barn. What he needed, he told himself, was a hard hike up the mountain. Maybe a night or two on his own. Get his mind clear. Get his sense of control and order back. Get the hell away from Daisy Saxon before she drove him completely crazy.

Daisy was worried.

Jericho had been gone for two nights already and, with no signs of coming back, he was about to make it three. He'd disappeared up the mountain with hardly more than a word to her or anyone else. Sam didn't know where he'd gone—or he simply wasn't saying—and the other guys were just as clueless.

They didn't seem concerned either. They only said that Jericho did this from time to time and she shouldn't worry herself over it. But how could she not?

She'd become accustomed to seeing him every day. To hearing him move around the house. To knowing that he was right down the hall from her every night. Without him there, something vital was missing. Even Nikki was moping around the house as if she'd lost her best friend.

The house was closed up for the night. There were no clients at the moment and the other employees lived in a separate log home on the other side of the compound. She and Nikki were alone and though she wasn't scared, she was uneasy. Wrapping her arms around her middle, she shivered in her short cotton nightgown and stared out her bedroom window at the moonlit darkness beyond the glass.

"Where are you?" she murmured.

How long was he going to stay out there on his own? Why was he gone? She'd so hoped they'd made a connection on their two days in the woods together. She remembered with perfect clarity that deep, lingering kiss that still had her waking up in the middle of the night with her body aching and her heartbeat racing.

How could he just leave? Doesn't he care if people worry?

Behind her on the bed, Nikki whined in sympathy.

But Daisy didn't want sympathy. She wanted Jericho. Home. Where he belonged. Funny, but she hadn't even realized until this moment that she'd already begun to think of this place as home. Strange how quickly she'd acclimated to being here. To this way of life. So completely different from life in the city, living on the mountain was slower yet so much more…fundamental. Here, everyone worked together to make sure life moved as it should. The employees at the camp were a family and she'd slid into their company so easily, she'd come to rely on all of them.

But when the head of their family was missing…

"Darn it, where *are* you?"

Chewing at her bottom lip, she ignored the growing chill in the room and wondered what it would be like here when the snow came. Would she still be here? Would Jericho still be avoiding her? Or would she be pregnant and already gone from this place?

The thought of that sent a curl of regret unspooling at the pit of her stomach. She'd never planned to stay here forever. But now that she'd been here a while, become a part of things, the thought of leaving left her feeling… empty.

But she would have her child, she reminded herself. She wouldn't be alone anymore.

She would have her own family again.

"If he ever comes back," she muttered.

Behind her, Nikki suddenly jumped onto all fours and let out a yip of excitement. Daisy turned to look at her dog, then swung around to gaze out the window again. Jericho, bathed in moonlight, stepped from the tree line and walked across the wide yard, stopping directly in front of the house.

Nikki leaped off the bed, hit the wood floor and skidded, her short nails clacking against the oak planks as she raced for the closed bedroom door.

But Daisy wasn't watching her dog. Instead, her gaze was locked on the man standing in the yard. Moonlight stretched his shadow across the grass and outlined him in a pearly light that seemed otherworldly. In the stillness, he tipped his head back, looked up at her window and met her gaze. Heat sizzled through her and a part of her was amazed that she could feel such an intense reaction from the man at such a distance. She lifted one hand and laid her palm against the cold windowpane as if she could touch him if she concentrated hard enough. And in that instant, something of her thoughts must have transmitted themselves to him because his features went hard and taut and a moment later, he was stalking toward the house with purposeful strides.

Daisy whirled around, grabbed up her robe from the end of her bed and pulled it on as she raced across the room. She threw the door open and Nikki burst free, flying down the hall and then the stairs, headed for the front door. The little dog got there just as Jericho opened it and when he stopped on the threshold, Nikki went up on her hind legs and waved her forepaws at him in celebration.

Daisy stood at the top of the stairs, breath caught in her chest as she watched him bend down, scoop up the dog and stoically accept Nikki's kisses.

"She missed me," he said, his voice low and rough.

"She's not the only one," Daisy told him. Her earlier frustrations and worry and anger were forgotten now in the rush of heat swimming through her system. Just looking at him made her knees weak. Locking her gaze with his fed her fantasies and sent her pulse rate into a gallop.

His mouth went straight and grim. He set the dog on the floor then closed the front door behind him.

"Why did you leave?"

"To get some distance from you." His eyes were stormy, dark, and flashed with emotions that shifted too quickly for her to make sense of them.

"How's that working for you?"

One corner of his amazing mouth lifted briefly. "Not well."

"I'm glad."

"You shouldn't be," he said and dropped his pack beside the door. Shrugging out of his jacket, he tossed it at the hall tree and didn't seem to care when it missed and fell to the floor.

Daisy's insides twisted as she drew one long, shaky breath. She hadn't expected this, she thought wildly. Hadn't thought that he would be the one to come to her. She'd expected to have to seduce him into bed. But looking into his eyes left her little doubt that Jericho King was a man on a mission.

And lucky her, *she* was that mission. She felt it. She sensed it in the very air surrounding them. It was bristling with tension, with a sexual energy and heat that was strong enough to light a dozen homes through a cold, dark winter.

She laid one hand on the banister and held on as she watched him walk slowly toward the staircase.

"I knew you were going to be trouble," he said tightly. "The minute I saw you, I knew."

"Is that right?"

"Tried to get rid of you, remember? Tried to talk you out of staying."

"You did," she agreed.

"But when you wouldn't listen, I decided to just ignore you," he admitted, taking the steps with a deliberate slowness. "Finally went out on the mountain just to get some space. Clear my head. Thought I could put you out of my mind, but you wouldn't go. You stayed."

Heat pooled in her belly then dipped lower, warming her through and setting up a tingling ache that throbbed at her center.

"I think about you even when I know I shouldn't," he told her as he came closer.

"I've been thinking about you, too," she told him and her heartbeat fluttered unsteadily. "And you were gone so long, I was worried about you."

He snorted. "You should be worried about *you*."

"You don't scare me." She lifted her chin and tossed her hair back from her face. The fire in his eyes glinted at her as he moved steadily closer. Daisy took a breath and held it, not sure she'd be able to draw another. He was big and powerful and looked just a little dangerous and, oh, her entire being was quaking with banked eagerness.

When he stopped on the step just below her, their eyes were level and he said softly, "I should, Daisy. I should scare the hell outta you."

She studied him for a long moment and saw past the desire and the heat in his eyes to the shadows lurking deep within. Shaking her head, she reached out to cup his cheek in her palm and whispered, "You're no danger to me, Jericho King."

He covered her hand with his own. "No," he agreed, "but I can't say the same for your virtue."

Daisy laughed, but the sound was cut off as Jericho grabbed her and slammed her close to his chest. Her head fell back and her eyes were linked with his when she nodded slowly, telling him silently that she wanted him as badly as he did her. Then she said, "My virtue isn't an issue. My need for you is."

"Thank God," he muttered and tossed her over one shoulder.

She yelped in surprise, but Jericho paid no attention. He'd damn near killed himself getting back to the lodge while the moon was still high. He'd wanted her to himself. He'd finally accepted that he wasn't going to get any peace until he'd satisfied his body inside hers. And tonight was the night. He slipped one hand beneath her nightgown and caressed her panty-covered behind as he hit the landing and started down the hall for his room.

"No more waiting," he told her. "No more thinking

and dreaming about this. Tonight, I'm going to make you scream my name until you're hoarse."

She shivered and a tiny moan escaped her throat. His own body tightened at the images racing through his mind and he hurried his steps. The little dog nipped along at his heels, but he couldn't have cared less. He reached his bedroom, walked across the wide space and tossed Daisy onto the mattress. She bounced, settled in atop the handmade quilt and then stared up at him through wide, whiskey-colored eyes.

He tore his clothes off, telling her, "I even stopped to bathe in the river so I wouldn't have to waste time with a damn shower once I got home."

She grinned and pushed herself up onto her elbows. "Must have been cold."

He shook his head. "Didn't feel a thing."

Then he was on the bed with her, pushing her nightgown up and over her head, baring her luscious breasts to his gaze, to his touch. He bent over her, took first one nipple then the other into his mouth, licking, nibbling, sucking, and felt her fingers thread through his hair, holding him in place.

His hands moved over her skin, fingers dipping below the elastic band of her panties, a tiny scrap of white lace. With one quick move, he snapped that band and tugged the lace free of her body. Then he touched her, covering her heat with the palm of his hand, feeling her body arch into him and listening to the soft sighs of expectation sliding from her lips.

"Jericho…"

"First time's going to be hot and hard, baby," he muttered against her breast. "I've been waiting for you too long."

"Yes," she said and met his gaze when he lifted his head. "Now, please. Fill me. I need you so much."

He didn't need to hear more. Jericho shifted position, knelt between her legs, then parted her thighs. He stroked her most sensitive skin with the tips of his fingers until she was writhing helplessly beneath him.

"Jericho, now…"

"Almost," he told her, watching her squirm, watching a passion-induced haze slide over her eyes.

Then, when he was satisfied that she was on the teetering brink of completion, he pushed his body into hers.

She gasped, lifting her hips to accommodate him, and he took advantage of her move, sliding ever deeper inside her. Her tight, hot body surrounded his and he groaned aloud at the sweeping satisfaction of finally being exactly where he'd dreamed of being.

This was all he had craved. This was what he needed above all else. Daisy. With her hot welcome, with her warm sighs and the soft ease of her lush body.

He levered himself over her, hands on either side of her head, and their eyes met and locked as he pumped himself into her. Plunging, claiming, again and again, his hips rocked against hers.

Her arms came around his neck, she locked her legs around his waist and pulled him deeper, tighter on every thrust. Breath mingled, mouths met and tongues twisted.

And when at last she tore her mouth from his and screamed his name, Jericho shouted in victory and allowed his body to explode into a pleasure so profound, it left him shattered.

Eight

They'd been at it for hours.

He was insatiable, Daisy thought with an inward smile. And very creative. Her body felt used and complete and was practically humming with stored energy. There was just something about incredible sex that made her feel strong enough to move mountains.

But even as that thought slid through her mind, she knew it was more. Knew that this long, incredible night had been about much more than simple sex. This wasn't just a case of needs being met, hungers assuaged. This was something else.

And that worried her.

She hadn't planned on loving Jericho.

But it seemed, she told herself, that it was too late to avoid it.

His body covering hers, she ran her hands up and

down his spine, loving the hard, warm feel of his skin against hers. His breath puffed across her throat and their heartbeats thundered in time.

She'd gone to King Mountain because of his connection with her brother. Because she'd felt that Jericho and the military owed her one. They'd taken her brother—her only family—from her and she'd come to collect on that debt. But now, it was so much more complicated than that. She'd come to care for him and during the long, sex-fueled night, she'd taken that last trembling step into love.

Which left her exactly *where?*

"You're thinking," he murmured against her skin. "I can practically hear the wheels in your head spinning."

She smiled and moved her hands up to thread through his hair. "Well, maybe you could think of something to do that would completely shut down my brain."

He lifted his head and grinned down at her. "Is that a challenge?"

"Do you need one?"

"Nope." He kissed her then slid his body down along hers, pausing along the way to taste her nipples, to run his tongue across her abdomen.

Daisy shivered as he moved over her, then she tipped her head back into the pillow as he knelt between her legs and lifted her hips from the bed. Her legs dangled and her hands fisted on the sheets as he lowered his mouth to her.

She watched him as he took her. As his mouth covered her and his tongue worked over that erotically charged bud of flesh. Again and again, he caressed that spot, sending tingles shooting through her system with complete abandon. His breath was hot, his tongue was wicked and as he took her, his hands kneaded her bottom until she was besieged with too many sensations to count.

Her heartbeat was frantic as she lay helplessly in his strong grasp. She rocked her hips into his mouth, claiming as much as she could of what he was doing to her. His eyes burned into hers and she couldn't look away. Couldn't tear her gaze from his as the world around her splintered and she called his name out one more time, her throat sore, her voice raspy.

And before the last of the tremors had rocked through her body, Jericho sat back on his heels, grabbed her up and settled her over his throbbing erection. In one fluid move, she sheathed him. Her arms went around him, her legs locked about his waist and his big hands were at her hips. He moved her on him, up and down, sliding into a hot friction that seemed to explode into flames that enveloped them both.

He caught her mouth with his and this time, when she called his name, he swallowed the sound and buried it under his own groan of completion.

Over the next few days, life on the mountain settled into a routine. A constantly changing routine in Jericho's opinion, but he seemed to be the only one bothered by it.

Daisy was imprinting herself not only on him, but also on his home. Clients arrived, were taken care of and left. Meals were not only healthier, but tastier, plus there was a variety that Kevin had never managed. She had become a part of the unit that lived and worked at the lodge. It was almost as if she'd always been there, and Jericho noticed that the guys spent a lot more time smiling than they used to.

Of course he noticed, because his frequent scowl was such a contrast.

Now, he walked into the great room and stopped on the threshold. Glancing around, he noted all the changes she'd made here, too. Nothing was safe from the woman. Daisy had raided the attic, where generations of King clutter were stored and she'd found what she called "treasures." Handmade quilts done by Jericho's grandmother and decorative pillows that Daisy had strewn across the utilitarian furniture. The room had a softer feel now, with scattered rugs and splotches of color dotting the area.

"She's nesting," he muttered and waited for the zing of panic to shoot through him. But it didn't come.

Why?

Was he getting so used to having her around that he didn't mind the fact that she'd taken his well-ordered male world and turned it on its head? Was he so enthralled by the nights they spent together that he no longer worried about getting too attached? If that were the case, it was time to put the brakes on.

Because no matter how much he enjoyed her, being with her, the bottom line was she didn't belong. And she wouldn't last. One hard winter would be enough to send the city girl screaming back down the mountain in search of sidewalks and coffee shops.

He scowled at the thought and knew that when she was gone, it wouldn't be easy on him. He'd miss her, damn it, which was something he hadn't counted on. Best to start preparing himself for it now, he supposed.

"Hi," she said from right behind him. "You're back early. I thought you said you were going up the mountain today to check the fencing on the ridgeline."

"I did," he said and stepped aside so she could pass. But she didn't move away. Instead, she inched in closer to him. Close enough that he caught the ripe peach scent of the shampoo she preferred. Close enough that he felt waves of heat reaching out for him and his body responded in an instant.

He'd thought that getting Daisy into his bed would be the one sure way to get her *out* of his system. Hadn't worked out that way. Rather than chasing her out of his mind, sex with Daisy had burned her into his brain. One whiff of her scent, one touch of her hand could have him hard as iron and as eager as a teenager in the backseat of a car.

Focus, he told himself. Focus on anything but her. Not as easy as it sounded. "We've got three lawyers showing up tomorrow. Everything ready?"

She gave him a half smile, filled with confusion at his sudden brisk tone, but said, "Yes, their rooms are ready and I've got their dietary requirements. I had Tim drive down the mountain to get a few groceries today, but—"

He held up one hand to stop the flow of words and asked, "Tim? I told him to check the climbing wall today, make sure it was sound after the last rain."

"Sam did that," she said, moving past him to plump pillows and toss them onto the couch again. "He said he didn't mind and Tim was eager to make the trip.

Something about stopping to say hello to his mom while he was in town…"

The reins of control were slipping out of his fingers and Jericho fought to get a firmer grip. "If I'd wanted Sam out slogging his way through the mud, I would have sent him."

Daisy turned around to face him. "What are you angry about?"

"Oh, I don't know," he said, tossing both hands high before letting them slap down against his thighs. "Maybe because I give orders that you change around to suit yourself?"

"Orders?"

Her voice sounded tight, but he was past caring. This was just a symptom, he told himself. Just one more sign that she was changing everything on him. She even had his men doing her bidding and forgetting all about whatever it was *he'd* told them to do. Well, it was time to remind her who was the boss around here.

"Yes, orders. You work for me, Daisy, not the other way around."

"I didn't say different, did I?"

"You didn't have to," he countered. "You do whatever the hell you want around here and expect the rest of us to just go along."

"I haven't heard any complaining," she snapped, folding her arms over her chest in a classic position of self-defense.

"You are now." He closed the distance between them with a few long strides. "Sam's too old to be pushing through mud. But you didn't think about that, did you?"

"He's hardly in his dotage, Jericho."

"And that's your decision to make, is it?"

"No," she argued, "it was Sam's decision and he made it. You're making a huge deal over nothing," she said and tipped her head to one side as she stared up at him. "So what's really bothering you? It's not Tim going to the store. Or Sam fighting with mud. What is it, Jericho? Just say it."

He scraped one hand across his face and blew out a frustrated breath. "I run this camp my way, understand? Stop countermanding my orders and everything will be fine." He glanced around the room, waved one hand at the feminine touches she'd added and grumbled, "And quit trying to girlie the place up while you're at it."

"Girlie?"

"Pillows, rugs, blankets..." He stopped and muttered, "Hell, it's getting to the point where I don't know what to expect every time I come into the room."

"Yes, well," Daisy said softly, "pillows and crochet work are dangerous entities..."

He snapped her an irritable look. "You know what I mean. Just do your job and nothing else."

"Uh-huh. Am I supposed to salute, too?"

"Wouldn't hurt!"

"You are the most impossible man," she said, shifting so that her hands were fisted on her hips. "Are you really that threatened by a few throw pillows and crocheted afghans? Do scented candles throw you into a tizzy?"

"This is still my house," he argued, even though he was beginning to feel like a damn fool.

"Nobody said it wasn't," she told him. "So why don't you tell me what's really bugging you, Jericho?

You're not afraid of me, are you? Afraid I'm getting too close?"

The fact that that was *exactly* what was worrying him only irritated him further. His head snapped up and his gaze fired into hers. Gritting his teeth, he hissed in a breath and said, "Nobody gets any closer to me than I want them to be. So if you're looking at me and seeing rainbows and picket fences, then you need to get your eyes checked."

Rather than being put off by his gruff voice, barely restrained temper and crappy attitude, Daisy smiled at him. Her eyes lit up and she shook her head as she walked toward him. Then laying both palms flat on his chest, she went up on her toes and brushed her mouth across his.

"I see you clearly, Jericho. I always have."

Temper drained away from him as if someone had pulled a plug. Hard to maintain anger when you were straddling a razor blade of desire and want. "I'm not the kind of man you need."

"That's where you're wrong," she said softly with another sly smile. "You're exactly the man I need."

When she went into his arms, Jericho held her tightly to him, and he had to wonder if she'd be saying these things if she knew that he still blamed himself for her brother's death.

A couple of days later, it was a cloudy afternoon with a chilly bite to the air as Jericho packed up his truck for an annual fishing trip with his brothers Jesse and Justice. While he worked, Jericho actively wished both of his brothers to the other side of the planet. For the past two days, Jericho had been treating Daisy as if she were a land mine with a tricky trigger mechanism. He wasn't sure why. It wasn't as if the woman had a short fuse or anything. She was usually so damn happy it was hard to spot a frown on her face. But his tension had been bleeding into her and now she was wary, as if she was no longer sure just how to treat him.

Ever since that confrontation in the great room, neither one of them was entirely comfortable around the other.

You're exactly the man I need.

Her words repeated over and over again in his mind, making him short-tempered and more irritable than usual. What the hell had she meant? She needed him? For what?

Sex?

Or had she meant something more? Was she building castles in the air around him? Because if she was, they were going to collapse. He couldn't be the man for her. There were too many secrets between them. Too many things left unsaid, and once she knew the truth, he knew he'd never see that smile of hers again. Never feel her squirming beneath him in the middle of the night.

And that was a hell of a thing, wasn't it? He'd begun keeping his secret to protect her. Now, wasn't he just protecting himself? Wasn't he keeping the truth from her so that he wouldn't lose what he'd found with her?

This never should have begun, he thought. Going down this road was a mistake from the first and he'd known it. Hadn't he tried to get her to leave? Hadn't he tried to keep his distance? Hell, he'd realized right away that nothing good could come of this, but Daisy

Saxon was a damn force of nature. She was unstoppable. Irresistible. He couldn't regret what he'd had with her the past few weeks, but he knew the memories of this time with her would haunt him for years after she was gone.

So what kind of bastard was he, to know all of this and still go to her bed every night?

"Idiot," he muttered darkly and tossed a folding lawn chair into the bed of the truck. "Keep your distance, but don't stop sleeping with her."

But damned if he could stop himself. What was a man supposed to do? Turn his back on a warm, beautiful, *willing* woman who wanted him as much as he wanted her?

Guilt threatened to rear up inside him, but he pushed it away. Daisy was here because she wanted to be. The fact that she didn't know the whole truth of her brother's death meant nothing. There wasn't a thing he could do to change reality and didn't know if he would if given the chance. Of course, he would spare her pain, but would he take away her brother's bravery? Brant's decision to volunteer for dangerous duty, just to keep him safe? No. He couldn't do that and honor the kid. And that young Marine deserved the honor he'd found in death. Hell, they all did.

What was really bugging him was that he hadn't told Daisy the whole story. When she'd asked about her brother's death, he'd dodged her. Told her only the bare minimum. Why? To save her grief? Or was it to save himself from having to see accusation shining in her whiskey eyes?

And did it matter? he demanded of himself silently.

Was the reason important when the result was that he was hiding the truth? He, who put such store in honesty, was deliberately keeping something from the woman who was dominating his every thought. So he had to wonder what was driving that. Concern for someone else or self-service?

But as his mind went round and round that question for what had to be the hundredth time, Jericho told himself to suck it up. To keep his mouth shut and to wait Daisy out. One day soon, she'd realize that he wasn't the man for her, that nothing was going to come of whatever it was that was between them…and she'd give up and go away.

Daisy? His mind argued. Daisy, who didn't know the meaning of the word *quit?* Fat chance.

His brothers' voices rushed to him on a cold wind and he shook his head and grumbled under his breath. He was in no mood for dealing with Justice and Jesse, but he didn't have a choice in the matter. Every year, his brothers came up to King Mountain for a weekend fishing trip, guys only, just before the onslaught of winter. It was out of season, but on private property they could fish all they wanted to. They never actually caught much, but it was a good chance for them all to sit and talk and catch up on each other's lives.

Any other time, he would have been looking forward to it. He'd missed quite a few of these trips when he was still in the military. Now that he was home, he wanted to reconnect with his family. He had to admit that Daisy had had a part in that, too. She'd reminded him all too often about just how important family was. And when she'd discovered that Jesse and Justice were coming for a fishing trip, she'd been excited at the idea of meeting his brothers.

And excitement for Daisy translated into cooking and baking. The kitchen was stocked now with every kind of food and dessert imaginable. She had been determined that the King brothers would feel welcome. Now, she was practically pushing all three of them out the door to get them started on their overnight trip.

Jericho had noticed his brothers noticing Daisy and had even caught an inquisitive glance or two being exchanged. He knew what they were thinking. That the last King brother had finally taken the plunge. Well, once they were at the lake, he'd just set them both straight on that score.

"This is great," Justice said, as he approached, letting his gaze roam over the property. "I like the changes you made to the big house."

"Thanks." Jericho jerked his head toward the barn. "I've got a new horse you should see, too."

"Yeah?"

His eyes lit up and Jericho almost laughed aloud. Justice was the patient one of the bunch of brothers. He was quiet, thoughtful, withdrawn. But you show him a horse and the rancher in the man stood up and roared.

Damn, it was good to see them, he thought, even though their timing sucked.

"We're not here to look at horses—we're here to fish and drink beer," Jesse told them both, tossing a tackle box into the back of Jericho's truck. "Bella and Maggie are having a girls' night in at the ranch—said they're planning a big family get-together, all of the cousins, God help us—for Christmas and Justice's housekeeper,

Mrs. Carey, is in hog heaven with both of the kids to look after. Justice and I barely escaped with our lives."

Jericho just shook his head at his youngest brother. A former professional surfer, Jesse now owned and operated King Beach, a sportswear and sports equipment company. He was also crazy in love with his wife and Joshua, their son. "Sounds dangerous."

"That's no joke," Justice said. "Yeah, Jesse's a little dramatic as always, but I can tell you, Maggie and Bella together…" He shuddered. "No man can stand against 'em. By the time we got out of there, the two of them were buried in discussions over menus and decorations and there was talk of having *us* stick around so we could help 'em decide things like…redecorating." He shook his head again at their narrow escape. "For some damn reason, Maggie figures we need to repaint the whole inside of the ranch for this shindig they're planning and Bella's right there with her."

"Too true," Jesse said. "She was showing me paint samples on the ride to the ranch and couldn't understand why I didn't give a damn about pomegranate or hydrangea for the breakfast room."

"It's white now. What's wrong with white, I ask you?" Justice demanded of no one. "Those women are on a roll and nothing's going to stop 'em. We're just lucky that Maura and Jefferson are safely in Ireland."

"Can't believe my brothers are such wimps. Letting their wives run the show."

"So says the single man," Jesse pointed out and reached down for the cooler. "Wait until it's your turn and then we'll talk."

"It's never going to be *my* turn, Jesse," Jericho told

him firmly. "Not a chance in hell I'll tangle myself up in marriage with anyone. Saw too much misery in the Corps. Even good marriages can end in pain, and I'm not interested in that, thanks."

"Just what I said," Jesse told him. "That changed when I met Bella."

"It was Maggie for me," Justice said, then added, "Your time will come, Jericho."

"Don't count on it," he answered. "I like my life just the way it is. I'm not looking for anything permanent and I'm not husband and father material."

"Didn't think I was either," Jesse said. "But now I'm married, with a son who makes me happy and Bella's pregnant again."

"And you're just now telling us?" Justice accused. "Congratulations, man. That's great news."

"Yeah." Jesse shook his head and gave them a bemused smile. "Who would have guessed a few years ago that I'd be so damn happy changing diapers?"

Even Jericho had to admit silently that he never would have pegged his surfing brother as the family type. But clearly, he was.

"Know just what you mean," Justice said with a grin. "Now that Maggie's pregnant again, looks like the Kings are having another population explosion."

"All right!" Jesse slapped his brother on the shoulder. "Now all we need is for Maura and Jefferson to make another one and for Jericho to get with the program."

Jericho shook his head. "For me, not a chance. For Jefferson and Maura, you might want to cut them some slack. Hell, Jensen's not even a year old, is he?"

"Neither's Joshua," Jesse pointed out. Then he asked, "So, how about it, Jericho? You really want to be the only King not working on the next dynasty?"

"One of us has got to stay sane, don't you think?"

"You always were a tough son of a bitch," Jesse said with a wide grin. "Not to mention too stubborn to know what's good for you." He hefted the cooler. "Damn, this thing weighs a ton. What's in it?"

"The bare essentials," Daisy announced from the back door. "There's beer, beer and, oh, just in case you get thirsty, some beer."

"My kind of picnic," Jesse said on a laugh.

She grinned back at him and for a second, Jericho felt like an outsider. He envied his brothers' easy way with Daisy. There were no undercurrents between them. No lingering sexual tension that ratcheted up every conversation they had. His guts were twisting and his mouth was dry just watching her.

She wore a dark green sweater with the collar of a white shirt poking out at the neck. Her jeans were worn, but clung to her legs like a lover's hands and she was wearing those boots she'd tried to wear on their survival trip. She looked damn good and had Jericho's heartbeat pounding so loud it was a wonder no one else could hear it.

He wondered, too, if she'd been there in time to hear him say he'd never marry anyone. Had she listened in to his brothers' talk about family and babies, and had she heard Jericho's refusal to be drawn into it all? He hadn't heard her open the door, so it was possible.

And though a part of him hoped she'd missed it, another part acknowledged that it might be easier all the way around, for both of them if she knew exactly where he stood on this.

Nine

"The other cooler has sandwiches." Daisy was talking to all of them, but her gaze remained on Jericho as she added, "Along with potato salad, macaroni salad, fried chicken and chocolate-chip cookies."

"Ma'am," Justice said and swept his Stetson off as he bowed, "you are a gift from above and we thank you."

"No pasties?" Jericho asked, voice soft enough he half didn't expect her to hear him.

He should have known better. Her whiskey-colored gaze landed on him, but her smile was less than brilliant. Had she heard him talking to his brothers? Or was this simply a sign that she was going to miss him while he was gone?

"Pasties, too," she said, "since I know how much you like them."

There was one long, simmering second that flashed

between them and it was as if his brothers weren't there. As if he and Daisy were alone on the mountain. And the depth of emotion rocking through him almost choked him. He hadn't counted on this, Jericho realized grimly. Hadn't counted on caring for her. The need for her had been so overpowering, he hadn't noticed when it became leavened with affection. With… Deliberately, he shut down that train of thought before it could leave the station.

He couldn't acknowledge, even to himself, that what he was feeling for her was anything more than a softening of a heart he hadn't realized was still there. What they shared wouldn't last. Couldn't.

Not only because, as he'd told his brothers, he wasn't looking for forever. But because there was still something she didn't know. He hadn't told her about Brant's last mission. Not yet. But, he told himself, that was exactly what he was going to have to do. As soon as he got back from this trip with his brothers, he'd be up-front with her. Tell her everything. Then she'd leave and things would get back to normal around here.

If he missed her the rest of his life, that was just something he'd have to deal with.

She laughed at something Jesse said and Jericho's gaze fixed on her. Everything inside him fisted up tight. The woman hit him on so many levels he couldn't even identify them all. He wanted her and at the same time wanted her gone. Needed her and resented that need. Cared for her, but fought against it at every breath.

How could one small, curvy woman instigate so many different emotions in a man? Especially one who'd made it his business to *never* feel deeply for anyone?

Hell, until Daisy had stumbled into his life, the closest Jericho had come to commitment was the two weeks he'd spent at his cousin Rico King's hotel in Cancún, with a brunette he barely remembered.

For years, he'd carefully steered clear of entanglements, firmly believing that military life wasn't suited to hearth and home and family. He'd thought then and still did that a man served his country best when there were no other distractions in his life.

Jericho had seen too many families disintegrate under the strain of long deployments. Or worse yet, he'd seen the damage done to wives and kids when their Marine didn't make it home. His friends had insisted that he was looking at it all wrong, of course. They claimed the strength they got from their families more than made up for the worry of leaving them. And true enough, there were plenty of military personnel who made it work, balancing career and family so well they made it look easy.

But Jericho had drawn a firm line for himself. He'd chosen to live a solitary life while in service.

What's your excuse now? a sly voice whispered in the back of his mind. He wasn't in the military anymore and still he kept people at a distance.

It was cleaner, he told himself. Less cluttered. Though those excuses sounded pitiful even to himself.

"So what's the big weekend plan?" Daisy was asking and Jericho came up out of his thoughts. Before he could speak though, Jesse was talking.

"To sit beside the lake and listen to my brothers' lies," he told her with a wink.

"The day you close your mouth long enough to listen

to anybody will be the day they open an ice rink in hell," Justice told him, giving Jesse a friendly shove.

"Well now, you and Jericho are so damned close-mouthed, it only looks like I'm doing all the talking." He turned his smile on Daisy again. "You can testify to that, can't you, Daisy? Jericho's about as talkative as a rock, wouldn't you say?"

She turned her gaze on him and Jericho felt the solid punch of her stare. Humor shone in her eyes again as she said, "I don't know about that. He doesn't seem to have much trouble when he's telling me how he wants things run around here."

He scowled at her, but it was more for form's sake than anything else.

"Giving orders doesn't count," Jesse told her, leaning one hip against the back of the truck. "Because I'm the youngest, I can tell you I've been taking orders from my brothers since I first opened my eyes."

"Not that you ever follow them," Justice reminded him and lifted the heavy cooler filled with food so easily, it might have been empty. He set it in the back of the truck and glanced at Daisy. "His wife, Bella, came to my house just looking for a little peace and quiet."

"Ha!" Jesse laughed shortly, then got a bemused look on his face. "My Bella? Peaceful? That'll be the day."

"Please," Justice said. "Your wife's a sweetheart. You want to see a woman with a temper, you take my Maggie on in an argument. You'll be lucky to get out with your hide still attached."

"You're pitching Maggie's Irish temper against Bella's Mexican temperament?" Jesse laughed again. "No contest, big brother. Bella's small, but she's tough."

Both men continued to compare their wives, each of them sounding so damn proud of the women in their lives that Jericho felt a moment's envy. Which was new for him. He was even tempted to jump in and tell them both that Daisy was more woman than either of their wives.

That thought startled him down to the bone. Usually, all he experienced when his brothers started talking was a pang of sympathy for the women who'd chosen to love his hardheaded brothers. Now though, since Daisy, Jericho could understand just what his brothers felt for their wives. Didn't make him feel any better to realize it though. Instead, it seemed to solidify for him the fact that he'd let Daisy get too close.

He'd allowed her to *matter*.

Jericho stood to one side, his gaze still locked with Daisy's as his brothers ragged on each other. The banter was familiar and comfortable. The only difference this time was that Daisy was here, so Jericho's mind wasn't really on keeping up with his brothers. Instead, all he could think was that he wished the weekend was over so that he could drag her upstairs, lock the two of them up in his room and forget about everything but her for the next twenty-four hours or so.

Yes, he'd decided to tell her everything, his mind argued, but that wasn't saying he couldn't have one more night with her first. If that made him a selfish bastard, then he could live with that.

"Yo, Jericho!" Jesse punched his arm. "You alive?"

"Yeah, I am, little brother," he said, tearing his gaze from Daisy long enough to give Jesse a hard stare that had once been known to freeze Marine recruits in their tracks. Naturally enough, Jesse didn't even flinch. Disgusted, Jericho told him, "Load up the rest of the gear so we can get moving."

"See?" Jesse pointed out to no one, "Still giving orders."

"You guys have fun," Daisy said with a laugh as she headed down the back porch steps and turned for the corner of the house. "Come on, Nikki," she called to the little dog clearly torn between walking with her or staying to stare longingly at Jericho. "I've got some chrysanthemums to stake. Guess I'll see you all tomorrow night?"

"We'll be back by supper time," Justice assured her.

She lifted one hand and kept walking, disappearing around the edge of the log house, with the dog pausing for one backward look before joining her.

"Staking flowers?" Jesse muttered with a shake of his head as he looked after her. "Why?"

"Do I look like a gardener to you?" Jericho asked with irritation. "How the hell would I know?" He scrubbed one hand across his chin. "I didn't even know we had chrysanthemums."

Jesse turned to the task at hand, tossing in sleeping bags and a camp stove, then he carefully set their fishing poles into the back of the truck, too. While he worked, Jericho simply stared off into space, watching the spot where Daisy had vanished.

"Something you want to tell me?" Justice asked quietly as he stepped up alongside him.

"Huh?" Jericho started and looked at him as though

he were crazy. But it wouldn't fool Justice. He'd always been the one of them to see things no one wanted him to see. Well, except when it came to his own life. Their oldest brother Jefferson had explained to Jericho just how badly Justice had screwed up his marriage to Maggie. And how close the couple had come to losing everything that was between them.

"I'm not blind, you know," Justice told him. "I can see how she looks at you—and just how you're looking back."

"You don't know what you're talking about." Damn it. He should have expected this, he told himself. Of course Justice would pick up on the tensions between him and Daisy. Of course he'd notice things Jericho would rather keep under the radar.

"Yeah? Then why is it you look like a man on the ragged edge?" Justice asked. "Hell, Jericho. You finally fall for a woman and you're not going to do anything about it?"

"Nobody fell for anybody," he argued, distinctly uncomfortable with the conversation.

"What's this?" Jesse sidled up alongside Justice and stuck his two cents in. "The Almighty Jericho King falling in love?" He laughed and reached out to shove Jericho's shoulder. "This is big news, man!"

"Will you shut the hell up?" Jericho snapped, shooting a glance at the spot where Daisy had last been seen just to make sure she wasn't in earshot. Now that Jesse had caught wind of this, there would be no keeping him quiet. "Nobody said anything about love."

"Didn't have to. Hell," Justice mused, "you practically set her on fire just looking at her."

"Lust isn't love, in case you didn't know that already," he told his brothers, sparing first one, then the other of them a hard glare meant to end the conversation once and for all. Of course, it didn't.

"It's a good start though," Jesse told him, his unabashed grin nearly splitting his features in two. "First time I saw Bella..." He paused for a heavily dramatic sigh, then said, "Well, not the first time. The first time, it was dark and I could hardly see her at all. The second time, she was wearing this ugly-ass tent dress, but the *third* time," he mused with a grin, "that's the one that got me."

"You're an idiot," Jericho told him. "And my sympathies to your wife."

Jesse's eyebrows lifted as he laughed, clearly unoffended. "She loves me."

"No accounting for taste," Justice put in.

"Hey," Jesse shot back, "we were ragging on Jericho, remember?"

"And now you're done. You talk too much," Jericho told him. "Always did. A bad habit you ought to try to break."

"Too late now," Jesse said with a negligent shrug. He walked back to the truck and took a seat on the tailgate. "Besides, it's part of my charm."

"Is that what that is?" Jericho lifted his gaze to the sky. They had a good four hours before sunset. Time enough to drive to the lake and set up camp. If he could get his brothers to back off and get moving. "So are we ready to go or what?"

"Changing the subject doesn't make anything go away, you know."

"I'm not changing the subject," he said tightly, with a glare for each of his brothers. "There is no subject because I'm not talking about it at all. Not with you two. Not with anyone. Because there's nothing to talk about."

"Are you crazy or just stupid?" Jesse asked from his perch on the tailgate. "A woman who not only looks like that and can cook *and* can stand being around your crab-ass attitude for longer than five minutes and you're not falling on your knees in front of her?"

Jericho sneered at him.

"He's over the top again," Justice said, with a little more heat in his voice than usual, "but Jesse's got a point. For God's sake, Jericho, you really want to spend the rest of your life a hermit on this mountain?"

"How am I a hermit? I've got people coming and going all the damn time."

"Key word there in that sentence," Jesse tossed in, *"going."*

Jericho snapped at him. "Who asked you to talk?"

Jesse pushed off the tailgate, stood up straight to face his older brother and said, "You ever notice that your attitude gets even crappier when you're wrong?"

"Just shut up, will you?" Jericho shook his head, looked at his more rational brother and asked, "Justice can I toss him in the lake?"

"You could try," Jesse goaded.

"Nah," Justice said, "Bella'd have a fit. And trust me when I say you don't want to see that woman angry."

"Amen," Jesse muttered.

"Fine. No tossing in lakes, but no more 'advice' from

you either," Jericho said and slammed the gate of the truck shut with enough force to rattle metal.

"Fine," Jesse agreed. "No more advice, even though you really need it."

"Get in the truck," Justice told him, then when Jesse was gone, he said, "He's right, you know. About Daisy. And you. You might want to think about this before you screw something good up. I know. I damn near did the same thing myself."

Jericho sighed, shoved one hand through his hair and said, "I'm glad you and Maggie made it work. Really. But this thing with Daisy, it's different."

"How?"

"There are things she doesn't know," Jericho said. "Things we haven't talked about. But even discounting that...bottom line?" Jericho said with a slow shake of his head. "We're way too different. I'm scotch, she's wine. I'm outdoors, she's in. Just wouldn't work because, like it or not, she doesn't belong here."

Daisy bit down on her bottom lip to keep from speaking up and giving away her position. She should have known better than to stand there and listen in on Jericho and his brothers. And she really hadn't meant to at first. But when she'd headed back for the house to get a pair of scissors to use to deadhead the flowers, she'd gotten caught back up in their conversation.

It had been fun listening to the three brothers go back and forth, making fun, teasing each other. She'd been reminded of how she and Brant had talked and laughed together, so she'd stayed hidden, enjoying the easy banter between them.

Then, when the conversation had shifted to her, she'd been too intrigued to leave.

Now, anxiety wrapped itself around her and she felt cold to the bone. She leaned back against the side of the house and curled her hands into fists at her sides. It took everything she had to stand her ground and not go rushing out into the yard, demanding that Jericho tell her what he'd been keeping from her.

What was it she didn't know?

What was he hiding?

"And why?" she whispered, glancing briefly down at Nikki who sat, head cocked, ears lifted as if considering Daisy's question.

But when no answers came, Daisy shifted her gaze to stare up at the sky. She didn't see the clouds sweeping across that wide expanse. Instead, she saw Jericho's ice-blue eyes looking down at her. In her mind's eyes, she saw his face, emotion charging his features as he covered her body with his. As they lay together in the shadows, talking and laughing after the loving.

And she saw him now, as he'd faced Justice and said, *She doesn't belong here.*

How could he still believe that? Hadn't she made a place for herself here? Hadn't she helped him with his clients, turned his stark, barren house into a comfortable home? Hadn't she spent every night in his arms?

Irritation spiked inside her, warring instantly with the regret and sorrow that had her system strangling. He thought *she* was stubborn? They'd spent every day of the past few weeks together. Worked together. She'd gone on one survival trip with him and his clients and not only had she kept up, but she'd also handled the cooking and made the camp's clients more comfortable. She'd proved herself, she knew she had.

Yet, he still held back.

Still stood to one side and pronounced that she didn't fit. Didn't belong. What would it take for him to admit that she *did?* Or would he, ever? If he was so determined to keep her out, would that ever change? Wasn't she just setting herself up for disappointment and pain if she remained, waiting, hoping he'd see the light?

"This is your own fault," she muttered as she listened to the rumble of the men's laughter. "If you hadn't fallen for him, then this wouldn't matter at all. You'd simply leave as you'd planned to do in the first place and you wouldn't have looked back."

But that was the trouble, she told herself. She would be looking back. Always.

Jericho laughed aloud at something one of his brothers said and the rich, deep sound of it sliced into her.

Nikki whined and Daisy bent to scoop up the little dog and cuddle her close to comfort both of them. At the moment, she wanted nothing more than to walk right out there and confront Jericho. She wanted answers. She wanted him to look her in the eye and try to say she didn't belong. That there was nothing between them.

"This shouldn't have happened," she told herself quietly, her voice lost in the sigh of the wind. "Daisy," she murmured, burying her face in Nikki's soft fur, "why did you have to fall in love with him? Why couldn't you have just slept with him and kept your heart out of the mix?"

Too late to regret that now, she thought, as pain whipped through her. She wished she could see Jericho's face. Would she see the lie in his eyes? Or would she see an indisputable truth written there?

But she stood her ground, because as long as he was with his brothers, it wasn't the time to confront him. She'd only look like the fool she felt for having been caught eavesdropping on them all.

She stayed put and waited until the truck engine fired up and the three men rode off down the long drive. Only then did she come around the edge of the house to look at the fantail of dust rising up in the wake of the truck.

Her heart ached as Jericho's words played over and over in her head. He was determined to feel nothing for her, she realized. It didn't matter that her own feelings had grown and changed since she'd first come to King Mountain. Didn't matter that she loved him—he wouldn't be interested.

She wrapped her arms around herself and held on, scraping her hands up and down her upper arms in a futile attempt to beat back the rising chill inside her. Until just a few minutes ago, she hadn't even been aware that she'd begun nursing dreams centered around Jericho. Dreams that had the two of them happily living together here on the mountain. Building a family. Raising their children and loving each other every night.

How hard it was to feel those nebulous dreams shatter and dissolve as if they'd never been. But through that pain, she managed to console herself with the fact that she'd done what she'd originally come here to do. She'd made love with Jericho King and if the gods were kind, she was already pregnant. She'd find out soon and then, while she still was able, she'd leave him here on his precious mountain and find another place to belong.

But not, she told herself, before she found out exactly what he was hiding from her.

Ten

By the end of the following week, Daisy felt as if her nerves were strung as tight as a newly tuned piano's strings. After his brothers left for home, Jericho had retreated into himself. He hadn't touched her, kissed her—had hardly *looked* at her in days. And the strain of that was beginning to take its toll. While she stood at her bedroom window looking out at the night, her mind raced even as she stood as if frozen in place.

Sensing a coming confrontation between her and Jericho, Daisy had made a trip into the local town and found the pregnancy test she'd been looking for. But buying it didn't mean using it. The tidy blue box was still sitting in the cupboard beneath her bathroom sink, unopened.

She knew why she was hesitating to use it, of course. If she wasn't pregnant, then she'd be staying on, whether

Jericho approved or not—she'd find a way to stay close. To fight his instincts to chase her off. If she was pregnant, then she could leave—just as he wanted her to. As she'd planned.

Which, she told herself sadly, was exactly why she hadn't used the test kit yet. She didn't want to go. Didn't want to leave Jericho, this place and the handful of employees that had given her such a feeling of family. She was a part of the life here now. She'd become one of them. She'd found her place in the world, found the one man she wanted above all others and she didn't want to lose any of it.

Giving up went against her very nature, she thought. But was it giving up to leave when that had been the original plan? And was it worth it to stay if Jericho never allowed himself to care for her? God, her head hurt.

"What're you doing?"

Nikki yipped in excitement from her perch on the bed and Daisy spun around to face Jericho when he spoke up from the doorway to her bedroom.

"Nothing," she blurted because he'd caught her off guard and at a vulnerable moment. She forced a smile that felt brittle and false. "Just thinking."

He walked into the room and didn't stop until he was no more than an arm's reach away. He ignored Nikki, who pranced to the edge of the bed, hoping for a scratch and head rub.

"I've been doing some thinking, too," he said and he didn't look any happier with his thoughts than she was with hers.

The time had come. Everything inside Daisy braced for whatever was next.

When silence spun out between them, Daisy took it for as long as she could and then felt what little patience she had left splinter and blurted, "For heaven's sake, Jericho, just say it."

His dark brows drew together and his mouth flattened into a grim line. "Say what?"

"What you came here to say," she challenged. "What you've been dying to say since the day I arrived. You want me to leave the mountain."

"You're wrong," he ground out. Shoving one hand through his hair, he stalked past her, looked out the window and, after a long minute, swiveled his head to lock his gaze with hers. "I don't want you to go…"

Her heart swelled and an instant later deflated as if someone had popped it with a needle.

"…which is why you have to."

She blinked at him, shook her head and finally managed to say, "That makes absolutely no sense."

"Doesn't have to," he told her flatly. "Like I said before, my mountain, my rules."

So cold. So hard. So distant. Not the man she'd come to know at all. He was already pulling away so fast she could hardly reach him. And that tore at her.

"So I'm supposed to just leave. Without an explanation. Without— Why, Jericho? Do I worry you that much?"

He laughed shortly, but there was no humor in the sound. "You don't worry me, Daisy. You just have to go."

"Why?"

"Don't make this harder than it has to be," he told her.

"Oh, I think I will." As she said it, as her spine

stiffened and her shoulders squared, she realized that she was going to fight to stay, not even knowing if she was pregnant or not, she was going to take a stand. Because looking up into his ice-blue eyes, Daisy knew he was something worth fighting for. What they had together was too important to let die without a battle.

He looked like the cold-eyed warrior he was, she thought. But her brother had been a Marine, too. Now, Jericho was about to realize that this Saxon could be just as tough as any combat-hardened Marine.

And she fired her biggest gun with her first salvo.

"I love you."

His features went blank and, if possible, his eyes became even icier, more remote. "No, you don't."

Anger, hot and alive, pumped through her and she stepped right up to him. Tipping her head back so she could give him a full power glare, she said, "You might think you know everything, Jericho King, but you do not get to tell me what I do and don't feel. I said I love you. And I meant it. Now you have to deal with it."

She didn't have to wait long for his response and, frankly, it was pretty much just what she had expected.

"You think I'm blind, Daisy?" He countered, looming over her. His voice was low, rough and sounded as if the words were being ripped from his soul. "You think I don't see what's really going on? It's not me you love. It's being here, with me, with Sam and the others. You've been lonely since your brother died and now you've made us the family you want back so badly."

She felt as if he'd slapped her. Perhaps there was some truth in his words, but it wasn't the whole picture, not by a long shot. Yes, she'd come here looking to find a family again. She hadn't expected to find love, but she had. And she wouldn't let him make that less than it was.

Honestly. She told him she loved him and he threw her feelings back in her face? What kind of man did something that stupid?

"You idiot. Do you really believe I'm that big a simpleton? Do you think I don't know the difference between love and longing?" She fisted her hands at her hips and leaned in, narrowing her gaze on him until her eyes were mere slits of fury. "Of course I was lonely. But I didn't just pick the first man I ran into to become the family I miss so much. I came here because you knew my brother. I didn't come looking for a husband or someone to cling to. I don't cling. I didn't mean to fall for you. It just…happened."

He frowned, but she wasn't finished.

"Of all the arrogant, foolish, stubborn men in the world, why is it you I had to fall in love with?" Shaking her head, she reached up and yanked at her own hair in frustration. "You're so determined to lock yourself away up on this mountain, shut away from anything or anyone who might matter to you that you absolutely refuse to see that not only do I love you, but you love me back!"

He took a step away, ground his teeth together so hard she could see a muscle in his jaw twitch. She watched as he fought for control and finally managed it. Only then did he speak.

"You know, I didn't ask for this. Didn't want it." He blew out a breath. "You're the one who showed up and wouldn't go away. You're the one who kept pushing and prodding me until I was in a corner."

"Poor you," she said with a slow shake of her head.

A smirk curved his mouth briefly. "Justice and Jesse don't know squat about tough women," he said. "You could give their wives lessons."

"Thank you."

"Not sure it was a compliment."

"I am. I'm not afraid to say what I want. To fight for what I want. Are you?"

He inhaled sharply, deeply. "If a man said that to me, I'd punch him," he admitted.

"Really?"

He didn't respond to that. "I made up my mind before I left with my brothers that when I came back, I was going to take you to bed and keep you there for twenty-four straight hours and then I was going to send you away. For your own good."

She rocked in place, shaken by his words. "But you haven't so much as touched me in days."

"Because when I got back and saw you again…I knew that if I touched you I'd never let you go. And I have to let you go."

Something small and sharp seemed to tear at her heart. "Why?"

He shook his head.

"There are things you don't know…"

"So tell me," she countered.

He scrubbed one hand across his face.

"Honestly, Jericho, does the thought of being loved really engender so much panic?"

"Not panic, no," he told her honestly, the shutters in

his eyes lifting slightly, the ice there melting just enough for her to see a glimmer of warmth shining out at her. "But second thoughts, even third…yes. You don't know what you're doing."

"You're wrong." She walked toward him, one deliberate step after another.

He stood his ground. Not backing away. Not turning from her. Just watching her with a fire in his eyes that melted the last of her anger and fueled another emotion entirely.

"No, I'm not," he said softly, gaze locked with hers as she approached. "If you knew what was good for you, you'd pack up your stuff and be off the mountain inside an hour."

"I'm not going anywhere."

"To tell the truth, never thought you would," he admitted and swallowed hard as he reached for her. "I may be damned for this one day, but God help me, I can't let you go. Won't let you go."

"What're you saying?" she whispered.

"I'm saying that right here, right now, I need you." He took a breath. "Not talking about a future or happily ever after. Don't ever count on a future. Right now is all I can offer."

"Then for now," she said, "that's all I'll ask for."

Jericho's arms came around her like a vise, holding her to him, pressing her body's length along his. She buried her face in the curve of his neck as he clung to her and he felt her warmth slide into him, filling all the cold, empty places he'd been living with for days.

She loved him and he was going to let her. For however long it lasted, he would take what she so wanted to give and give her what he could in return. He'd never thought of himself as the "forever" kind of man, but he knew that for right now, he was where he belonged. With the woman he wanted above all else.

When he cupped her face with his palm and turned her mouth up to his, he kissed her with a depth that left him hungry for what he found only with her. But an instant later, that moment was shattered by a single shout from outside.

"Fire!"

The barn was burning and the next few hours passed in a blur.

Heat, shifting light thrown by wind fed writhing flames, the shouts of men and the screams of terrified horses filled the night air. Jericho directed his men, shouting orders over the noise. The volunteer fire department had been called out, but no one was standing around waiting. Hoses were dragged from every area of the yard, and water was aimed at the flames licking along the sides and climbing toward the roofline of the barn.

They fought to get the fire under control to prevent it from spreading not only to the other buildings but to the forest itself. It had been a long dry summer and the only thing they had going for them was the fact that it had recently rained.

The crackle and hiss of the fire sounded like demons chattering in the shadows. And that was what it felt like as well—as if hell had come to the mountain. The heat was amazing and Jericho felt sweat pouring down his back as he made run after run into the barn, leading the horses out. The terrified animals refused to cooperate, so the process took far longer than it should have. But he was intent on getting every animal out of the barn alive.

Just as he'd been intent on keeping Daisy safe.

"Stay in the house!" he'd shouted at her when the first call for help had sounded out. Immediately, he'd raced away from her, fully expecting her to hear and *obey* him, for God's sake.

Naturally, she didn't.

She paused only long enough to close the bedroom door, making sure Nikki couldn't get out and be injured, then she was on his heels as he ran downstairs for the front door. Before he could shout at her again, she'd yelled, "Don't waste your breath, Jericho. This is my home, too, and I'll help save it."

Then she had bolted out of the house and he'd had no choice but to follow after her. Still he'd kept as close an eye on her as possible throughout the battle with the fire.

She was tireless, he thought as the mountain fire department roared up the drive and more men joined the struggle. Daisy handled one of the ranch garden hoses, shooting streams of water on the flames as the men beat at the fire with wet blankets. She never quit. Never flagged. She stood her ground alongside the others and faced whatever fears were choking her without once turning from them.

And as the night wore on and sparks flew into the night, winking from brilliance to darkness, Jericho at last realized the truth.

He loved her.

Loved her with everything he was.

It wasn't about lust. Wasn't about not wanting her to go. It was so much more. He'd tried to tell himself she was just a clumsy, pretty city girl. But there was grit and strength and purpose in her. She was the woman for him.

The only woman.

By the time the fire was contained, Daisy was in the kitchen making boatloads of coffee for the men. Jericho found her there, face sooty, clothes grimy, her hair tangled—and he thought she'd never looked lovelier to him.

"More coffee's on the way," she said, with a quick glance at him.

"That's good. The men are sucking it down as fast as you take it out there."

"Fire's really out?"

"Completely," he said, walking to her, laying his hands on her shoulders and turning her around to face him. "Fire chief thinks it was an electrical thing. Started in one of the wall panels. But we got lucky." He pulled her in close, wrapped his arms around her and felt himself settle for the first time in what felt like forever. "No one was hurt. The animals are safe and we'll rebuild the barn. Structure's still sound. Just going to take—"

"A coat of paint?" she murmured wryly.

He chuckled, kissed the top of her head and said, "A little more than that, but it'll be good."

"And I'll be here to see it?" She tipped her head back and looked up at him. "No more talking about me leaving?"

"No," he told her, wiping away some of the grime from her cheek with the pad of his thumb. "I don't want you to go. Ever."

She smiled at him. "That's the nicest thing you've ever said to me, Jericho King. But you already said it before."

"This is…different. I've got plenty more to say, Daisy Saxon," he admitted. "Starting with—"

"Don't."

The proposal that had leaped to the tip of his tongue stayed locked inside when she shushed him by laying her fingertips against his mouth. Confusion rushed through him. Hell, he knew she'd guessed what he was about to say—so why did she stop him? "Daisy…"

"Before you say anything else, there's something I have to tell you," she whispered.

From outside came the clatter and noise of the men working to put away the firefighting equipment and getting the animals settled down again. They'd have to put the horses up in one of the outbuildings for the night. It wouldn't be a long-term solution but for right now… Jericho dragged his mind back from the logistical problems facing him and instead focused on the woman watching him with a wary regret in her eyes.

"What is it?" His voice was low, his chest tight with the pressure of his breath backing up in his lungs. "What's wrong?"

"Nothing's wrong," she assured him and took a deep breath herself, as if trying to find her own balance before continuing the conversation. "But I have a feeling you were about to ask me to marry you…"

"And you don't want to marry me?" Shock pumped

through him. Daisy, the woman to whom commitment was essential? The woman who longed for family was now going to turn down a proposal from the man she claimed to love? This had to be the weirdest situation he'd ever found himself in.

Jericho had never considered proposing to anyone before. Now that he was ready, the woman he loved was heading him off before he could say the words? What the hell was going on? "You said you love me."

"I do," she said quickly. Reaching up, she cupped his face in her hands and speared her gaze into his. "Oh, Jericho, I do love you. Completely. But I can't marry you until I'm completely honest with you. I think we both need to be truthful with each other. So I'll go first. I can't let you ask me the question until you know the real reason I came here."

"What?" The tension in the kitchen was alive and pulsing around them. So Jericho did what he always had when faced with a problem. He charged right at it. "What do you mean, the real reason?"

She blew out a breath, squared her shoulders and said, "I came here planning to seduce you, Jericho. I wanted a baby and I wanted *you* to be the father."

Eleven

Everything in him went cold and still.

It was as if he were standing outside himself, a silent observer to a scene that had him both furious and baffled.

"You what?"

When she pulled back from him, he let her go. It was better to keep a distance right now. He didn't know what he was feeling and his brain was racing from one thought to another.

"I wanted a family, Jericho," she said, filling a thermos with the freshly brewed coffee. Her hands weren't entirely steady though, and some of the hot, dark liquid spilled onto the countertop. "Brant was all I had. When I lost him..." She stopped, capped the thermos and turned to him. "I was crazy with grief for so long. Weeks, months, all I could do was mourn him. Mourn the loss of my family. When I finally came up for air and realized that I needed to keep living, I knew I didn't want to live alone."

He didn't know what to say to that so he held his silence and waited. It didn't take her long to continue.

"You called me, remember?"

He nodded.

"You offered to help me for the sake of Brant. Because of the connection you two had had."

"Yeah, but I don't remember offering you a child."

She flushed and even through the grime and soot on her face, Jericho could see the pink stain color her skin. "No, you didn't. That was my idea. Don't you see? The Marine Corps stole my family. Brant died for his country, but with him gone, I was so alone. I hated it. It tore at my heart until I thought I would die from the pain."

Something inside him softened toward her. He knew what it was to experience loss. Hell, he'd seen grief destroy people. The fact that Daisy had not only risen above it but found the strength to go on was admirable. But that didn't explain the rest of it. Then she was talking again and Jericho told himself to listen.

"When I decided to have a child, I knew I wanted you to be the father," she admitted. "You and Brant were friends. He admired you so much. And frankly, I thought, Jericho King is part of what took Brant from me—so what could be better than having you be the father of my new family?"

"I don't believe this," he muttered, rubbing the back of his neck hard enough to tear off a layer of skin. When his gaze snapped to hers it was hard and brutal. "So all of this was a scheme? You've been playing me from the start?"

Before she could say anything, he answered his own question on a short laugh. "Of course you have. Damn me, I was sucked in, too. I actually believed you were exactly who you said you were. Hell," he added, throwing his hands high and wide, "I even felt bad for 'taking advantage of you.' There's a joke."

"Jericho, let me explain—"

"No," he said sharply. "Answer one question. Did your plan work? Are you pregnant?"

She took a deep breath and folded her hands across her middle as if already protecting something precious. "Yes. I took the test when I came in to make the first batch of coffee."

"Bullshit," he said. "We used protection."

"Not the first night."

Jericho's world rocked precariously around him. His mind raced back to that first night when he'd come home to her and had been blinded by everything but the staggering hunger rampaging through him. No, he hadn't used a condom. Hell, he'd been doing good to find the damn bed. He'd been blind for her. Conscious only of the need pounding in his veins.

So he couldn't blame her entirely. He wanted to, God knew, because she'd tricked him. She'd made him believe. Made him trust and now she had shown herself as a liar.

"That's perfect," he muttered, turning from her to stare out the window at the men still working in the compound. From upstairs came Nikki's frantic barks and yips as she demanded to be freed from captivity. And behind him stood a woman who was carrying his child.

"Jericho—"

"What the hell am I supposed to do with this?" he asked and didn't really expect an answer.

"I'm sorry I lied to you," she said softly, "but I'm not sorry I came here. I was looking to find a family and instead I found *love*." She took another breath and added, "Jericho, everything changed for me after I'd been here just a few days. I knew then that it wasn't just a child I wanted. I wanted *you*. I love you."

He snorted. "Handy. How you confess your love for me right after you find out you're pregnant."

"I told you before I knew."

He laughed again. "And of course I believe you."

"Why are you so angry?" she asked, taking a step toward him. "Because I lied to you or because I'm pregnant?"

Jericho didn't have the answer to that. He could hardly believe that he was going to be a father, for God's sake. That was a hard piece of truth to hand a man. Wasn't he allowed a few minutes to take it in? To try to decide what he was feeling?

"I'm not talking about this now," he muttered and snatched up the thermos she'd prepared. He turned and headed for the back door, but her voice stopped him before he could leave.

"Jericho, I'm not the only one with secrets. And nothing's changed. I still love you. And you love me."

He looked into her eyes and saw worry glittering in those whiskey-colored depths. But he couldn't assuage it. Couldn't give her what she needed. Not right now. "I don't even know you," he said and walked out to rejoin the men.

The next morning, he was gone.

She'd spent the night alone in her room, with only Nikki for company. She felt cold and lost and when she caught herself blindly reaching for him across an empty bed, the tears came.

How had this all become so confused? So twisted inside and out? In the long, sleepless hours of the night, Daisy had had time to think. To realize that she'd never really considered how her plan would affect Jericho.

Stupid, she knew, but in her quest to have a family, to become pregnant, she'd never stopped to think how her decision would affect him.

Three days later, Jericho was still gone and Daisy was no closer to figuring out exactly what it was she should do next. Walking into the kitchen, Nikki right alongside her, she put one hand to her abdomen and thought about the child already growing inside her.

Soon, she would have a baby. A family. But would that family ever be complete without her child's father?

Nikki walked to the door, sat down and stared at it. Just as she had since Jericho left, as if she could make him appear with the power of her mind. Funny, Daisy thought, she and her dog were in the same boat. Both of them missing the only man either of them wanted.

The back door opened suddenly and she started, gaze shifting quickly, heartbeat accelerating, stomach pitching with an infusion of hope. Nikki yipped in excitement, then drooped to the floor. Daisy knew just how she felt. The expectation she'd felt so briefly drained away as Sam stepped into the room. He must have seen the disappointment she felt written on her face because he gave her a wry smile.

"Sorry," he said as he closed the door behind him. His eyes were kind and an understanding smile curved his mouth. "You don't have to worry about him, you know. He does this occasionally."

"Does what?" she asked. "Disappear?"

He shrugged and answered, "Yeah. You know that. He'll go up into the high country whenever he feels things closing in on him. Sometimes he's gone for days, sometimes longer."

"Longer." Fabulous. How would she ever last without seeing him? Talking to him? Making him listen to her? Jericho was a former Marine. He knew all about survival and getting by in the woods with no more than a piece of string and a knife. He could stay gone for weeks.

"It's none of my business what's going on between the two of you," Sam said softly, "but whatever it is, you'll work it out."

"Not if he doesn't come back."

"He'll be back."

"I wish I was so sure," she told him, moving across the room toward the refrigerator. She opened it, pulled out a bottle of water and opened it. After a long drink, she admitted, "He's furious, Sam. What if he doesn't come back?"

The older man gave her a smile. "He will. This is home. He's never been able to stay away too long. Besides, he loves you."

"I don't know about that."

"Well, I do," Sam said and walked to the coffeepot. Getting down a heavy mug, he poured himself a cup, took a sip and sighed. Then he continued, "I've known Jericho for years and I've never seen him the way he is with you."

That was something, Daisy thought, hope beginning to rise inside her again. If Sam had seen something in Jericho change and grow, then maybe what they'd found together would be strong enough to get past what she was sure Jericho saw as a betrayal.

Oh, God, she had betrayed him. Hadn't meant to, but she could see now how it would feel to Jericho. How he might not be able to trust her. How he might think she was using him. And how could she change his mind if he didn't come back?

"Thank you," she said, taking a seat at the high breakfast bar. Late morning light spilled through the windows, dazzling against the appliances. Outside, the sounds of construction rang out. Hammers, saws and the shouts of men as they worked together rebuilding the damaged section of the barn.

"That means a lot to me, Sam. But the truth is, I really hurt him. I didn't mean to, but I did just the same."

"He's a big boy with thick skin. He'll get over it."

"I hope you're right."

"Usually am," he said with a quick grin. Then his features sobered and he stared down into his coffee for a long moment before he looked at her again. "I haven't said this to you before, but you coming here was a good thing, Daisy."

"I'd like to think so," she admitted. It would make her own sense of guilt much easier to bear. God, she kept seeing the flash of emotion in Jericho's eyes and it all but choked her. She'd been so happy when she saw the positive pregnancy test. So pleased that she'd gotten her wish. That she was carrying Jericho's baby.

Then, when she was sure he was going to propose, she hadn't been able to let him go through with it. Not without telling him the truth. Now she didn't know what to do. What to feel. She had her baby, but had she lost Jericho forever?

"How can it be a good thing," she said quietly, "if my coming here has made him so miserable?"

"Everybody gets mad, honey. Can't go through life without wanting to kick the furniture once in a while. But I've noticed that the only people who can really set us off are the ones who matter."

"You think?"

"I'm not the only one who's noticed the change in Jericho, you know." He locked his eyes with hers as if trying to impress upon her just how important what he was about to say was to him. "He's easier with everyone. Like a heavy weight's been lifted off his shoulders. When your brother died, it tore him up some."

Tears welled in her eyes at the mention of Brant and the reminder that her brother and the man she loved had once been close. "I know they were friends."

"They were," Sam agreed. "But it was more than that. As often happens to those who serve together, Jericho and Brant became more brothers than friends. Suppose he already told you how hard it hit him when that kid died. Guess you know how Jericho struggled for a long time with wondering whether he might have prevented Brant's death."

A ball of ice dropped into the pit of her stomach. "Prevented it?"

"You always wonder, you know," he said, shifting his gaze to the commotion on the other side of the window. "Hell, years later, I still see faces in my sleep. Of the men I served with. The ones I saw die and I ask myself... could I have done something different? Could I have changed that somehow?"

Was that all it was? she asked herself. Was Jericho haunted by the images of what might have been? Or was there more to it? Had he had the opportunity to save her brother? Her breath came faster now as she listened and, though she wasn't sure she wanted the answer, she had to ask the question.

"Why did Jericho think he could have saved Brant?"

The older man whipped his head around to meet her gaze, and he must have seen that she'd known nothing about this. That he'd told her something that Jericho had been keeping from her. And panic flickered briefly over his features before they once again became carefully blank.

"Uh," he said, setting the coffee mug down onto the counter. "Don't mind me, my mouth starts running, there's no telling what might come out of it. I better get out there, ride herd on those guys and make sure they're hammering everything together right."

"Sam..." She hopped off the high kitchen stool and stared at him. Her heartbeat was staggering wildly, as if it couldn't quite find the regular rhythm. Her breath was whooshing in and out of her lungs and her mind was screaming. It was all she could do to keep her voice low and controlled. "Tell me. Did Jericho let my brother die?"

"No, he did not," the older man said tightly. "But I can see I spoke out of turn. Whatever else happened is for Jericho to tell or not as he sees fit. I admire you a lot, Daisy. But this is not my story to tell. Now, excuse me, I'm going back to work."

Stunned, she simply stood there, speechless. What did it mean? Was this the secret Jericho had been keeping from her? What had happened on the day Brant died? What was Jericho hiding?

Alone in the bright, cheerful kitchen, with sunlight pooling all around her, Daisy felt as if she were at the bottom of a deep, dark hole.

Sam would have been surprised to know that Jericho hadn't gone to the high country at all. Instead, he'd steered his Jeep down the mountain and had driven directly to Justice's ranch. He'd needed to talk to somebody, to try to straighten out everything that was in his head and he had known that Justice would talk straight and say exactly what he was thinking—whether Jericho liked it or not.

"You really are an idiot, aren't you?" Justice shook his head in disgust and took a long drink of his beer.

"Thanks. Now I remember why I came to you." Jericho jumped up from his chair and stalked the perimeter of the ranch office. He'd always liked this room. It was purely masculine and the one spot Justice had been able to defend from Maggie's influences. Every other inch of the ranch had been transformed or redecorated, but here, Justice drew a line.

Jericho slapped one hand on the fireplace mantel, looked over his shoulder at his brother and said, "You wouldn't be mad?"

"Hell, yes, I'd have been mad." Justice lifted his booted feet to the corner of the desk and crossed them at the ankle. "I *was* mad when Maggie showed up with Jonas in her arms and claimed he was mine."

"He is yours."

"Yeah, but I didn't believe her."

"So who's the idiot?" Jericho countered.

"You are. I'm a recovering idiot. There's a difference."

"Damn it, Justice," he complained. "She seduced me for my sperm!"

"Sneak up on you in the night, did she?"

"Not funny."

A short bark of laughter shot from his brother's throat and had Jericho scowling at him. "The hell it's not. You can't be seduced if you're not willing. And if you're so damned protective of your sperm, why didn't you have the little suckers corraled?"

He didn't have an answer for that one, so he turned around, stared into the dancing flames in the hearth and tried not to grind his own teeth into powder.

"You're not listening," he ground out. "She tricked me. Right from the beginning. Lied to me. Used me."

"Yeah, well, welcome to the world. People lie sometimes." Justice took another drink of his beer, balanced the can atop his flat abdomen and reminded his brother, "But when it mattered, when it really counted, she told you the truth. Besides, if you're looking for perfection, Jericho, you're not gonna find it."

"Yeah, she did," he agreed, remembering the look on her face when she'd told him. When she'd seen his reaction. Well, damn it, he'd like to know what man would have reacted differently. "I never planned on a family, you know," he said, talking to himself as much as Justice. "Wife. Kids. I never wanted anyone so dependent on me that my death could destroy them. I never wanted to cause anyone that kind of pain."

"Just *this* kind of pain then?" Justice argued. "That girl loves you, Jericho. She's carrying your baby and she loves you and you walked out. You turned tail and ran out the minute she really needed you. The minute you were actually tested."

Well, that didn't set well with him. He hadn't thought of his leaving in those specific terms. But now that he had, he was forced to admit that Justice was right. He'd walked out not only on the woman he loved, but on his own child, too. What did that say about a man's honor?

"There's something else to think about, too," Justice said. "Didn't you tell me that there was something you hadn't told *her?*"

That brought him up short. In all the mess with Daisy and his fury at her deception, he hadn't stopped to consider that he'd been keeping secrets, too. *And if you're keeping secrets, isn't that the same damn thing as lying?*

Hell.

"So maybe, Jericho," his brother mused aloud, "it's time to swallow that damn pride of yours, go home and talk to the woman you love before you do something so stupid she gets away from you altogether."

* * *

Daisy should have left.

She knew it.

Staying at Jericho's house only made his absence tear at her even harder. But how could she leave before she faced him? How could she go on with her life until she knew exactly what it was he'd been keeping from her?

How could she go on with her life without him?

That was the real question and one she didn't have an answer to.

She'd buried her emotions in cooking. There were now so many casseroles, desserts and stews stored in the freezers, no one at the camp would have to shop for supper for two years at least. And still, she was unsettled.

Nikki was on the couch beside her, curled into a ball, when suddenly she jumped straight up, gave a loud, sharp bark and jumped to the floor. Her nails clattered on the wood planks as she raced to the front door.

Daisy's insides twisted into knots as she stood up. Jericho was home. At last.

The door swung open, but Daisy stood her ground and listened as Jericho's deep voice rumbled out.

"Missed me, huh?" he asked and Nikki's soft whines answered him. "Yeah," he said, "crazy thing is, I missed you, too, CB."

Confused, Daisy frowned slightly and the frown was still on her face when he walked into the great room with Nikki held against his chest.

"Hi," he said.

"Hi yourself," she said, then asked, "What's CB?"

He shrugged, patted the little dog's head, then set

her onto the floor where she ran circles around him. "Coyote Bait."

"Not very nice," she told him.

"She doesn't seem to mind."

He walked farther into the room and it occurred to her that they were behaving like polite strangers. A corner of her heart ached for what they'd lost.

"How are you?" he asked. "How is the baby?"

"We're both fine. You?"

"Same."

He scrubbed one hand across his jaw, something Daisy had noticed he did whenever he was stalling, looking for the right words to say. So she waited to hear what he would come up with.

"You pissed me off," he finally said. "But I guess you figured that out."

"Yes, though you hid your feelings so cleverly, I deduced it when you left and didn't come back."

"Right." He nodded. "I shouldn't have done that. And so you know, it didn't do any good anyway because I took you with me when I left."

"Jericho—" Daisy started.

"No, don't say anything." He walked toward her and stopped just a few feet from her. "Not until I've told you something I should have told you long ago."

She swayed a little, then locked her knees to keep herself standing. This was what she'd been waiting for. What she'd been dreading. What had kept her dreams filled with images of her lost brother, tangling with visions of Jericho and all he'd come to mean to her. Now she was both terrified of learning the truth and determined to hear it.

"You mean about Brant's death?"

Surprise flickered in his eyes. "What do you know about that?"

"Not enough," she said. "Sam—"

"Damn it."

"Don't you be mad at him," she said quickly. "He thought you'd already told me whatever it is that you're keeping from me and when he realized you hadn't, he wouldn't say anymore."

Outside, night was falling and the setting sun was painting the sky in brilliant colors. Crimson-stained clouds studded the horizon and Daisy realized a storm was brewing. Well, that was appropriate because another kind of storm was building right here.

"What happened to my brother?" she demanded, moving right up to him, fixing her eyes on his. "How did he really die?"

Pain shot across his eyes, but Daisy wouldn't be moved. She had to know. Was she in love with a man who was the cause of her brother's death? Had she created a child with a man she should hate?

"You know how he died," Jericho said softly, staring into her eyes.

"I don't know why."

"Ah, hell." Jericho peeled off the worn brown leather bomber jacket he habitually wore and tossed it onto the couch. He wore a red T-shirt with the words *King Adventure* stenciled on the left breast pocket. Folding his arms across his chest, he braced his feet in a wide stance and said, "All right. Here we go." Watching her as if he couldn't bear to look away, he said, "Brant volunteered for a dangerous mission and I could have stopped him from going."

"He volunteered?"

"Yeah." Now it was as if he couldn't stand still. He walked past her to the hearth, then turned around and came right back again.

He looked at her, but Daisy thought he was really looking into the past. A past that was haunting them both.

"He knew it was dangerous. The captain called for volunteers and Brant's hand shot up." He smiled in memory and shook his head. "The kid knew no fear. He was eager to serve. Proud to serve."

"Yes, he was," Daisy said and nearly sighed with relief as the knots inside her began to loosen. She couldn't say why because she didn't know the whole truth yet, but looking up at Jericho now, she knew with a bone-deep certainty that this man would have done anything to keep her brother safe. There was simply no way he could have been responsible for Brant's death.

"And why do you think you should have stopped him?"

"Because he was a kid," Jericho snapped irritably. "Sure of himself and not cocky with it either, but he was just a damn kid."

Her brother's face rose up in her mind and Daisy saw what Jericho was obviously not seeing. Her brother had been young, yes. Too young to die and, God, she would always wish that he'd come home, married, had had a family and lived to be a cranky old man. But that hadn't happened, so she would deal with reality.

What she wouldn't do was take away from her brother's sacrifice by playing 'what if?'

"I could have stopped him," Jericho muttered thickly, spearing his gaze into hers. "Could have gone to the captain, recommended he choose someone else. Done... something."

"I have one question, Jericho, and I want you to give me your gut reaction answer, okay?"

"Yeah. What is it?"

"Was Brant ready for that mission? Trained? Capable?"

"Absolutely," he said without hesitation.

And the last of the knots inside her fell free. Daisy took a deep breath, sighed it out and moved toward the man she loved to distraction. Reaching up, she laid one hand on his cheek and said, "Then you have nothing to regret."

"But—"

"You know, it's ironic," Daisy told him thoughtfully. "I raised him, and you're the one who made him into a man. Yet you're the one thinking of him as a boy."

Jericho's jaw dropped and his eyes went wide. A hundred different emotions chased each other across his face as seconds ticked past.

"It wasn't your fault, Jericho," she whispered, leaning into him, willing him to believe her. "Brant made his choices. He was a Marine and he took the same chances any of you did. You can't take that away from him now by putting the blame for his death on yourself."

"You surprise me. Endlessly," he said.

"Good." She smiled. "I understand how you feel, believe me. But you could have told me this before."

He grabbed her and yanked her close. He dipped his head, buried his face in the curve of her neck and inhaled her scent as if he were taking one long, last breath. "I've carried that around with me for so long…"

"Time to let it go. Time to think about the future, not the past."

"Our future," he said, lifting his head to kiss her once, twice. He threaded his fingers through her hair, skimmed his gaze over her face as though he were burning her image into his brain. "I love you, Daisy. I want you. I want our baby."

"Jericho…"

"Stay, Daisy," he said. "Marry me and stay."

She sighed, smiled and whispered, "Okay."

Epilogue

One month later...

"You noticed it's snowing, right?"

Jericho grinned at his wife and pulled her up close to him. "Yeah, I noticed. Pretty, isn't it?"

It really was. Their campsite was alongside the lake and the snow was falling in huge, soft tufts. Silence reigned in the white darkness and the only sound came from their whispered conversation and the hiss and snap of their fire.

"Gorgeous. And cold," Daisy said, burrowing in even closer. "Don't forget cold." She turned her face up to his. "Tell me again why we're taking a honeymoon camping trip in late October?"

"To be alone," he reminded her, using one hand to toss another piece of wood on the campfire in front of them. "Most of the King family is still at the lodge. My family doesn't like leaving a good party in a hurry. Some of them will probably still be there when we get back."

"I like them all."

"Yeah," he said, "me, too. But I'm just as glad they're not here at the moment."

"True."

Nikki hadn't been happy about being left behind, but she was so busy being spoiled by Bella, Daisy didn't think the little dog would miss them for long. Besides, this trip was about them. Newlyweds. That word made her smile. Behind them, a tent stood, waiting for them to snuggle in and Jericho had already told her of his plans for just how to spend their first night on the trail.

"Hotels are nice, too," she whispered, then sighed as he skimmed his fingers across the tip of her nipple. Even through the heavy sweater she wore, she felt the heat of his touch and knew she'd have gone anywhere with him.

"Our first 'date' was at a campfire, remember?" he teased.

"Some date. You were trying to get rid of me."

"Nope, I was trying to keep my hands off you," he confessed. "Now, I don't have to."

Daisy looked at her gold wedding band in the firelight and when it winked at her, she smiled in appreciation. "It was a nice wedding, wasn't it?"

He sighed, dropped his forehead to hers and said, "Yeah, yeah, it was. Almost worth what you, Maura, Maggie and Bella put us all through for the past month getting the camp ready for the wedding."

Daisy laughed and snaked both arms around his middle. "Almost? Almost?"

Jericho grinned at her and couldn't imagine his life without her. She'd brought him closer to his family. She'd eased his mind, his heart, and she'd opened up his soul to the possibilities of real love. He'd spend the rest of his life thanking whatever kind fates had sent her to him.

"Definitely worth it," he amended.

"Oh, and Maggie told me that Justice has some ideas about how we can open up the camp to inner-city kids…"

Yep, she'd brought a lot of changes, he thought and smiled as he watched her animated features brightening at the idea of a new challenge. She was the perfect woman for him. If he could just get her to stop talking.

Being a military man, he used diversionary tactics, sliding one hand up under the hem of her sweater to cup her breast.

"Oh, my…"

"Talk later?"

"You bet. But, Jericho," she sighed as he stroked his thumb across her nipple, "there's just one more thing you should know about me."

"Hmm? What's that?"

"I really don't like camping," she whispered.

"Bet I can change your mind," he said, smiling against her mouth.

"I don't think so…"

He shifted, drawing her into the privacy of their tent,

lifting the hem of her sweater and gliding his mouth along her skin to the swell of her breast.

"Okay," she admitted, "maybe you can change my mind…"

* * * * *

This attraction felt so right, but it was so incredibly wrong.

Jared was her article subject, her employer, one of the most powerful entrepreneurs in Chicago. She had absolutely no business becoming attracted to him.

He reached out to brush a stray lock of hair from her temple. His touch was electric, arousing, light as a feather but shocking as a lightning bolt.

Thunder rumbled in the distance, and the first fat raindrops clattered on the roof.

"I'm going to kiss you," he told her.

She drew a sharp breath. "You think that's a good idea?"

He moved slightly closer. "It's not the smartest thing I've ever done. But I've never wanted anything more."

SEDUCTION AND THE CEO

BY
BARBARA DUNLOP

Published in Great Britain 2011
by Mills & Boon, an imprint of Harlequin (UK) Limited,
Eton House, 18-24 Paradise Road, Richmond, Surrey TW9 1SR

© Barbara Dunlop 2010

ISBN: 978 0 263 88213 1

51-0511

Harlequin (UK) policy is to use papers that are natural, renewable and
recyclable products and made from wood grown in sustainable forests. The
logging and manufacturing processes conform to the legal environmental
regulations of the country of origin.

Printed and bound in Spain
by Blackprint CPI, Barcelona

For my amazing husband—cowboy, pilot and
businessman

Barbara Dunlop writes romantic stories while curled
up in a log cabin in Canada's far north, where bears
outnumber people and it snows six months of the year.
Fortunately, she has a brawny husband and two teenage
children to haul firewood and clear the driveway while
she sips cocoa and muses about her upcoming chapters.
Barbara loves to hear from readers. You can contact her
through her website at www.barbaradunlop.com.

Dear Reader,

Welcome to book number one in the MONTANA MILLIONAIRES: THE RYDERS series from Desire. I love writing about siblings, and I hope you enjoy reading Jared's story in *Seduction and the CEO*, along with his brother Royce and his sister Stephanie's stories over the next couple of months.

The idea for this series goes back a long time. When I was ten years old, my parents took me to visit my aunt and uncle's ranch during the summer school break. Even at that young age, I spun fanciful stories about the people living and working on the cattle ranch. I thought the cowboys were exotic and exciting, and I loved the space and isolation that gave such a sense of community.

Montana is one of my favorite states, and since the source for my hero is my husband—a pilot, a cowboy and a business owner all rolled into one, the stories came together naturally.

Happy reading!

Barbara

One

Journalist Brandon Langard's blunder was the talk of the bullpen at *Windy City Bizz*. The odds-on favorite for a promotion to feature writer, he'd struck out in his attempt to get an interview with Jared Ryder.

Melissa Warner and the rest of the sixth-floor magazine staff watched the fallout with morbid fascination. The managing editor's door was closed tight, but through the interior window, it was obvious Seth Strickland was shouting. His eyes snapped fire, and his face had turned a mottled purple. Brandon's head was bent and still, his shoulders hunched.

"They've already designed the cover," photographer Susan Alaric stage-whispered over the low barrier between her and Melissa's desks.

"That's because Brandon swore it was a done deal,"

said Melissa, remembering his swagger last week when he'd announced the plum assignment.

"Nothing wrong with that man's confidence," Susan returned with an eye roll. Brandon's habit of bragging, flirting and ogling the female staff had long since alienated them.

"I was sure he'd pull it off," Melissa had to admit. Brandon might be obnoxious, but he was also driven and hardworking. And like all the journalists at the *Bizz,* he knew an in-depth article on Chicago's most elusive entrepreneur and bachelor would clinch the promotion to feature writer.

That Jared Ryder had made a fortune in the Chicago real estate market fit *Windy City Bizz*'s mandate for business news. That he was the heartthrob of half the city's female population suited the magazine's new focus on circulation numbers.

Seth became even more animated, gesticulating with both arms as he rounded his cluttered desk to confront Brandon face-to-face. The occasional word filtered through the closed door. "…incompetent…unreliable… reckless…"

"Ouch." Susan cringed.

Melissa experienced a fleeting twinge of pity for Brandon. But then she remembered how he'd eavesdropped on her conversation with the Women in Business organization last month and presented the story idea as his own. She still owed him for that one. Or rather, he still owed her.

She paused on that thought.

It was true. He *did* owe her one. And maybe it was time to collect.

It would serve him right if she swooped in on this particular story. And why not? Seth clearly needed the Jared Ryder interview. And Melissa would kill for a chance at that promotion.

Through the window, Seth stopped talking. His breathing went deep, his nostrils flared, as he set his jaw in a grim line. Brandon bolted for the office door, and Melissa saw her chance. She quickly came to her feet.

Susan glanced up quizzically, assessing the determined expression on Melissa's face. She obviously came to the right conclusion.

"Do it," she begged with a grin. "Oh, *please* do it."

Melissa's heart upped its rhythm. She swallowed hard, trying not to think about the career-limiting consequences of failure. If she promised the interview and didn't deliver, she'd be in more trouble than Brandon.

Still, as Brandon yanked Seth's door open, she tamped down her fear and made her move.

Her colleagues' gazes hit her from all sides as she made a beeline for the editor's office. Some probably guessed her plan. Others would be simply shocked to see her approaching Seth before he had a chance to calm down. His tirades were legendary. They normally sent the staff scurrying for cover.

Brandon peeled off to the right, studiously avoiding eye contact with anyone.

Melissa rapped on the still-open door. "Seth?"

"What?" he barked, without looking up, rustling through a pile of papers on his cluttered desk.

She took a couple of steps into the office, clicking the door shut behind her.

His round face was flushed all the way to his receding hairline. There was a sheen of sweat above his bushy brows. His white shirt was rumpled, sleeves rolled up. And his tie was loose and dangling in two sections over his protruding belly.

"I can get you the interview," she stated outright, standing tall, her three-inch pumps giving her a slight height advantage.

"What interview?"

"The Jared Ryder interview."

"No. You can't."

"I can," she insisted, voice firm with the confidence she'd learned facing down five older brothers. "I will. What's the deadline?"

"Ryder left Chicago this morning."

"No problem. Where'd he go?"

Seth glared at her without answering.

"I can do it, Seth."

"He turned Langard down flat."

"I'm not Langard."

"You're not," Seth agreed in a tone that told her she'd never be as good as Brandon Langard. Then he picked up his phone and punched in a number.

"Give me a chance," Melissa insisted, closing the space between the door and his desk. "What can it hurt?"

"We're out of time."

"A week," said Melissa. "Give me a week."

"Is Everett available?" Seth asked into the phone.

Everett was publisher of the *Bizz,* the head honcho, the guy who approved the lead headlines and the cover copy.

"Can we at least talk about it?" she pressed.

"Nothing to talk about. Ryder ran off to Montana."

That information took Melissa by surprise. "What's Jared Ryder doing in Montana?" Surely he wasn't building a skyscraper in Butte.

"He's holed up at his ranch."

Melissa hadn't known he had a ranch. Sure, there were rumors he was once a cowboy. But there were also rumors he was once a spy.

Seth gauged her confused look and raised his bushy brows. "You didn't know he had a ranch."

She couldn't argue that one.

"It's the foundation of the entire Ryder conglomerate. How're you going to save my ass when you didn't even know he had a ranch?"

"Because I will," said Melissa with determination. Just because she didn't happen to know Jared was a cowboy didn't mean she couldn't get an interview. "I'll fly to Montana."

"He hates the press. He really hates the *Bizz.* He'll probably run you off his land with—" Seth's attention went to the telephone. "Everett?"

"I can do it," Melissa said, feeling her big chance slip away.

"I have a situation," Seth said to Everett.

"I'll get on the ranch," she pressed in an undertone,

her mind scrambling. "I'll go undercover. I *will* get you the story."

Seth's attention never left the telephone. "It's the Jared Ryder interview." He paused, face flushing deeper, while Everett obviously voiced his displeasure.

"Have I ever let you down?" Melissa went on. She hadn't. But then, she'd never tackled anything this big, either.

"Yes. I know I did," Seth said to Everett.

"Please," said Melissa, leaning forward. "I'll buy my own plane ticket."

Seth shoulders tensed. "Langard *was* the best I—"

While Everett obviously weighed in again, Melissa searched her mind for fresh arguments.

"I grew up with horses," she blurted out. Well, one horse, really. It had lived in a field, on the edge of suburbia, across the street from her new house. She'd nicknamed it Midnight. "I'll—"

Seth's glare warned her to shut up.

"—get a job on the ranch."

Seth smacked his palm over the mouthpiece. "Do you know who this is?"

She gave a small nod.

"Get out."

"But—"

"Now."

Melissa pursed her lips.

Seth's gaze glittered dark with warning as he went back to Everett. "The Cooper story can take the cover."

Melissa debated a split second longer. But bravery

was one thing, stupidity quite another. She'd pushed Seth as far as she dared.

She retreated, and Seth's voice followed her back to the bullpen. "I'll get a photographer on it right away."

Like Brandon had done only minutes before, she avoided eye contact as she made her way to her desk.

"Susan," Seth bellowed from behind her.

With a darting look of pity at Melissa, Susan rolled back her chair, came to her feet and headed for the editor's office.

Melissa dropped into her own chair and stared at the randomly bouncing colored balls of her screen saver. She could have gotten that interview. She knew she could have gotten that interview.

"It's Lorne Cooper on the cover," said Susan as she slipped back into her seat.

Melissa nodded with resignation. "The sports-gear king." There was a new megastore opening on Murdoch Street, and "Cruisin' Cooper" was sponsoring a bicycle race to celebrate.

"The article's written. All it needs is an update and some new art."

Melissa pulled herself closer to her computer screen and hit the space bar. "It was written by R. J. Holmes," she pointed out, voice laced with self-pity. R.J. was one of the newest journalists on staff, and he was beating her out for a cover.

"I guess Seth wasn't feeling charitable toward Brandon."

"Or toward me." Melissa's screen powered up on a search engine.

"What've you got ready?"

"Myers Corp. or the Briggs' merger."

Susan didn't answer.

"I know," Melissa conceded, randomly poking the *H* key. "They're even lamer than Cooper." Not that any old cover story would clinch the promotion. There was only one story that would catapult her into the feature writer's job.

She backspaced to erase the *H* and typed Jared Ryder into the search engine.

In a split second, it returned a list of options that included the home page of Ryder International, Jared's speech last month to the Chamber of Commerce, contact information for his new office tower and a link to the Ryder Ranch.

Curious, she clicked the ranch link.

A brilliant green panorama of trees, meadows and rolling hills appeared in front of her. The sky was crackling turquoise, while a ribbon of pale blue meandered through the meadow, nearly kissing a two-story, red-roofed house surrounded by pens and outbuildings.

So that was what Montana looked like.

A row of thumbnail pictures lined the bottom of the screen. "Natural beauty," advertised one caption. "Surrounded by wilderness," read another. "South of Glacier National Park."

Susan shut down her own computer, rising to sling three cameras over her shoulder. "Gotta get to work."

"Have fun," Melissa offered, clicking on a thumbnail

of summer wildflowers. Red, purple, yellow, white. They really were quite gorgeous.

Susan grinned as she pushed a drawer shut with her hip. "I will. Headshots today. Then there's a gala Friday night, and I'm going to hitch a ride on the channel-ten chopper for the bike race Sunday."

"Shut up," Melissa griped as Susan rounded the end of the desk.

Melissa would be sitting right here all week long, in the stuffy, hot office, combing through the minutes of various City Hall committees, looking for permits or variances or financial-policy news, anything that might lead to an interesting business story.

"What's that?" asked Susan, nodding to the computer screen.

Melissa refocused on the verdant green and bright flowers. "Montana," she answered. "Where *I'd* be if Seth had half a heart." *Or half a brain.*

She clicked on an area map. There was an airport in Missoula and everything.

"Not my cup of tea," said Susan, popping a jaunty plaid hat on her curly brown locks.

"Not mine, either," Melissa admitted, gathering her own straight, blond hair into a knot at the nape of her neck in an effort to let the building's weak air-conditioning waft over her hot skin. "But I'd fly there in a heartbeat to meet Jared Ryder."

"So do it," said Susan.

"Yeah, right."

"Why not?"

Melissa swiveled to face her coworker. "Because Seth turned me down flat."

Susan shrugged. "Tell him you're doing City Hall research from home. Then get on a plane."

Oh, now that seemed brilliant. "Lie to my boss and ignore his orders?"

"He'll forgive you if you get the story." Susan's lips curved in a conspiratorial grin. "Trust me."

Melissa let the hair slip out of her hand. The idea was preposterous.

Susan leaned in and lowered her voice. "If you don't get the story, somebody else will."

"At least it won't be Brandon."

"Result will be the same."

"Flying to Montana could get me fired," Melissa pointed out.

"It could also get you promoted." Susan straightened.

"Easy for you to say."

Susan shrugged the cameras into a more comfortable position, then adjusted her cap. "Up to you. But no risk, no reward. My biggest payday was when those vandals let the lions loose at Lincoln Park."

"That was insane," Melissa reminded her. Susan had been clinging to the branches of an oak tree with a hungry male lion pacing below when the animal-control officer had darted the thing.

Another shrug.

"Are you suggesting that if I don't put myself in mortal danger, I'm not trying hard enough?"

Susan patted Melissa's shoulder. "I'm suggesting if

you don't torpedo Brandon and go after that promotion, you're not trying hard enough."

Point made, Susan winked and sauntered away, while Melissa drummed her fingertips on the desktop.

She glanced at the pictures of the Montana ranch. Then her gaze shifted to the spacious window cubicle reserved for the new feature writer.

She pictured Seth's expression when she presented the article. She pictured Brandon's face when he learned of her coup. She pictured her byline on the cover of the *Bizz.* Then just for good measure, she pictured herself at the podium, accepting a Prentice award next January. She could wear her black-and-gold-layered gown, with the teardrop medallion she'd found last week in that funky little art gallery on Second.

Take *that,* Brandon Langard.

Her life would be perfect. All she had to do was talk her way onto the Ryder Ranch.

Body loose in the saddle, Jared Ryder held his horse Tango to a slow walk across the wooden bridge that led to his sister Stephanie's place. Her jumping-horse outfit was built on Ryder land up on the Bonaparte Plateau, about ten miles into the hills from the main spread at Spirit Lake. Tango's ears twitched and his body tensed as he took in the nearly hundred head of horses grazing in the fields and milling about in the pens clustered around the main riding arena.

Jared was feeling just as twitchy as his horse. Far from the haven he'd always known, the familiar sights and sounds of Montana brought a crush of memories. And a fresh surge of anger roiled in his belly.

His instinct had been to stay far away from the ranch this week. But his sister, Stephanie, needed him. Besides, Chicago had its own problems at the moment.

Ryder International had just signed a long-term lease to rent space to the City of Chicago in the Ryder office tower that was under construction on Washington Street. For some reason, the mayor had insisted on parading Jared from charity ball to art gallery opening. Jared had been out in public so often that the tabloids started to believe there was a reason to take his picture and stuff a microphone in his face.

It was beyond frustrating. He was a businessman, not a politician or a celebrity. And his personal life was none of their damn business. The reporter from *Windy City Bizz* camping out at the end of his driveway Monday night was the last straw. When he got back to the city, he was looking into restraining orders and disguises.

But for the moment he had no choice but to come to terms with the home front. He cleared the main equestrian barn, and a cluster of people on horseback at the riding arena came into view. His appearance caught their attention. One horse and rider immediately broke free from the group, trotting down the dirt road to meet him. Both Jared and Tango tracked the pair's progress past the pens, dotted outbuildings and sparse trees.

"The prodigal returns," sang his twenty-two-year-old sister, Stephanie, pulling her mare to a halt, raising a cloud of dust in the July sunshine. Her smiling, freckle-flecked face peeked out from her riding helmet. Her long legs were clad in tight jodhpurs and high, glossy brown boots, while a loose, tan blouse ballooned around her small frame. Her unruly auburn hair was tied back in a ponytail.

"I think you're confusing me with Royce," said Jared, watching her closely. She might not know what he knew, but they'd all been shaken by their grandfather's death three months ago.

He halted Tango, who eyed the mare with suspicion.

"At least Royce makes it to my competitions," Stephanie pointed out, shifting in her stirrups. "He was there to watch me win last week at Spruce Meadows."

"That's because he lives on his jet plane," Jared defended. His brother, Royce, routinely flew from New York to London, Rome and points east, checking out companies to add to the Ryder International empire. Royce was mobile.

"I live in a boardroom," Jared finished.

"Poor baby," Stephanie teased. She smiled, but Jared caught the veiled sadness in her silver-blue eyes. Stephanie had been only two when their parents died, and Gramps was the closest thing to a parent she'd known.

"Congratulations," he told her softly, reflexively tamping down his own anger to focus on her needs. He'd been fifteen when they lost their parents, and he liked to think he'd had a hand in raising her, too. He was immensely proud of her accomplishments as both a rider and a trainer.

"Thanks." She leaned forward to pat Rosie-Jo, her

champion gray Hanoverian, briskly on the neck, but not before Jared caught the telltale sheen in her eyes. "Want to see our trophy?"

"Of course," he answered. There would be plenty of time later to talk about their grandfather.

"We've got a few hours before the meeting." She drew a brave breath and squared her shoulders, shaking off the sadness as she turned the horse to draw alongside Jared.

Together they headed toward her two-story blue-gabled ranch house.

The annual meeting of the Genevieve Memorial Fund, a charitable trust named in memory of their mother, would take place today. Each year, it was scheduled to coincide with the anniversary of their parents' deaths. Picturing his parents, Jared felt his anger percolating once more. But he had to suck it up, be a man about it. There was absolutely no point in disillusioning his younger brother and sister.

"I saw *you* in the Chicago paper last week," Stephanie chimed in as they left the river behind them.

"That was a picture of the mayor," Jared corrected. He'd done his best to duck behind the burly man.

"They named you in the caption."

"Slow news day," he told her, remembering the flashbulbs outside the gallery and how the reporters had shouted inane questions as he'd helped Nadine into the limo.

Stephanie's expression turned calculating, her tone curious. "So who was she?"

"Who was who?" he asked, pretending he didn't

know exactly where his baby sister was headed. Raised in a male-dominated household, she'd been lobbying for *somebody* to please marry a nice woman since she was seven years old.

"The bombshell in the picture with you."

"She was my date," he offered, letting the statement dangle without elaboration.

Stephanie pasted him with a look of impatience. "And?"

He forced her to wait a beat longer. "And her name is Nadine Romsey. Sorry to disappoint you, but she's not a bombshell. She's a lawyer with Comcoe Newsome."

Stephanie's interest grew. "Looks *and* brains. This must be something serious."

"It was a business arrangement. The mayor invited me to the party, and there were people attending that Nadine wanted to meet."

Stephanie pouted. "But she's so pretty."

"And you're so hopelessly romantic."

"Will you take her out again?"

"Only if she needs to get into another party." He admired Nadine, but he didn't have any romantic interest in her.

Stephanie compressed her lips in frustration. "You've written her off after one date? You know, you're never going to meet a woman if you don't get out there and—"

"I'm 'out there' 24/7, little sister." He gestured around the spread. "That's what pays for all of this."

Stephanie pointed her nose in the air. "Ryder

Equestrian Center brought in a million dollars last year."

Jared snorted a laugh. "While you spent four million."

"We also provided dozens of marketing opportunities for the firm, and we improved your corporate image. That is priceless."

"You rehearsed that, didn't you?"

"You should get married, Jared."

"Aren't you a little old to be angling for a mother figure?"

"I'm looking for a sister now. You should find someone young and fun. Who likes horses," she added for good measure, kicking her mare into a faster walk.

Jared shook his head. Between the revelation his grandfather had spoken on his deathbed, the mayor and the media, and Ryder International's accountant's concerns that the company was expanding too fast, Jared didn't have a scrap of emotional or intellectual energy left over for romance.

As he followed Stephanie past the open door of a stable, a sudden tingle spread up his spine. He turned sharply and locked gazes with a blond-haired, green-eyed beauty who stood just inside the main doorway. She was wearing blue jeans and a crisp white shirt, and she held a manure fork in both hands.

She quickly glanced away, but his radar pinged.

What was it?

He stared at her a little longer.

It was the makeup. Her makeup was subtle, but she was definitely wearing some. And he'd bet her blond highlights were from a salon, not the sunshine. Her collared shirt was pressed, and the hands that held the manure fork were soft, bare, no gloves.

"Who's that?" he asked his sister.

Stephanie turned and followed the direction of his gaze.

"Why? You think she's pretty?"

Anyone could see the woman was gorgeous. But that wasn't the point.

"I think she's a rank greenhorn," he said.

"Her name's Melissa…something. Webster, I think. You want me to introduce you?" The calculating flare was back in Stephanie's eyes.

"Stop," Jared ordered.

His sister grinned unrepentantly.

"What I want you to do," he continued with ex-aggerated patience, "is to hire experienced staff. We're blowing enough money on this place as it is."

"She needed a job," said Stephanie. "She's from Indiana."

He wasn't sure what the hell Indiana had to do with anything. While he watched, the woman awkwardly scooped a pile of horse manure from the wooden floor and dumped it into a wheelbarrow. "If she needed a million dollars, would you give it to her?"

"She didn't ask for a million dollars. She's on her way to Seattle. She needed money for bus fare."

"You're hiring transients now?"

"She's mucking out our stalls, Jared, not signing the company checks."

"I'm not worried about embezzlement. I'm worried about labor cost efficiency."

He was also worried something wasn't quite right. Why would a woman that polished take a menial job for bus fare?

She could be running away from something, he supposed. Or she could be running from some*one*. Which seemed more likely. An ex-boyfriend? Someone's angry wife? It had better not be the FBI or the state troopers.

He considered her delicate profile, trying to decide if she was a criminal. She tackled the next pile of manure, her city-soft hands sliding up and down the wooden handle.

"She's going to get blisters," he voiced the thought out loud.

"You want to give her some gloves?" asked Stephanie.

"Somebody better," he conceded. Aimless wanderer or criminal on the run, if they were going to employ her, the least they could do was make sure she avoided injury.

"Hey, Melissa," Stephanie called.

The woman paused and glanced up.

"Grab some gloves out of the storeroom."

Melissa gave her hands a puzzled look.

"She hasn't a clue," said Jared, hit with an unexpected flash of pity. Maybe she was running from an angry ex. He quickly reined in his thoughts. None of his business.

"You *sure* you don't want me to introduce you?" Stephanie singsonged.

Jared turned Tango toward the house. "You going to show me your trophy or what?"

"Can't blame a girl for trying."

"Yes, I can." But Jared glanced over his shoulder one last time as they moved away. Manure fork balanced in the crook of her elbow, the woman named Melissa was wriggling her fingers into the pair of stiff leather gloves. The fork slipped and banged to the wooden floor. The sound startled a horse. The horse startled the woman. She tripped on the fork and landed with a thud on her backside.

Their gazes met once more, his amused, hers annoyed.

He turned away, but the flash of emerald stayed with him as he followed Stephanie to the hitching rail in front of the house.

Two

By the end of the day, the bruise on Melissa's left butt cheek had settled to a dull ache.

While she swept the last of the straw from the stable floor, a late-model Bentley rumbled its way to the front of the farmhouse. The glossy black exterior might be dusty, but it was still one impressive automobile. And the chauffeur who jumped out of the driver's seat was crisp in his uniform.

She moved into the oversize doorway, leaning on the end of the broom handle while she waited to see who would emerge from the backseat.

It was an older man, distinguished in a Savile Row suit. He was tall, with a head of thick silver hair. He nodded politely to the chauffeur, then headed up the stairs to the wraparound porch, where both Stephanie and Jared appeared to greet him and usher him inside.

The chauffeur shut the car door. He glanced curiously around the ranch yard before moving to open the trunk. Melissa peered at the house, but there was no way to guess what was going on inside. The man might be a friend, or perhaps he was a business associate.

Jared's sister's house seemed like an odd location for a business meeting. Unless, of course, somebody wanted to keep the meeting a secret.

Now *that* was an interesting possibility. Was there something clandestine in the works for Ryder International?

As the chauffeur had before her, Melissa glanced curiously around the yard. Several young riders were practicing jumps in the main ring, their grooms and trainers watching. A group of stable hands were loading hay into a pickup truck beside the biggest barn, and three cowboys were urging a small herd of horses across the river with a pair of border collies lending a hand. Nobody was paying the slightest bit of attention to the Bentley.

Then another vehicle appeared and pulled up to the house. This one was an SUV, larger but no less luxurious than the Bentley.

A thirtysomething man with dark glasses and curly dark hair stepped out of the driver's seat. He looked Mediterranean, and he was definitely not a chauffeur. He wore loafers, well-cut blue jeans, an open white dress shirt and a dark jacket. He also offered a polite greeting to the Bentley driver before striding up the stairs of the porch.

Melissa's journalistic curiosity all but ordered her to investigate. She leaned her broom up against the stable wall and started across the yard. She told herself she'd put in a good eight hours today. It was close to dinnertime, and the Bentley was at least vaguely in the direction of the cookhouse. She'd have a plausible excuse if anyone questioned her.

Ironically she'd been disappointed not to get a job down at the main ranch. The foreman there had all but sent her packing this morning when she'd told him she was a stranded traveler. Luckily Stephanie Ryder had been there at the time. The younger woman had taken pity on Melissa and offered her a job at the Ryder Equestrian Center. Melissa had been plotting ways to get back to the main ranch when Jared and his horse had wandered into the yard. Talk about good luck.

Now she was looking for more luck. She smiled brightly at the chauffeur, smudging her palms along the sides of her thighs, wishing she wasn't covered in dust and sweat, and was wearing something other than blue jeans and a grime-streaked shirt. She wasn't the greatest flirt in the world, but in the right party dress, she could usually hold a man's attention.

"Very nice car," she ventured in a friendly voice as she approached.

The man pushed the trunk closed and gazed critically at the Bentley. "I suppose dust is better than mud."

She guessed he was about her own age, maybe twenty-five or twenty-six. He was attractive, in a farmboyfresh kind of way, with blond hair, a straight nose and a narrow chin. He was clean-shaven, and his hair was neatly trimmed.

She slowed her steps, taking in the Montana license plate and committing the number to memory. "Did you have a long drive in?" she asked pleasantly.

"Couple of hours from Helena."

Helena. Good. That was a start. "So you work in Helena?"

"Three years now."

She stayed silent for a moment, hoping he'd elaborate on his job or the company. She scanned both his uniform and the car for a logo.

"Your first time at Ryder Ranch?" She tried another approach.

He nodded at that. "Heard about it, of course. Everybody in the state knows about the Ryders."

"I'm from Indiana," she supplied.

"Grew up south of Butte myself." He gave the dust on the car another critical gaze. "There a hose around here someplace?"

She had no idea. "I guess you meet interesting people in your job?" She struggled to keep the conversation focused on his employment.

"I do some." He glanced around the ranch yard while a horse whinnied in the distance, and a tractor engine roared to life. Unfortunately he didn't pick up the conversational thread.

But Melissa wasn't giving up, not by a long shot. She moved in a step closer, tossing back her hair, hoping it looked disheveled, instead of unruly.

Her actions caught his attention, and he glanced at the ground.

She lowered her voice as she gave him her brightest smile. "I'm a little embarrassed," she cooed. "But should I know the man you dropped off?"

The chauffeur looked back up. He didn't answer. Instead, he swallowed hard, and his neck flushed beneath the collar of his uniform.

"I only ask," she continued, tilting her head to one side, surprised it took so little to rattle him, "because I don't want…"

He worked his jaw.

She paused, waiting for him, but he didn't make a sound.

She suddenly realized his gaze wasn't fixed on her. He was focused on a spot behind her left shoulder. Her scalp prickled.

Uh-oh. She twisted her head and came face-to-face with Jared Ryder.

It was clear he was annoyed. He was also taller than she'd realized, and intimidating, with that strong chin and those deep blue eyes. He wore a fitted, Western-cut shirt and snug blue jeans. His shoulders were broad, his chest deep, and his sleeves were rolled halfway up his forearms, revealing a deep tan and obvious muscle definition.

"Don't want to what?" he asked Melissa, his tone a low rumbling challenge.

She didn't have a quick answer for that, and his deep blue gaze flicked to the silent chauffeur. "There's coffee in the cookhouse." He gave the man a nod in the appropriate direction.

The chauffeur immediately took his cue and hustled away.

Jared's tone turned to steel, the power of his irritation settling fully on Melissa. "I'd sure appreciate it if you could flirt on your own time."

"I…" What could she tell him? That she wasn't flirting? That, in fact, she was spying?

Better to go with flirting.

"I'm sorry," she told him, offering no excuses.

He gave a curt nod of acknowledgment, followed by a long assessing gaze that made her glad she was only pretending to be his employee.

"I don't know why Stephanie hired you," he finally stated.

Melissa wasn't sure how to answer that, or even if he expected an answer. The only thing she did know was that she was determined to take advantage of the opportunity to talk to him alone.

"You're Stephanie's brother?" she asked, pretending she hadn't been poring over his press coverage on the Internet.

"She tells me you grew up around horses," he countered, instead of answering the question.

"I did." Melissa nodded. Technically it was true. She gestured to the northern paddocks. "You obviously grew up around a lot of them."

"My qualifications aren't at issue."

"Stephanie seemed fine with mine." Melissa valiantly battled the nerves bubbling in her stomach. "I saw the main house yesterday. The one your grandparents built. Were you born on the Ryder Ranch?"

A muscle ticked in his left cheek. "Since you're obviously not busy with anything else, I need you to move my horse to the riverside pen. The one with the red gate."

"Sure." The brave word jumped out before she had a chance to censor it.

"Name's Tango." Jared pointed to a paddock on the other side of the driveway turnaround where a black horse pranced and bucked his way around the fence line. Its head was up, ears pointed, and it was tossing his mane proudly for the three horses in the neighboring pen.

Melissa's bravado instantly evaporated.

"You can tack him up if you like," Jared continued. "Or he's fine bareback."

Bareback? She swallowed. Not that a saddle would help.

"Melissa?"

Okay. New plan. Forget the interview, it was time for a quick exit.

"I…just…" she stammered. "I…uh…just remembered, I'm off shift."

His brows twitched upward. "We have shifts?"

"I mean…" She blinked up at him. What? *What?* What the hell did she say?

She rubbed the bruise on her left butt cheek, making a show of wincing. "My fall. Earlier. I'm a little stiff and sore."

"Too stiff to sit on a horse?" He clearly found the excuse preposterous.

"I'm also a little rusty." She attempted to look contrite and embarrassed. "I haven't ridden for a while."

He cocked his head, studying her all over again. "It's like riding a bike."

She was sure it was.

"Tack's on the third stand. Don't let him hold his breath when you cinch the saddle."

As far as she was concerned, Tango could do any old thing he pleased. She wasn't going to stop him from holding his breath. Quite frankly she'd rather chase lions around Lincoln Park.

"I really can't—"

"We fire people who can't get the job done," Jared flatly warned her.

The threat stopped Melissa cold. If she got fired, she'd be thrown off the property. She could kiss the article and her promotion goodbye. And if Seth found out she'd been here, she could probably kiss her job at the *Bizz* goodbye, too.

"I hope you won't," she said in all sincerity.

Jared searched her expression for a long moment. His voice went low, and the space between them grew smaller. "Give me one reason why I shouldn't."

"I've been working really hard," she told him without hesitation.

"Not at the moment," he pointed out.

"It's six o'clock."

"We're not nine to five on Ryder Ranch."

"I'm prepared for that."

He edged almost imperceptibly closer, revealing tiny laugh lines beside his eyes and a slight growth of beard along his tanned square jaw. "Are you?"

She ignored the tug of attraction to his rugged masculinity. "Yes."

"You'll pull your own weight?"

"I will."

"You can't depend on your looks around here."

Melissa drew back in surprise.

"If I catch you batting those big green eyes—"

"I never—"

He leaned closer still and she shut her mouth. "You mess with my cowboys, and your pretty little butt will be off the property in a heartbeat."

A rush of heat prickled her cheeks. "I have *no* intention of messing with your cowboys."

A cloud rolled over the setting sun, and a chill dampened the charged air between them.

Jared's nostrils flared, and his eyes darkened to indigo in the shifting light. He stared at her for a lengthening moment, then his head canted to one side.

How his kiss might feel bloomed unbidden in her mind. It would be light, then firm, then harder still as he pulled her body flush against his own. A flash of heat stirred her body as the wind gusted between them, forming tiny dust devils on the driveway and rustling the tall, summer grass.

The ranch hands still shouted to one another. Hooves still thudded against the packed dirt. And the diesel engines still rumbled in the distance.

"See that you don't," he finally murmured. "And move my damn horse."

"Fine," she ground out, quashing the stupid hormonal reaction. She'd move the damn horse or die trying.

Later that evening, in Stephanie's dining room, Jared struggled to put Melissa out of his mind. His sister had obviously hired the woman out of pity. Then Jared had kept her on for the same reason. He wasn't sure who'd made the bigger mistake.

"We've had thirty-five new requests for assistance this year," said Otto Durand, moving a manila file to the top of his pile. Otto had been a board member of the Genevieve Memorial Fund for fifteen years. He was also the CEO of Rutledge Agricultural Equipment and a lifelong friend of Jared and Melissa's parents.

"We do have the money," Anthony Salvatore put in, flipping through a report. "Donations, they are up nearly twenty percent." Anthony was a distant relative, the son of Jared's mother's cousin. The cousin had met and fallen in love with Carmine Salvatore on a college trip to Naples, and their only son had held a special place in Genevieve's heart.

Stephanie replaced the empty bottle of merlot on the large oblong table as the housekeeper cleared away the last of the dinner dishes.

Although Royce was stuck in London until Saturday, the remaining four board members of the Genevieve Fund were empowered to make decisions on this year's projects.

"I like the school in West Africa," said Stephanie.

"Most of the kids in that region are from agricultural families."

"Mom would like that," Jared acknowledged, then caught Stephanie's fleeting wince. This year in particular, he knew his sister felt a hole in her life where her mother should have been.

Along with their grandfather, he and Royce had struggled to keep their mother's memory alive for her, showing videos, telling stories, displaying mementos. But there was a loneliness inside her that they couldn't seem to fill. It had always manifested itself in hard work and a driving need to succeed. Jared only had to look at the row of equestrian jumping trophies along the mantelpiece to know how hard she pushed herself.

"Yes to the West Africa school." Otto put a check mark on page three of his report. "And I think we can all agree on increasing the animal shelter contributions. Now, the South American clinic project?"

"I still think it's too dangerous," said Jared. He knew his brother, Royce, had advocated for the project after meeting a British university student who'd worked in the mountainous region. But there were too many unknowns, too many frightening stories coming out of the area.

"The rebel activity has been down in that area for six months now," Anthony put in. "And we will use a contractor with experience in the area."

"What about security?" Jared countered. It wasn't the first time the Genevieve Fund had worked in an unstable part of the world, but the other projects had a multiagency, multinational presence, and security had been provided by experts.

"We will hire our own security," said Anthony.

Jared wasn't going to be easily convinced. "For the cost of private security, we could take on two other projects."

"None that are as critical as this one," said Anthony, warming up to the debate. The two of them settled into a familiar rhythm of point counterpoint, each trying to convince Stephanie and Otto of the merits of their respective positions.

Jared acknowledged it was a worthwhile project, while Anthony acknowledged the security circumstances were less than ideal. Still, on balance, Jared felt the situation was far too dangerous, and he made that clear in no uncertain terms.

Finally Anthony threw up his hands in frustration. "I am going for some air."

Fine with Jared. It would give him a few minutes alone with Stephanie and Otto to solidify his case.

Stephanie stood to stretch, while Otto dropped his pen on the report in front of him, speaking before Jared had a chance. "Maybe we should go with Anthony and Royce on this one."

"And if somebody gets kidnapped or killed?" It was a worst-case scenario, but it was also a realistic one.

"They have signed a ceasefire," Otto said.

"Not worth the paper it's printed on. It's Sierra Benito, for goodness' sake. The political situation could turn on a dime." Jared's gaze caught Anthony's profile through the gauzy curtains.

"How many kidnappings last year?" asked Stephanie.

"Too many," replied Jared.

"Nothing since December," said Otto. "I don't want to go against you on—"

"And I'm not looking for risk-free," Jared stressed. "And I don't mind spending the extra money on security. But do we *really* want to take Royce's advice on what's dangerous and what's not?"

Neither Otto nor Stephanie had an answer for that.

In the sudden silence Jared caught another movement on the porch. But this time it wasn't Anthony's profile. It was…

"Excuse me for a moment." He rose from his chair, ignoring their looks of surprise as he crossed to the front door.

"We still have the family home in Naples," Anthony was saying to Melissa as Jared pushed open the screen door. "And I visit it as often as possible." Anthony had planted his butt against the log railing of the porch, one arm bracing him on each side while Melissa stood in front of him.

"I've always wanted to see Italy." She sighed. "The Colosseum, Vatican City, the Sistine Chapel."

Jared scoffed. Pretty big dreams for a woman who couldn't even make it to Seattle.

Anthony levered himself forward to standing, and Melissa didn't back off.

"I would love to show you Venice," he said in a voice that promised more than a tour of the Grand Canal.

Jared wasn't sure who he should warn—Melissa that

Anthony was a player, or Anthony that Melissa's only life skill appeared to be flirting.

"I assume you moved my horse?" he said, instead, causing her to turn her head. Once again she looked both guilty and surprised to see him. And once again he was stabbed in the solar plexus with a shot of unwelcome attraction.

He determinedly shook it off.

"Melissa and I were discussing the treasures of Italy," Anthony offered conversationally, but the set of his shoulders and the tightness around his mouth told Jared that he didn't welcome the interruption.

Too bad.

"You're supposed to be thinking about Sierra Benito," Jared reminded him, moving through the beam of the porch light, transmitting his clear intention to join the conversation.

"Business can wait," said Anthony.

Jared made a show of glancing at his watch. "It's been a long meeting already."

"Give me five minutes. I will be right in."

But Jared had absolutely no intention of leaving.

Melissa glanced back and forth between the two men. Her expression hadn't changed, but the interest in her eyes was obvious.

"Since Melissa's here—" Jared angled his body toward her "—maybe she has something to contribute. What do you think? Is Sierra Benito too dangerous for a humanitarian project?"

Anthony jumped in. "I am sure Melissa doesn't want to discuss—"

"Do you mean right in Suri City?" she asked. "Or up in the mountains?"

Her answer surprised him. Most people had never heard of Sierra Benito, never mind its capital city.

"A little village called Tappee," he told her.

Her head shook almost imperceptibly, but the small motion emphasized the bounce to her silky blond hair. "Horrible conditions up there. The villagers live in abject poverty."

Anthony chuckled and swung an arm around her shoulders. "I welcome you to the debate, Senorita Melissa."

Jared steeled himself against the urge to rip her out of Anthony's arms. It was a ridiculous reaction. The half hug was a friendly gesture, nothing more.

"Do you have any idea what the gold miners do to the villagers?" Melissa asked. She didn't react to Anthony's hug—didn't lean in, didn't shrug him off, either.

"Do you have any idea what the rebels do to the gold miners?" Jared asked around the clamor of emotion inside his head.

What the hell was the matter with him?

What did he care if Anthony hugged Melissa?

She shook her head in disgust. "I can't believe you're going to exploit them."

Jared jerked back at the accusation. "Exploit *who?*"

"The villagers."

"I'm not going to exploit the villagers." Jared's gaze caught on Anthony's hand and held.

Melissa was wearing a white cotton shirt. It was thin

fabric, hardly a barrier between Anthony's fingertips and her shoulder. Why didn't she shrug him off?

She scoffed. "Right. You'll subcontract the exploitation to Madre Gold to Tomesko Mining."

"That's a leap in logic," he pointed out.

"There's no other reason to go to Tappee."

"We are building a medical clinic," Anthony put in.

"Not necessarily," Jared countered with a warning glare.

Melissa glanced from one to the other with surprise and more than a little curiosity.

"How do you know anything about Tappee?" he couldn't help but probe, watching her closely for signs of…he wasn't even sure what.

"I read the *Chicago Daily,*" she answered with a blink, and her green eyes went back to neutral. "There was a story last year about a mining engineer who was kidnapped by rebels."

"The company paid a million dollars." Jared took the story to its conclusion. "And they killed the guy, anyway."

"That was more than a year ago," said Anthony. "And we are not going there to mine."

"You think they care?" asked Jared. "Do you honestly believe they won't take any Westerner hostage?"

"I believe they do care," said Melissa.

"Yeah?" Jared challenged. "Is that conclusion based on your vast travel experience with the American national bus system?"

"Do not be rude," Anthony cut in, anger clear in his tone.

Well, Jared was angry, too. He'd had about enough of the argument, and he'd had about enough of watching Anthony maul Melissa. He grabbed his Stetson hat from a peg on the wall and crammed it on his head.

"I'm going to walk Melissa back to her cottage," he announced, linking her arm and moving her firmly out of Anthony's grasp.

"What in the hell…" Anthony began.

"*You* need to get back to the meeting," Jared ordered over his shoulder, propelling Melissa toward the stairs. It took her a second to get her feet sorted out under her, but he made sure she didn't stumble.

He could feel Anthony watching them as they crossed the darkened yard toward the driveway lights. Jared knew he was going to get an earful back in the house, but he didn't care. He could give just as good as he got.

He marched her forward at a brisk pace. He didn't know which cottage Melissa had been assigned, but single women were usually on the river side of the arena, so he took a chance and turned right.

"Why do I get the feeling this isn't about walking me back to my cabin?" asked Melissa.

Jared gritted his teeth, struggling to bring his emotions back under control. "Why do I get the feeling you're not here to earn money for a bus ticket?"

Three

Melissa ordered herself not to panic. There was no reason to assume he knew the truth. But even as she mentally reassured herself, the roots of her hair prickled in dread.

His pace was brisk, his large hand still wrapped around her upper arm. It felt strong and uncompromising as steel. She wondered if he intended to march her all the way to his property line.

"First the chauffeur." Jared's angry voice cut through the night air. "Then Anthony." He sucked in a tight breath. "And I can guess what went on with the damn horse."

The last took Melissa by surprise.

The *horse?* Why would she interview his horse?

"Ride it yourself?" Jared taunted.

Melissa struggled to make sense out of the accusation. She hadn't ridden the horse herself, but how could that possibly be relevant?

"Or did you get a little help?" he finished on a meaningful lilt.

He obviously already knew she had. There was no point in lying about that. "I got one of the cowboys to help me. Rich or Rand or Rafe…something…"

"I'll just bet you did." The contempt in Jared's voice was crystal clear.

"So what?" Her confusion was starting to turn to annoyance. Rafe had, in fact, offered to help her. The whole operation hadn't taken more than fifteen minutes of his time.

"So *what?*" Jared jerked her to a stop and rounded on her, glaring from beneath his battered tan Stetson.

Melissa caught her breath while she searched his hard expression in the shadowed light. Why was the horse such a salient detail? Shouldn't he be more upset about the way she'd pumped Anthony for information?

Unless…

It suddenly hit her that she'd jumped to the wrong conclusion. She wasn't caught. Jared was angry about her interaction with his cowboys.

"Is there a company ban on cowboys helping stable hands?" she asked.

"No, but I'm thinking about banning *fraternization.*"

His obvious euphemism was more than a little offensive. "You think I had time to *fraternize* with Rafe before dinner?"

Something flickered in his eyes. It might have been regret. "I think flirting is your only life skill."

"It's not." For starters, she had a university degree. She owned real estate. And she had a good job, soon to be a great job if she could pull off this interview.

"Do tell," he challenged.

"I'm intelligent, articulate and organized."

"You couldn't even organize a bus ticket to Seattle."

"Buying the bus ticket ahead of time wasn't the point."

"What was the point?"

"I'm experiencing America."

"By batting your eyes and swaying your hips?"

She held up her blistered palms. "By shoveling your stable for eight hours."

He reached for her wrist, moving her hands under the beam of a yard light, and his expression tightened. "You put something on this?"

"Work gloves." And she wished she'd thought to do it sooner.

"I'm serious."

She pulled her hand from his grasp. "I'm fine."

He took in her body from head to toe. "I don't think you're cut out for manual labor."

She subconsciously shifted her injured hands behind her back. "I told you I was fine."

"You know how to operate a computer? Type? File?"

Oh, no. She wasn't giving up her ranch job. "I've never worked in an office," she lied. "Besides, I only need bus fare. I'll be out of your hair in a week." At least that part was true.

"You might not last a week."

"I lasted a day."

"Maybe." He paused. "But you know those guys you're flirting with are going to eventually expect you to put out."

"No, they won't." She wasn't flirting anywhere near that seriously.

Jared grunted his disbelief.

The man was an alarmist. But he didn't have the worst idea in the world.

Instead of arguing with him, she sidled forward, tucking her hair behind her ears and lowering her voice to a sultry level. "So how far do you think I'll have to go?"

He brows quirked up. "You're flirting with *me?*"

She leaned in. "Is it working?"

He shifted, letting his crooked hip and cocked head transmit his indolence. "All depends on what you're after."

What she wanted was the story of his life. And she was definitely prepared to bat her eyes a little to get it. "An exemption from riding your horse," she said, instead. "He's scary. Where'd you get him?"

"He's a direct descendent of Renegade."

Melissa tilted her head and widened her eyes, letting the silence go on for a moment.

"My great-great-grandfather's stallion," said Jared. "The pair of them settled this valley back in 1883."

"I thought your grandparents built the original

house." She'd seen the impressive structure when she first arrived this morning.

"The house, yes." He nodded downriver. "The original cabin's been abandoned for decades."

"So you're the fifth Ryder generation to live here?" Her article wasn't going to focus on the family history, but Melissa found herself fascinated by the thought of such deep roots.

"I'm the fifth," said Jared. "Tango's somewhere in the twenties."

"You've kept records?"

"Of course we've kept records." His tone told her she should have known that.

To cover the blunder, she turned and started walking down the rutted driveway, continuing her way toward the Windy River and the little white cottage she'd been assigned this morning. "How many horses do you have now?"

Jared fell into step beside her. "Several hundred. Several thousand head of cattle."

"Is the ranch still profitable?"

He hesitated, and she could feel him looking down at her. "Why do you ask?"

She kept her focus on the quarter moon riding above the silhouetted mountain range across the river. "You went into construction."

"How did you know that?"

"I heard people talk. Around the ranch."

"Gossip?"

"No," she quickly denied. "Just chitchat. You're here. You're usually in Chicago. People commented on it over lunch." Truth was, Melissa had carefully orchestrated the conversation that had revealed that information and more, but there was no need to mention that to Jared.

"You seem to know a lot about me."

She dared to look up at him. "You're the boss. People naturally care about what you do."

"They shouldn't."

She couldn't help but smile at that. "Maybe not. But that's not the way life works."

"It's gossip," he stated. "Plain and simple."

"It's curiosity," she corrected. "And it's interest. And respect."

He ground out an inarticulate sound.

"You can't make millions of dollars and hope to stay under the radar," she told him.

"How do you know I make millions of dollars?"

"How many acres you got here?"

"Five thousand."

"I rest my case."

"Most cattle ranches lose money these days."

"Most construction companies make money these days."

Jared didn't answer. They came up on the short bridge over the froth of a narrow spot in the river. A dirt driveway jutted off to the south, winding through a grass-and-wildflower carpet dotted with aspen and oak trees, which fronted the staff cabins. It looked exactly like the picture on the ranch Web site. This morning it had taken Melissa's breath away.

"Which is yours?" Jared asked, nodding to the neat row of white cottages.

"Number six."

"I'll walk you down." He turned on the driveway, and Melissa was struck by how easily he fit into the surroundings. He had a smooth, rolling, loose-limbed stride, and his booted feet never faltered on the uneven ground. A few lights burned behind curtained windows.

"Very gentlemanly of you." She hoped to keep him talking as long as possible.

"Wouldn't want you to run into a cougar." He seemed to be teasing, but it was hard to tell.

She decided to assume the ranch staff weren't in mortal danger this close to the buildings. "I'm more afraid of rogue cattle," she returned.

"The range bulls are up in the hills right now."

"Good to know. So how long are you in Montana?"

"About as long as you."

"Something you have to get back to?" She tripped on a tree root, and he quickly grasped her arm to steady her.

"Why do you ask?"

"Just making conversation. You seem to like it here."

He gazed around. The Windy River roared its way past, while an owl hooted in a faraway tree. A pair of truck lights flashed in the distance beyond the barns, while several horses whinnied to each other on the night air.

Melissa surreptitiously slowed her steps, not wanting to arrive at her cottage while Jared was still willing to talk.

"I've always liked it here." But his jaw was tight and his voice seemed strained.

Melissa sensed an undercurrent. "Why did you leave?" she dared.

"To make money," was the quick response.

"Cowboys need millions?"

"A spread this size needs millions. The past few decades have been hard on Montana ranchers. It'll change in the future. It has to. But for now…"

Her footsteps slowed to a stop. There was no help for it, they'd arrived at her front porch. She turned to face him, scrambling for ways to prolong the inevitable. She wasn't likely to get another chance like this for the rest of the week.

"So for now you're building office towers to keep your cattle ranch and horse-jumping operation in the black."

"How did you know I was building office towers?" The man was entirely too observant for her comfort level.

"Somebody also mentioned it at lunch today," she said, bluffing.

Jared stared into her eyes for a long slow moment. Then his index finger went to her chin and he tipped her face to the starlight. "There's something about you, Melissa."

"I'm a decent flirt?" Better to feed into his misconception than to let him start thinking about other possibilities.

He gazed at her a moment longer. "That must be it."

He paused again, his expression going unexpectedly intimate. "So you going to put out now?"

His voice was smooth, his dark eyes sensual, and his lips full and soft. Melissa let herself envision delivering with a kiss. Would it be soft and sweet? Strong and sure? Sensual? Sexy? Or downright erotic?

"You really are frighteningly good at this." His gruff voice interrupted her fantasy.

She blinked. "Huh?"

His jaw tightened, and he took a step back. "I can see why you've got so many men at your beck and call."

She shook her head. "I don't—"

"Be careful, Melissa," he warned. "Not all of them will walk away."

And with that, he turned on his heel.

She thought about calling out to protest. Her flirtation was normally light and inconsequential. She'd never let herself get carried away. This was the first time she'd ever even considered taking the next step.

And she wouldn't have actually kissed him.

There was far too much at stake. All she wanted was some information on his business, his life, his background.

And she had some.

Melissa couldn't help but smile.

Jared might think she was shameless, but at least he didn't know she was a journalist, and she'd obtained more useful material for her article.

Ignoring the anger in his stride, and the stiff set of his shoulders as he made his way back down the dirt driveway, she skipped up the stairs to her cottage. She needed to make notes right away.

"What did you do to tick Anthony off last night?" Stephanie's voice startled Jared as he tightened Tango's cinch in front of her house midmorning. The meeting had ended late last night, and it had been simpler to sleep here than ride ten miles to the main house at the cattle ranch in the dark. Anthony and Otto had left immediately after breakfast.

He took one final reflexive look at Melissa cleaning tack inside a shed across the driveway. The woman was taking an inordinately long time on a basic bridle. Then he slipped the cinch buckle into place and turned to face his sister.

Stephanie was dressed in dressage clothes, obviously ready for another day of training with Rosie-Jo. They had a competition coming up, but Jared couldn't remember the details.

"I told him to stop flirting with the help," Jared answered.

"What help?"

"Melissa." He pulled the right stirrup into place. "I don't know why you hired that woman. She's completely useless."

"She needed a job," said Stephanie.

"We're not running a charitable organization."

Stephanie stuffed one hand on her hip. "Actually we are."

Jared rolled his eyes, grasping the saddle horn to

wiggle it and test the placement. "Then she can apply through the Genevieve Fund."

"Don't be such a hard-ass."

"I'm not a hard-ass. I'm a realist." He nodded toward Melissa. "She's been working on that same bridle for half an hour. And mark my words, she's going to cause trouble between the cowboys."

"The cowboys are full-grown men."

"My point exactly."

"They're responsible for their own behavior."

Jared gave his sister a meaningful glare. Men were men. And flirtatious women were trouble. "Like I said, I'm a realist."

Stephanie set her helmet on the end post of the hitching rail and gathered her auburn hair into a ponytail. "I'm not going to fire Melissa."

"Well, I'm not going to be responsible for the fallout," he warned.

"Who said you had to be responsible? Besides, aren't you going back down to the cattle ranch today?"

Jared gently positioned the bit in Tango's mouth. "Thought I'd stay at your place for a few days."

There was a moment's silence, and he braced himself.

Her tone hardened. "I'm perfectly fine, big brother."

"I know you're perfectly fine," Jared allowed. He was sure she felt that way for now.

"This is no different than any other anniversary."

Jared didn't argue the point. But they'd just lost their grandfather, and Stephanie was hurting. No matter how hard she pretended otherwise, the siblings' annual reunion and visit to the family graveyard would be particularly difficult for her this year. He usually stayed down at the main house at the cattle ranch, since it was larger. But Stephanie couldn't leave her work and her students at the equestrian center, so he'd stay here instead.

"When's Royce showing up?" he asked, instead.

"Saturday. You should get back down there and help McQuestin." Stephanie referred to their aging cattle ranch manager.

"McQuestin doesn't want my help."

She plunked her helmet on her head and set her lips in a mulish line. "I don't need a babysitter."

Jared leaned back against the hitching rail, crossing his arms over his chest while he faced his sister. "Maybe I need you."

Her pale blue eyes immediately softened. "You *do?*"

He nodded. It wasn't a lie. He needed to be with her right now. It was the only way he'd be sure she was okay.

She moved forward and placed a hand on his arm. "I know you miss Gramps. Do you still miss Mom and Dad?"

Jared nodded again. But this time, his lie was outright. He didn't miss his parents. He was angry with his parents. Furious, if the truth be known. But that was his burden, the secret passed down by his grandfather. His only choice was to preserve their memories for his siblings.

Stephanie's eyes shimmered and she blinked rapidly. "Then you should stay."

Jared covered her hand with his. "Thank you."

"You want to watch me jump?"

"Sure." He nodded. "I'm going to check the pasture land at Buttercup Pond. Clear my head a little. I'll swing by later in the morning."

Stephanie nodded. Then she swiped the back of her hand across one cheek and headed for the main arena.

Jared tugged Tango's lead rope free and swung up into the saddle. The ride to Buttercup Pond to establish his cover story would take him a couple of hours. But his real mission was across the Windy River. Since his grandfather's deathbed revelation in April, he couldn't get his great-great-grandparents' cabin out of his mind.

The walk to the Ryders' great-great-grandparents' cabin took longer than Melissa had expected. At last she came around a bend of the river to see two cabins. One, made of logs, was nearly collapsing with age. The other was obviously newer. It was larger, made from lumber, with glass windows still intact and peeling white paint on the walls and porch.

A single story, it was L-shaped, with a peaked, green shingle roof. The rails had sagged off the porch, but the three steps looked safe enough, and the front door was a few inches ajar. The buildings were surrounded by a wildflower meadow that nestled up against steep rocky cliffs, jutting into the crystal-blue sky. The river glided by through a wide spot, nearly silent compared to the rapids upstream.

Melissa pulled out her cell phone, clicking a couple of pictures, wishing Susan was along with her camera.

Then she gingerly climbed the three stairs. She pressed the front door, slowly creaking it open. A dank, dusty room was revealed in the filtered sunlight through the stained windows. It held a stone fireplace, an aging dining table and chairs, and the remnants of a sofa. The floorboards were warped and creaky. Through a doorway, yellowed linoleum lined a small kitchen. Curtains hung in shreds over two of the windows.

Melissa let herself imagine the long-ago family. Jared's great-grandfather must have grown up here. Was he an only child? Did he have brothers and sisters? Did Jared have cousins and more-distant relatives around the country?

She made a mental note to research the family's genealogy.

On the far side of the living room, next to the kitchen door, a narrow hallway led to the other side of the house. The floor groaned under her running shoe–clad feet as she made her way through. Her movement stirred up dust, and she covered her mouth and nose with her hand to breathe more easily.

The hallway revealed two bedrooms. One was stark, with plywood bunks nailed to the wall and a hollow cutout of a closet. But the second was a surprise. Intact yellow curtains hung over the window. The bed was obviously newer than the other furnishings, and a brightly colored quilt was shoved against the brass footboard, while the remnants of two pillows were strewn at the head.

"Can I help you?"

The deep voice nearly scared Melissa out of her skin. Her hand flew to her heart as she whirled around to see Jared standing in the bedroom doorway.

"You scared me half to death!" she told him.

"Shouldn't you be working?"

"It's lunchtime. I thought you were a *ghost.*" Her heart was still racing, and adrenaline prickled her skin, flushing her body, then cooling it rapidly.

"Still very much alive," he drawled, expression accusing. "What are you doing here?"

"I was curious."

He waited.

"Last night. You mentioned your great-great-grandparents and, well, I like old buildings."

"So you walked two miles?"

"Yes."

"On your lunch hour?"

"I wanted to come while it was light."

He sighed in disgust and gave his head a little shake. "You're flaky, you know that? Instead of eating, you take off on a whim to see a dilapidated old building. How are you going to work all afternoon?"

"I'll manage," she offered, already hungry and quite willing to concede his point. But she didn't have a lot of time to waste.

"You'll be passing out by two."

She could have argued, but she had more important

questions. "What's with this room?" She gestured around. "It seems newer."

Jared's gaze fixed on the disheveled bed for a long beat. His eyes hardened to sapphire, and a muscle ticked next to his left eye. "Must have been a staff member sleeping here."

"You think?" She wondered why they hadn't fixed up the rest of the house.

He seemed to guess her question. "I imagine they ate at the cookhouse with everybody else."

He turned his attention fully to Melissa and held out a broad callused hand. "Come on. I'll give you a lift home."

"You drove?" Why hadn't she heard the engine?

"I rode Tango."

She instinctively shrank back.

"Don't tell me you're afraid to ride double on him."

"Of course not." She sure hoped there wasn't a trick to riding double.

"Then let's go. You need to eat something."

"I'll be fi—"

"No, you won't. Skipping lunch was a stupid decision. Honestly, I don't know how you've managed to stay alive this long." He reached out and grasped her hand, tugging her out of the bedroom and down the hall.

"Did your great-grandfather have siblings?" she dared to ask.

"He had a sister."

"That explains the bunk beds."

"Yes, it does."

Melissa blinked in the strong sunlight, her focus going immediately to where Tango was tied to the porch.

Jared mounted, then maneuvered the horse flush against the railingless platform, holding out his hand.

Melissa took a deep breath. She braced herself against his forearm, then arced her right leg high, swinging her butt to land with an unladylike thud, off-center behind the saddle on Tango's broad back.

The horse grunted and stepped sideways.

Jared swore out loud, reached back to snag her waist and shoved her into place as her arms went instinctively around his body and clung tight.

"Sorry," she muttered against his back.

"You're a klutz," he told her. "On top of everything else, you're a klutz."

"I never learned to ride properly," she admitted.

"You need to learn some life skills," he responded. "I don't even care which ones. But damn, woman, you've got to learn how to do *something*."

He urged Tango into a fast walk. The motion and play of muscles were unsettling beneath Melissa's body. She kept her arms tight around Jared, slowly becoming aware of the intimacy of their position. Her breasts were plastered against his back, his cotton shirt and her T-shirt little barrier to the heat of their bodies. Her cheek rested against him, and every time she inhaled, her lungs were filled with his subtle, woodsy musk scent.

She was quickly getting turned on. Arousal boiled in the pit of her belly and tingled along her thighs. Her nipples had grown hard, and for a mortifying moment, she wondered if he could feel them.

"Where do you live in Indiana?" he asked, voice husky.

"Gary."

"You have a job there?"

"Not yet." She'd decided claiming to have a job would raise too many questions about why she needed money, and how she had enough time off to travel across the country.

"An apartment?"

"I've been staying with friends." Not having a job meant she couldn't claim to be paying rent. Unless she had investments or family money. In which case, she wouldn't need to earn money for a bus ticket.

As embarrassing as it might be, she had to pretend to be as big a loser as Jared had decided she was in order to maintain her cover story.

He grunted his disapproval, and she felt a twinge of regret that she couldn't set the record straight. But it wasn't her job to impress Jared Ryder. And it sure wasn't her job to be attracted to him. She'd have to fight her instincts on both fronts.

Four

Near the cookhouse, Jared helped Melissa down from Tango's back. She staggered to a standing position, and he could see the pain reflected in her expression as she stretched the muscles in her thighs. If the woman had ever been on a horse before, he'd eat saddle leather.

"*There* you are," came Stephanie's accusatory voice.

Jared felt a twinge of satisfaction at the thought of Melissa getting her comeuppance. But then he realized Stephanie was talking to him. He'd obviously missed her jumping practice.

"I gave Melissa a lift," he explained.

Stephanie looked at Melissa. "Are you hurt?"

"No, I was—"

"Downriver," Jared quickly put in. "Walking."

The explanation earned him a confused look from Melissa.

Too bad. He'd worry about that one later. For now, he didn't want to plant any thoughts about the old cabin in Stephanie's head.

Stephanie looked from Jared to Melissa, then back again. "Well, you missed a no-fault round," she told him, putting her pert nose in the air.

"I guess you'll just have to do it again."

"You think it's easy?"

"No," he acknowledged. "I think it's very, very hard. But I also know you're a perfectionist."

"I wish," Stephanie retorted. But Jared knew it was true. You didn't become one of the top-ten show jumpers in the country without a strong streak of perfectionism.

He handed Tango's reins to Melissa. "He's all yours. When you're done taking off the tack, put him back in the red-gated pen."

Melissa glanced down at the leather reins. Then she looked at Jared, her eyes widening with trepidation.

Yeah, he thought so.

He gave a heavy sigh and took back the reins. "Or I could give you a hand," he offered. "Then you can grab something to eat."

He felt Stephanie's curious gaze behind him, and he twisted his head to give her an I-told-you-so stare. If she wanted him to have time to watch her jump, she shouldn't have hired such a hopeless case.

He wrapped the reins around the horn of his saddle,

clipped a lead rope onto Tango's bridle, then walked the few steps to the hitching rail in front of the stable.

"You can start with the cinch," he called over his shoulder, and Melissa quickly scrambled into action, hoofing it across the loose-packed dirt of the pen.

Stephanie watched them for a moment longer. Then he saw a small, hopeful smile quirk the corners of her mouth before she turned away.

Great. His good deed was obviously not going to go unpunished. He was helping Melissa out of pity, not out of attraction. She might be a gorgeous woman, but he liked his dates with a little more gray matter and a whole lot more ambition.

She came to a halt a few feet back from Tango's flank. Her hands curled into balls by her sides, strands of her blond hair fluttering across her flushed cheeks as she blinked at the tall black horse.

"The cinch," Jared prompted, releasing the reins and gently drawing the bit from Tango's mouth.

Melissa didn't make a move.

He flipped the stirrup up and hooked it over the saddle horn. "The big, shiny silver buckle," he offered sarcastically.

She took a half step forward, then wiped her palms down the front of her jeans.

Jared turned, planting his hands on his hips.

She pursed her lips, reaching her hand toward the buckle. But Tango shifted, and she snapped it back.

"He's not going to bite you."

"What if he kicks me?"

"Just don't do anything sudden."

"Oh, that makes me feel a whole lot better."

This was getting ridiculous. "You know, you might want to think about another line of work."

"I was perfectly happy scooping out pens."

"Nobody's happy scooping out pens."

"I was."

"Well, that's a dead-end career." He took a step forward and captured her hand.

She tried to jerk away.

"The trick is," said Jared in the most soothing voice he could muster, "to let him know what you're doing." He urged her reluctant hand toward Tango's withers. "That way, nobody is surprised."

"Is 'surprised' a euphemism?"

"I mean it literally."

Tango craned his neck to see what was going on.

"Your touch should be firm," Jared advised, keeping himself between Melissa and the horse's head. He gave Tango a warm-up pat with his free hand before placing Melissa's palm on the horse's coat. "That way, he knows you have confidence."

"I don't have confidence."

"Sure you do." He let go of her hand, and she immediately pulled it back from the horse.

Jared drew a frustrated sigh. "I've seen five-year-olds with more guts than you."

She glared at him.

"Lots of them," he affirmed.

Her glare lasted several seconds longer, but then she squared her shoulders, screwed up her face and turned to the saddle.

"Buckle first," Jared instructed as her small soft fingers tackled the leather. "Now pull the strap through the rings."

It took her a minute to get the mohair strap untangled and dangling straight down.

"You want to take the saddle and blanket off together. Grab it front and back. Lift, don't drag it. Then carry it into the stable. I'll show you where to put it."

He stepped back to give her some room.

Tango was sixteen hands, so it was a reach for Melissa to get a firm grip. But she grabbed the saddle, lifted, pulled back, stumbled in the loosely packed dirt and nearly fell over backward.

Jared quickly wrapped his arm around the small of her back, averting disaster. Her waist was small, her body and frame light. No wonder she was such a wimp when it came to physical work.

"You okay?" he asked reflexively.

"Fine." She firmed up her grip on the heavy saddle and straightened away before he could get used to the feel of her in his arms. But not before he realized how easily he could get used to the feel of her in his arms.

He wondered if she danced. Then for a second he allowed himself to imagine her in a dress. A dress would suit her, something silky and flowing, maybe a bright blue or magenta. Despite her hesitancy in the stable yard, something told him she'd have self-confidence in a different setting.

She all but staggered into the stable, and he was forced to give her points for grit.

"Third rack from the end," he instructed, following with the reins.

She plunked the saddle down.

"You can clean it after lunch," he told her.

She nodded, obviously out of breath. Then she dusted off the front of her navy tank top.

"But first we move Tango."

"Of course we do." Her tone was sarcastic as she turned to face him.

"You ticked off at me? For helping you?"

She studied his eyes. "No." But the tone told him she was.

"You can always quit."

"I'm not going to quit." Her annoyance was replaced by defiance as she started for the stable door. "Let's go."

"You want to lead him from the left," Jared called after her as he hung up the reins, positive now that she'd never been near a horse before today.

Tango wasn't intimidating. He was an incredibly well-trained, twelve-year-old saddlebred, solid as a rock and not the least bit flighty or malicious. Any horseman, groom or stable hand would recognize that in an instant.

He came through the doorway to find Melissa sizing up Tango from about five feet away.

"Talk to him," Jared advised. "Then give him a pat and undo the rope."

"Is there a trick to it?" she asked, apparently having given up any pretext of knowing what she was doing.

"Which part?"

Over her shoulder, she cut him an impatient glare, and he was forced to tamp down a smile.

"Pull the end." He demonstrated, tugging the quick-release knot. Then he handed her the rope. "Stand on this side. Make sure he can see you. Don't let the rope trail." Jared got her positioned properly. He didn't know how much she'd have to work between here and Seattle, but she stood a much better chance of avoiding starvation if she had a clue about what she was doing.

Melissa started walking, and Tango fell in easily beside her. Her face was pinched and pale, and there was clear tension across her slim shoulders as she made her way toward the ranch road, but at least she was making the effort.

A couple of Stephanie's border collies streaked toward them, obviously assuming there was work to be done. Melissa tensed, and Jared put an arm around her. "They won't hurt you."

"I know."

"You do?"

"They look…friendly." But her voice was slightly higher pitched than normal. "Will they scare Tango?"

"Tango's bomb-proof."

The dogs circled the small group a couple of times, then settled in back of Tango's heels, obviously up for whatever the job might be.

Melissa led the horse in silence down the slight slope of the dirt road, curving east toward the river and a row of horse pens. Stephanie was teaching a junior jumping class in the main arena behind them. The Ryder farrier was working on a yearling with the help of two cowboys who were trying to teach the twitchy colt the proper etiquette for hoof care. Meanwhile, stable hands moved hay, filled water troughs and repaired fences.

There was an endless cycle of work on a horse ranch. When he was in the city, Jared missed the predictable rhythm. In his corporate life, he was putting out one fire after another. He couldn't plan a single day, never mind a season.

"Did you come to an agreement about Tappee?" she asked as they approached the red-gated pen.

Jared shook his head, increasing his pace to unlatch the gate in front of the horse. "Stephanie voted with me, but Otto sided with Anthony."

"Otto?"

"Otto Durand."

Her forehead furrowed as she cautiously led Tango through the gate. "I don't understand."

Jared pulled it shut and flipped the latch. "There's a clip under his chin. Release the lead rope."

She reached cautiously under the horse's head. But she found the clip and clicked it free.

Tango instantly reacted to the familiar sound. Knowing he was free, he bolted, spraying clods of dirt at Melissa.

It was all Jared could do not to laugh at the horrified expression on her face.

She sputtered out the dirt while the horse rolled onto his back, relieved to be free of the saddle.

"What don't you understand?" he asked, instead.

She brushed away her hair and rubbed the back of

her hand over her face. "I don't understand why you had to vote. Aren't you CEO of Ryder International?"

"This isn't a Ryder International project."

"Oh. I thought…"

Jared cracked the gate open to man-size so they could exit the pen. "It's the Genevieve Fund."

Melissa raised her brow in a question.

"The Genevieve Ryder Memorial Fund," Jared explained. "It's a charitable trust named after my mother."

"Is your mother…?"

He nodded. "She was killed twenty years ago."

Her forehead creased. "I'm sorry."

Jared shrugged, brushing past the sharp stab of conflicting emotions that tightened his chest. "It's been twenty years."

Melissa's green eyes were round and soft. Her voice dropped to a husky level that somehow hit him in the solar plexus. "I'm still sorry."

They stared at each other in silence, and once again he was struck by the intelligence in her eyes. Only this time, it was laced with compassion. There was something he didn't understand about this woman, something lurking just beyond his comprehension.

"There are five members of the Genevieve Fund board," he told her, leaning an arm on a fence rail, forcing the frustrating dilemma from his head.

"Who's the fifth?" She mirrored his posture.

"My brother, Royce."

"I take it he gets to break the tie?"

"He'll be here on Saturday."

"Does he work on the ranch or with the construction company?"

"Neither. He works for Ryder International, but he's involved in acquisitions, not in the day-to-day business."

"So he was the one who found Saxena Electronics?"

And there it was again. "How do you know about Saxena?"

"I told you, Jared." She smoothed her mussed hair back from her forehead. "I read the newspapers."

"And you remember obscure facts like that?"

She shrugged. "Sometimes it's a blessing. Sometimes it's a curse."

"Ever heard of Bosoniga?"

"Little country in West Africa." She grinned, revealing flashing white teeth. "Is this a quiz?"

"We're building a school there."

Her head bobbed up and down. "Good choice. The monarchy is stable, so poverty and infrastructure will be your only problems."

He lifted his hand, then brought it down again on the rough wood of the fence, struggling to make Melissa's lifestyle add up in his head. "Why don't you have a real job?"

"Define a real job."

"An office, where'd you put that brain of yours to work from nine to five."

"I don't think they'd let me wander across the country."

"How long have you been wandering across the country?"

Her mouth tightened imperceptibly, and something flashed in the depths of her eyes. Fear? Pain? He was reminded once again that she could be running from something or someone.

But then the look was gone.

"Not long," she answered. "Do you think Royce will side with his family or with Anthony and Otto?"

"Anthony is our cousin."

"Really?"

He nodded. "Royce is a risk taker. He'll offer to fly down to Tappee himself."

"He's a pilot?"

Jared choked out a laugh. "He's definitely a pilot. I think he likes flying around the world more than he likes investigating companies."

"Can I meet him when he gets here?"

Jared tensed. A chill hit his body, and a warning sparked in his brain. "Why?"

She drew back, obviously reacting to his expression.

"You planning to flirt with him?" Jarred pressed. He shouldn't have let his guard down. He didn't know anything about this woman.

She emphatically shook her head. "He likes to travel. I like to travel." Her words came faster. "I was thinking you could be right. Maybe I should find a real job and save up some money. I mean, seeing America is fun and all, but it might be fun to see some of the rest of the world—"

"In my brother's jet?"

"No. *No*." She smoothed her hair back again. "I'm not going to flirt with your brother. I just thought…"

Jared waited. He truly did want to know what she thought.

She let go of the fence rail and took a step forward. "I thought he might be a lot like you. Smart and interesting."

He stared down as she moved closer. "I can't believe you're doing this." But what he really couldn't believe was that it was working. She was flirting with him, using her pretty face and killer body to gain an advantage. And it was *working*.

He was pathetic.

"You misunderstood," she told him in a soft voice. "I have no designs on Royce. I don't even know Royce. And if my mission was to land myself a rich man, do you think I'd be scooping horse poop on a ranch in Montana? No offense, Jared, but Manhattan is a whole lot closer to Gary, and their per capita count of rich eligible men is pretty darn high."

Jared watched her soft lips as they formed words, took in her feathery hair lifting in the light breeze, her bottomless green eyes, almost a turquoise, like the newly melted water of a glacial lake. She was stunningly gorgeous and intriguingly intelligent.

"So how stupid do you think I am?" Her voice dropped off into silence. The thuds of Tango's footfalls echoed around them.

"I don't think you're stupid at all," Jared admitted. "That's the problem."

* * *

Melissa had overplayed her hand.

Sitting at the end of a long table in the quiet cookhouse, spooning her way through a flavorful soup, she knew she'd made Jared suspicious. She should never have asked to meet Royce. And she should have been content to let him think she was slow-witted.

Her enthusiasm for getting the story, along with her stupid ego, had both gotten in the way. She'd just *had* to show off her knowledge of Bosoniga and Tappee. Like some schoolkid trying to impress the teacher. "Bosoniga has a stable monarchy," she mocked under her breath. Why didn't she just wave her university degree under his nose and challenge him to guess why she was out on the road playing vagabond?

She dropped the spoon into her soup.

Was she trying to sabotage the story?

"Melissa?" Someone slid into the chair next to her, and Melissa looked over to see Stephanie set a white stonewear cup on the table.

At two in the afternoon, the cookhouse had grown quiet. Faint voices could be heard from the pass-through to the kitchen. Coffee, biscuits and oatmeal cookies were still available on the sideboard in case anyone needed a snack. And a helper was setting the three empty tables for dinner.

"Hello," Melissa greeted Stephanie politely.

The younger woman's auburn hair was pulled back in her signature ponytail. She'd removed her riding helmet, but still wore the white blouse, tight jodhpurs and high boots that were the uniform of a show jumper.

Stephanie grinned happily. There was a freshness about her, Melissa thought. Maybe it was the freckles or maybe it was the complete lack of cosmetics. Or it could have been the perky upturned nose. But Stephanie looked young, carefree, almost mischievous.

"I saw Jared helping you with Tango," she began, her expression friendly and open as she turned the cup handle to face the right direction.

Melissa nodded, even while her stomach tightened with guilt. She couldn't help but like Stephanie, and she was sorry the woman was caught up in her charade.

"It was very nice of him," Melissa acknowledged. Then she paused, choosing her words carefully. "My horse skills are…" She let out a sigh, feeling like a heel for lying to Stephanie in the first place. "I guess, I, uh, exaggerated my skill level when I first talked to you." She cringed, waiting for the reaction.

But to her surprise, Stephanie waved a dismissive hand. "Whatever."

Melissa gazed at her. "But—"

"It doesn't take a rocket scientist to shovel manure."

"You're not mad?"

"Nah." Stephanie lifted the stonewear mug and took a sip of the steaming coffee. "I imagine people exaggerate on their résumés all the time."

"I guess they do," Melissa agreed, relieved—yet again—that she wasn't about to get fired.

"So what do you think of him?"

"Tango?" Was Stephanie going to try to get her to ride the horse?

"No, Jared."

"Oh." Melissa caught the speculative expression in Stephanie's eyes.

Oh.

Oh, no.

This could not be good.

"He seems, well, nice enough," Melissa offered carefully. Truth was, she thought Jared was demanding and sarcastic. Okay, in an intriguing, compelling, sexy kind of way.

Stephanie nodded cheerily. "He's a great guy. Lots of women seem attracted to him. I mean, it's hard for me to tell, being his sister, but I imagine he's pretty hot."

Melissa turned her attention back to her soup. "He's a very attractive man."

"You should have seen the woman he dated last weekend. They had their picture in the paper in Chicago. She was a knockout. A lawyer."

Melissa spooned up a bit of soup. She was not going to be jealous of some smart knockout lawyer in Chicago. Who Jared dated was absolutely none of her business.

"I told him he should see her again. But he's not interested." Stephanie gave a shrug. "So, really, he's not committed in any way, shape or form."

Melissa fought a smile. Again, there was an endearing quality to Stephanie. She was probably only four or five years younger than Melissa, but she seemed so innocent and untarnished. Maybe it was from living in the protected world of rural Montana.

"Honestly, Stephanie, I think I frustrate your brother."

Stephanie shook her head. "We can change that."

"I'm only here for a few days, remember?" The last thing Melissa needed was for Stephanie to give Jared a reason to avoid her. And she sensed that was exactly what would happen if he guessed his sister's intentions.

"He thinks you're pretty."

The assertion took Melissa by surprise.

"He told me," Stephanie continued. "The first time he saw you."

"This is a bad idea, Stephanie. Jared and I are from completely different worlds." And she was spying on him. And he was going to despise her in about three weeks when the article hit the newsstands.

"So were my parents."

"Stephanie, really."

"My dad was a rancher, and my mom grew up in Boston."

Melissa knew this was exactly the point where she should press Stephanie for some information. But for some reason, she couldn't bring herself to do it.

"My mom was gorgeous and classy. Blonde, like you." Stephanie sighed. "I wish I looked more like her."

"But you're beautiful," Melissa immediately put in, meaning it completely.

Stephanie wrinkled her little nose. "I have freckles and red hair. And, you know, I haven't bought myself a dress in three years."

"Well, that's easy to fix."

"I bet you own a lot of beautiful dresses." The speculative look was back in Stephanie's eyes.

"Very few," said Melissa. She pinned Stephanie with an earnest expression. "Promise me you won't do this, Stephanie."

Stephanie reached out to grasp Melissa's forearm, taking a careful look around the room. "I can be very discreet."

Given the woman's exaggerated spy-versus-spy room check, Melissa sincerely doubted that.

"I'll chat you up a bit," Stephanie continued. "You are gorgeous, and I can—"

"Jared is not, I repeat, not interested in me. You'll only embarrass us both if you try to match us up."

Stephanie took another sip of her coffee, a dreamy faraway expression in her eyes. "I promise, Melissa. I won't do a single thing to embarrass you."

Five

Melissa had waited all morning for a chance to privately warn Jared about Stephanie's matchmaking plans. She could hardly walk up to the front door of Stephanie's house and knock. And Jared, as far as she could tell, hadn't come out of the house.

Standing over a tub of water in the tack room, she had a decent view of the front porch. Her hands were red and slippery from the glycerin soap, but at least the job was straightforward: wash the tack, dry the tack, polish the tack. She'd worked her way through a decent-size pile of leather.

When lunchtime came along without a sign of Jared, she started to worry. If Stephanie was already matchmaking, he was probably plotting his escape from the equestrian center. If she didn't do something soon, there was every possibility that he'd leave before she got anything more for her story.

She had to find a way to get hold of him.

She clicked through the possibilities in her brain until finally she came up with a viable plan. If she could somehow get her hands on his cell number, she could talk to him without Stephanie knowing.

She pulled her hands from the warm water, shook them off and dried them on a towel. Her cell phone was in her taupe canvas tote bag, and it didn't take her long to get directory assistance and the Chicago number for Ryder International. The receptionist put her through to Jared's assistant.

"Jared Ryder's office," said a friendly female voice.

"I need to speak to Jared Ryder," Melissa opened, hoping the office would give her his cell phone number.

"I'm afraid Mr. Ryder is not in the office today." The voice remained friendly and professional. "Can I help you with something?"

"Do you happen to have his cell phone number?" Melissa mentally crossed her fingers that the woman would be willing to give it out.

"I'm afraid I can't provide that information. Is there someone else who can—"

"Would you be able to get a message to him?" Melissa moved to plan B.

Some of the patience leached out of the woman's voice. "Can I get your name, please?"

"So you can get him a message?" Melissa's hope rose.

"He may not get it until next week."

"I need him to get it today. Right away if possible."

"If I could just have your name."

"It's Melissa. Melissa Webster." She used the alias she'd used on her résumé.

"And what is the message regarding?"

Good question. Melissa racked her brain. She sure couldn't say she was a reporter, but if the subject didn't seem important, the secretary might not send it to Jared right away. "Saxena Electronics," she offered impulsively.

"You're from Saxena?" The skepticism was clear.

Melissa could only assume most Saxena employees had East Indian accents. "I'm affiliated with them," she lied. "The message is that Melissa Webster needs to talk about Saxena right away. In private," she added, ending with her cell phone number.

"I'm not sure—"

"Please believe me that it's important," Melissa put in quickly.

The woman hesitated on the other end of the line.

"There's no risk," Melissa pointed out. "If it's not important, he'll just ignore it, right?"

"I'll see what I can do."

"Maybe a quick text or an e-mail?"

"I'll see what I can do." The voice had turned stony.

It was definitely time to back off. "Thank you," said Melissa with as much gratitude as she could muster. "I really do appreciate this."

The professionalism and the formality came back. "Thank you for calling Ryder International."

"Thanks for your help," Melissa offered once more before hanging up.

Then she plunked her phone back in her bag, readjusted the clip that was holding her hair back and pulled her damp tank top away from her chest. She hated to go to lunch looking like this, but it was a long walk back to her cottage, and there was no way she could skip the meal.

As the days went by, her respect for cowboys and stable hands had risen. They worked extremely hard. A salad or a protein shake might cut it in an office, but out here, calories were essential.

She dried the last of the washed tack, laying it out on the bench to be polished later. Then she slung her canvas bag over her shoulder and headed for the cookhouse while she waited to see if Jared would call.

A couple of steps out the stable door, Jared startled her, blocking her way. She stopped short.

"What the hell?" he demanded.

She glanced around. "Is Stephanie with you?"

"What was this about seeing me in private?"

She didn't see Stephanie anywhere. "I'll explain in a minute. Is there somewhere we can talk?"

Jared hesitated. Then he nodded at the stable. "There's an office up those stairs."

"Great." Melissa turned, and he followed her in.

They tapped their way, single file, up the narrow staircase. It opened to a short hallway with three doors.

"Far end," Jared rumbled. "And this better be good. My secretary was scrambling the Saxena team for damage control. She thought you were warning me of a hostile takeover."

Melissa cringed. "Sorry. Did you call them off?"

"Of course I called them off." His boots were heavy on the wood floor behind her. "This better not be some flirting thing."

"It's not flirting." Melissa stopped at the closed door.

Jared reached around her and pushed it open to reveal a small desk, a couple of filing cabinets. Three open, curtained windows showed a cloud-laden sky, and a comfortably furnished corner with armchairs, low tables and lamps. Through the window, Melissa could see a crowd of people at the arena. She assumed it was a jumping class and that Stephanie was there.

"Take a seat." Jared gestured to a worn, brown leather armchair.

Melissa sat down, and he took the chair next to it. They were separated by a polished pine table, decorated with three small, framed horse portraits.

He leaned back, crossing one ankle over the opposite knee and folding his arms over his chest. "What's going on?" he asked directly.

Melissa took a deep breath, giving herself a second to compose her message. "It's Stephanie."

"What did you do?"

"I didn't do anything."

"She lost patience with you? Fired you?"

"No." Melissa sat forward. "Will you let me finish?"

He waited.

"Your sister, for some reason, has decided I'm…well, a good match for you."

Jared planted his feet and sat forward. "What did you say to her?"

"Nothing. This is about her, not me. I was minding my own business. She saw you helping me yesterday. Apparently the first time you saw me you said I was pretty."

"I never—"

"Well, Stephanie thinks you did. And she's a determined and romantic young lady, and she thinks she can subtly throw us together without you noticing. I was guessing you'd catch on, and I thought you'd appreciate a heads-up."

Jared's mouth thinned into a grim line. His hands moved to the arms of the chair, and he gave his head a subtle shake. "It's worse than I thought."

Melissa waited for him to elaborate.

He fixed his gaze on her. "If she's targeting *you,* things are really getting out of hand."

"Excuse me?" Melissa couldn't help the defensive tone in her voice. "I'm the bottom of the barrel?"

"No, you're not the bottom of the barrel." He paused. "But you're definitely from the unlikely half of the barrel."

"Is that supposed to make me feel better?"

"The last person she targeted was a lawyer."

Melissa nodded. "She told me."

"Just how long was this conversation?"

"Not long." Melissa shifted back in her chair. "For the record, I tried to talk her out of it."

Jared's expression turned thoughtful, and he glanced toward the window and out to the arena. "Did she seem…upset?"

Melissa shook her head. Stephanie hadn't seemed remotely upset. "I'd call it enthusiastic, even excited."

He stood up and walked toward the closest window, looking through the opening to the crowd in the distance. "It's about Sunday."

Melissa stood with him. The clouds were thickening in the sky and the wind was picking up.

"It's got to be," he continued.

"What about Sunday?" she dared to ask.

Jared kept his gaze glued outside. "The twentieth anniversary of our parents' deaths. And the first time my grandfather won't be here to commemorate it with us."

Melissa took a few steps toward him. "Your grandfather died?"

Jared nodded. "In April. It hit Stephanie pretty hard."

"I can imagine," Melissa said softly, her sympathy going out to the whole family.

"Look at her jump." Jared nodded toward the arena, and Melissa shifted closer to where she could watch Stephanie on her big gray horse.

"Perfect form," he continued as the two sailed over a high, white jump rail. "She's talented, driven, unbelievably hardworking. Only twenty-two, and she'll be a champion before we know it."

"Then she was only two when your parents died?" Melissa ventured.

"Only two," Jared confirmed with a nod, and his voice turned introspective. "And despite her success, all these years all she ever wanted was a mother."

Melissa didn't know what to say to that. Her own parents had moved to Florida only a couple of years ago. She saw them every few months, but she still missed her mother.

"I don't blame her," she offered.

"I understand the desire," Jared allowed. "But ever since she was old enough to understand, she's pestered the three of us to get married. Poor Gramps. And poor Royce. He was afraid to bring a date home in high school for fear of how Stephanie would embarrass him. She goes into matchmaking mode at the drop of a hat."

"You could get married, you know," Melissa offered reasonably, only half joking. "You're what, early thirties?"

"Thirty-five."

"So what's the holdup? I bet you meet eligible women every day of the week."

Jared frowned at her. "I'm not getting married for the sake of my sister."

"Get married for yourself. Hey, if you get proactive, you'll have your choice of women. If Stephanie gets her way, you're stuck with me."

It obviously took Jared a stunned minute to realize Melissa was joking. But then he visibly relaxed.

"What about you?" he asked. "Would you get married to keep your siblings happy?"

Melissa coughed out a laugh. "I have five older brothers. Trust me, no husband in the world will be good enough."

"Would they scare a guy off?"

Melissa smiled at that. "They range from six-one to six-four. All tough as nails. Adam's a roofer, Ben and Caleb are framers, Dan's an electrician and Eddy's a pipe fitter."

A calculating look came into Jared's eyes. "You think they'd be interested in jobs with Ryder International?"

"I'm afraid they're all gainfully employed."

His eyes squinted down as he stared at her, and she braced herself for sarcasm about her own dismal career status. It was going to be hard not to defend herself from his criticism.

"Might be worth marrying you for the union connections alone."

The words surprised a laugh out of her. She played along. "Plus, Stephanie would have a mother." She played along. "Well, more like a sister, really. I'm only four or five years older than she is, you know."

"Not a bad plan." Jared nodded and pretended to give it serious consideration. "Stephanie's pretty convinced the family would benefit from a few more females in the mix."

"Smart girl," said Melissa.

"Can't argue with the logic," Jared agreed. "It's her methods that cause the trouble."

As they spoke, Stephanie sailed over her final jump, completing a clean round.

"She really is good," said Melissa.

"You don't know the half of it." Jared turned from the window.

He paused, and they came face-to-face, closer than she'd realized. Sunlight streamed in, highlighting his gorgeous eyes, his strong chin, his straight nose and the short shock of brown hair that curled across his forehead.

The force of his raw magnetism drew her in, arousing and frightening her at the same time. He was all man. He had power, looks and intelligence, and she suddenly felt inadequate. She wasn't ready to work at his ranch or write an article about him. The phrase *out of my league* planted itself firmly in her brain.

For a second she let herself fear his reaction to the article. But then she banished the fear. It was her job to get the story, and she'd be far away from Montana by the time it ran in the *Bizz*.

The world outside darkened, and his eyes turned to midnight, sensuality radiating from their depths. The humidity jumped up, only to be overtaken by a freshening breeze.

There were shouts from outside as the wind swirled and a storm threatened. Doors banged, horses whinnied, and plastic tarps rattled against their ropes.

Meanwhile, gazes locked, Jared and Melissa didn't move.

The wild clamor outside matched the cacophony inside her head. This attraction felt so right, but it was so incredibly wrong. Jared was her article subject, her employer, one of the most powerful entrepreneurs in Chicago. She had absolutely no business being attracted to him.

He reached out to brush a stray lock of hair from her temple. His touch was electric, arousing, light as a feather but shocking as a lightning bolt.

Thunder rumbled in the distance, and the first fat raindrops clattered on the roof.

"I'm going to kiss you," he told her.

She drew a breath. "You think that's a good idea?"

He moved slightly closer. "It's not the smartest thing I've ever done." He stroked his thumb along her jaw, tipped her chin. "But probably not the stupidest, either. Might not even make the top three."

"What were they?" she asked.

"The stupidest things?"

She gave a slight nod.

"I don't think I'll be telling you that right now."

"Maybe later?"

"I doubt it." Done talking, he leaned in and pressed his warm lips to hers.

It was a gentle kiss, a tentative kiss. There was a wealth of respect and more than a couple of questions contained in the kiss.

She answered by softening her lips. One of her hands went to his shoulder, steadying herself, she lied. Truth was, she wanted to hang on, press closer, turn his inquiry into a genuine kiss.

He easily complied, stepping forward, parting his lips, one hand going to the small of her back, the other tunneling into the hair behind her ear. He tipped his head, deepened the kiss; she plastered herself flush against him, feeling the hard heat of his body, counterpoint to the wind and rain that rushed in through the open window.

Warning sirens clanged inside her head.

It wasn't supposed to happen like this.

She was supposed to maintain a journalistic detachment. Plus, hadn't she come up here to warn him about Stephanie? Not to flirt. Or worse, seduce. What on earth was she *thinking?*

He broke the kiss, but moved instantly into another. Melissa didn't have time to decide if she was relieved or upset before she was dragged away on another tidal wave of desire.

The world disappeared—the horses, the people, the wind and rain. Nothing existed except Jared's kiss, the rough texture of his hands, the heat of his hard body and the fresh, earthy, male scent that surrounded her and drew her into an alternative universe.

His thumb found the strip of skin between her tank top and blue jeans. He stroked up her spine, sending shivers of reaction skittering both ways. His hand slipped under her shirt, warm palm caressing the sensitized skin, working higher, closing in on the scrap of her bra.

His tongue touched hers, tentatively at first, but then bolder as she responded, opening to him, tipping her head to give him better access to her mouth. His hand caressed the back of her head. Her arms tightened around his neck. She went up on her toes, struggling to get closer.

A clap of thunder boomed through the sky, rumbling the building, lightning dancing in the clouds rapidly engulfed the ranch. The rain grew steady, blurring the world, cooling the air and clattering like a freight train against the cedar shakes above them.

Jared pulled her tighter still, leaving her in no doubt about the effect the kiss was having on him. It was having the same effect on her. It was wild, untamed, sexy and all but unstoppable.

He shifted, moving her away from the open window and the driving rain that was dampening their clothes. He backed her into the wall, and his leg slipped between hers. The friction sent a shot of desire through her body, and a moan found its way past her mouth.

Jared whispered her name, his kisses moving from her mouth to her cheek, her temple and neck. He moved aside the strap of her tank top, the thinner strap of her bra, kissing his way to her shoulder, where his warm tongue lingered, laving the sensitive skin.

Her legs grew weak, and she braced herself against the wall, clinging to Jared's strong shoulders, even as she kissed his chest through the damp cotton of his shirt. He'd crooked his knee, and she rested the core of her body against his strong thigh. A pulse throbbed through her veins, and there was no mistaking where she wanted this to lead.

"We have to stop," she forced herself to gasp.

His lips paused mid-kiss on her bare shoulder. "I'm not sure why," he breathed. He straightened, bracing his hands against the wall, arms on either side of her, gazing down with passion-clouded eyes.

"Did I do something wrong?" he asked.

She was all but shaking with reaction, afraid to move for fear she'd throw caution to the wind and lose herself in his arms. "This is nuts," she told him, struggling to bring her voice back to normal, forcing herself to drag her hands from his shoulders.

His thigh was still braced between hers, still pressed intimately against her body, still drawing a completely inappropriate reaction from her.

"Why?" he asked.

"I don't know," she nearly wailed. What had happened? Why had they combusted like that? They barely knew each other.

"I mean, why is it nuts?"

"Because…" She struggled over the question, not finding a satisfactory answer. At least, not one that she could share with him. "It's you, and it's me. And we're…" She couldn't find the words.

"Attracted to each other?" he finished for her.

"Apparently," she responded dryly.

He let his thigh fall away, and she nearly groaned with the sensation.

"Stephanie would be pleased," he pointed out.

Melissa's gaze darted to the window, suddenly wondering who had seen what before they moved away. What if Stephanie had seen them?

"Nobody saw a thing," said Jared, guessing her concern. "They were too busy running from the storm."

The rain had turned to a steady drum, while thunder and lightning punctuated the darkened sky. The yard was empty, everyone having taken shelter in one of the buildings. Horses were huddled in small groups, most of them under run-in shelters, some in the larger pens moving into the shelter of the trees. Tarps still billowed, cracking and snapping in the wind.

Jared gently stroked his thumb across her swollen bottom lip, making her desire flare all over again. "Our secret is safe."

She gazed into his eyes, unable to hide her renewed longing. And try as she might, she couldn't bring herself to walk away.

His eyes darkened further and his voice went husky. "You want to make it an even bigger secret?"

Six

Before Melissa could even open her mouth, Jared knew to retract the question.

"I'm sorry," he quickly told her. "That was way out of line."

He was her boss. Just yesterday he'd threatened to fire her, more than once, if memory served. He had absolutely no business propositioning her. It was unprincipled, immoral, probably illegal in most states.

"It wasn't—"

"It *was*." He forced himself back, hands tightening by his sides as he put some distance between them. The torrential rain was still dripping through the open windows, and he slammed one window shut, then the next and finally the third, taking some of his frustration out on the inanimate objects. He'd never felt this way before, never desired a woman so quickly and thoroughly. Yet he was wrong to feel this way, and he had to make it stop.

"Jared?" Her voice was tentative, and he felt like a complete jerk.

He latched the final window, then turned back to face her. Her hair was wet, messy from his hands. The damp blue tank top clung to her breasts, highlighting her nipples. Her eyes were round, sea-foam green and confused.

"I'm mad at myself," he assured her. "Not at you."

She took a step forward. "It was my fault, too. How about we forget it happened?"

"Can *you* forget it happened?" He'd give it a shot, but he wasn't holding out much hope.

"Sure." She nodded, offering a small smile. "Easy."

She seemed sincere, and he tried not to be offended. Maybe he'd imagined their explosive passion. Maybe to her it had been a simple ordinary kiss. He gave himself a split second to ponder exactly who the hell else she'd been kissing like that, but then he acknowledged that it was none of his business.

He took a deep breath, forcing himself to relax. "Sure," he forced out, adjusting his damp shirt and raking his fingers through his hair. "We'll just forget it ever happened."

Melissa glanced down and plucked at her own wet shirt. Then she quickly folded her arms across her breasts. Just as well, Jared told himself. Her clinging clothes were turning him on. So were her swollen lips and messy hair.

"You have a comb?" he asked.

She shook her head. "It's in my bag downstairs."

He realized they couldn't risk leaving the room with her looking like this, so he steeled himself against the inevitable reaction and moved toward her.

Her arms stayed protectively crossed over her breasts, so he reached for the hair clip. "I'll just…" He raked spread fingers through the mess, straightening out the worst of it, wondering how he'd ever manage to get the clip back in.

A voice called from the hallway. *"Jared?"* The door burst open, and Stephanie instantly appeared.

He and Melissa both jumped guiltily back, her covering her breasts, him holding her hair clip.

Stephanie stopped abruptly. "I'm sorry." But she didn't look sorry in the least. A broad grin grew on her face and her eyes sparkled in delight.

Barry Salmon and Hal Norris halted behind her. All three of them stared at the incriminating scene.

Jared inwardly groaned. Why the hell hadn't he kept his hands to himself? Melissa's reputation was about to tumble over the falls and be washed down the Windy River. Why the hell hadn't he kept his hands to himself?

She was the first to speak. "It's not what you—"

But he cut her off. "I was inviting Melissa to join us for dinner," he told Stephanie, giving the two cowboys a warning glare.

"I knew it!" Stephanie beamed.

"The rain blew right in the windows," he went on, to

explain their appearance. Then he handed Melissa the hair clip. "Thanks for your help."

She gave him a puzzled expression. "There's no need—"

He stopped her with a stare. There was every need to protect her reputation, not to mention his own. She'd be gone in a week. In the meantime, he'd rather have the ranch staff think they were dating than carrying on a clandestine affair in the stable office.

He turned to his sister. "Did you need me for something?"

"Royce just called," said Stephanie. "He's at the airport."

"A day early?" That surprised Jared. He hoped nothing was wrong.

"And McQuestin called," Hal put in. "Some of the herd's still in the south canyon, and there's a risk of flooding down there."

"Hal and Barry are going to take half a dozen men," said Stephanie, but her goofy gaze was still on Melissa.

Jared knew he'd have to deal with his sister's let-down later. But at the moment, seeing the pure joy on Stephanie's face, he was inclined to wait until they got through the graveside visit on Sunday. He wondered if Melissa would be willing to go along with the charade. It would definitely distract Stephanie from missing their grandfather.

"Do you need me?" Jared asked Hal. He hadn't played cowboy in a few years, but he was ready and able if they needed an extra hand.

Hal shook his graying head. "Should be done by dark."

Jared gave the man a nod of acknowledgment. Then he looked at Stephanie. "I'll be right down."

She all but winked in return as she pulled the door shut.

"What are you *thinking?*" Melissa demanded as the footsteps receded down the hall.

"That you cared about your reputation." He stated the obvious.

"This isn't 1950."

"It's also not Vegas. It's Montana."

"People don't kiss in Montana?"

"They didn't know we were just kissing."

"But…" Melissa took a step back.

"Your lips," he told her softly. "Your hair, your clothes. You look like you just tumbled out of a haystack."

"But we didn't do anything."

"We thought about it," he told her gruffly. "And it shows."

Her glance went down to her chest. "Oh."

"Yeah. Oh."

Melissa swiftly pulled her hair to the base of her neck and fastened it with the clip. "What about Stephanie? You know what she's going to think."

Jared nodded. "I wanted to talk to you about that."

Melissa raised her brows.

"Would you mind playing along for a few days? Have dinner with us, pretend you like me, just enough to make Stephanie think there's a possibility we'll fall for each other."

Melissa seemed genuinely astonished. "Why? Why would you do that to your own sister?"

"You saw how excited she was," Jared pointed out.

"Yes. And I know how disappointed she's going to be when she finds out the truth. Not to mention how ticked off she's going to be at you."

"Who says she has to find out?"

"I'm leaving in a few days."

"That's perfect," he said. "It'll get us through Sunday. Then we'll act like it didn't work out. She'll be disappointed, sure. But she'll also be past the hard part of commemorating our parents' deaths and remembering how much she misses her grandfather."

"I don't think you can postpone grieving."

"Sure, you can." You could postpone it. You could ignore it. And you could replace it. With, for example, anger.

Melissa shook her head. "I'm not comfortable with this."

Then, he'd simply have to make her comfortable with it. "How much are we paying you?"

"Minimum wage, why?"

"I'll double it."

"You want me to ignore my principles and fake being your girlfriend for two times minimum wage?"

"Triple."

"Jared."

"Name your price."

"It's not about money. It's about integrity." For some reason her voice trailed away on the final word. Her gaze focused on the window as she watched the rain streak down the pane of glass. "Do you really think it's best for her?"

"I do." He moved up behind her. He couldn't help but admire Melissa's decision-making process. "Do you think you could pretend to like me?"

He saw her smile in the blurry reflection of the window. "I'm a pretty good liar."

"Good to know." He restrained himself from resting his hands on her shoulders, even though he longed to touch her again.

She turned, and his desire ramped up. "What do you want me to do?"

Jared bit his tongue over the loaded question, but his expression obviously gave him away.

"You." She poked him squarely in the chest. "Have to promise to behave yourself."

"I will. If you tell me what that means."

Her eyes narrowed. "It means…" She seemed to stumble. "It means not looking at me like you're the big bad wolf and I'm carrying a basket of goodies."

"It'll probably help the charade," he reasoned.

"It'll make me jumpy."

"It should," was his blunt answer.

"Jared," she warned.

"I'll behave myself," he promised. "But it'll help if you do a couple of things for me."

"What?"

"Wear a gunnysack, and a veil, don't talk in that

sexy voice and, for the love of God, quit smelling so decadently delicious."

Back inside her cottage, Melissa was all but shaking with reaction to Jared's words. And to his kisses. And to the overwhelming opportunity he'd unknowingly handed to her.

She was having dinner with his family. Dinner with the Ryders—a private meal where she could ask as many questions as she liked, about growing up, their ranch, their charity trust, their businesses.

She already knew the article would show them in a positive light. Both Jared and Stephanie were hardworking, successful people. The fact that they commemorated their parents' deaths was admirable, and their grandfather's recent death would add a poignancy that readers would lap up like kittens with fresh cream.

She lowered herself into the armchair beside the cottage window, struggling to frame her thoughts. It was Friday today. She'd planned to give herself one more day, maybe two at the most, to gather facts at the ranch. Then she'd have to rush back to Chicago and write the article in time to have it sitting on Seth Strickland's desk for Monday morning.

But that timetable was out the window now. Her greatest interview opportunities would be in the next couple of days. Which meant there was no way to be ready Monday morning. Which meant she'd have to call Seth and confess.

She drew a breath, squeezing the fabric-covered arms

of the chair as she tried to still her racing heart. She could only hope her editor's excitement over the article would overrule his anger that she'd lied to him.

She glanced at her watch. Two o'clock. That made it three in Chicago. No time to lose. She pulled her cell phone out of her bag, pressing the buttons for his number. It rang three times, but then jumped to voice mail, giving her no choice but to leave a quick, vague message.

She replaced the phone in her bag when, over the sound of the continuing rain, she heard footsteps on the front porch. She glanced through the window to see Stephanie, a dripping white Stetson pulled low on her head, waving cheerily through the pane.

Melissa sighed inwardly. She wasn't ready for this. Being undercover to get a story was one thing, but leading Stephanie on was another thing entirely.

But Stephanie had seen her, and Melissa had no choice but to open the door. She crossed to the little foyer.

"Hi," said Stephanie, beaming as she entered the cottage.

Melissa couldn't help but smile in return. The young woman's grin was infectious.

"I told you so," Stephanie sang, hanging her hat on one of a long row of pegs on the wooden wall.

The entry area of the cottage was practically laid out. There were pegs for coats and hats. A small bench beneath, with room for footwear under it, and a bright, woven Navajo rug decorating the wooden floor.

The foyer took up one corner of the small living

room. The rest of the room boasted a simple burgundy couch, a leather armchair, a small television and two low tables with ivory lamps.

There was a compact kitchen beside the living room, a table and two kitchen chairs under the front window, and a door to a bedroom/bathroom combination on the far side. Melissa had to admit, she adored the brass bed and the claw-foot tub. And the oak tree outside the bedroom window rustled in the night breeze, while the muted roar of the river outside filled in the background.

Melissa took a step back to stay out of the way of Stephanie's wet raincoat. Not that she wouldn't have to change clothes, anyway. Standing in front of the open window with Jared had been...well, it had been amazing, of course. But mostly it had been foolish. And not just because she'd ended up with wet clothes.

Stephanie kicked off her boots. "Do you know how long it's been since Jared invited a woman home for dinner?"

Melissa knew she needed to dial Stephanie's excitement level way down. "He didn't exactly—"

"Never," sang Stephanie. "He's never invited a woman home for dinner."

"Your equestrian center is not his actual home," cautioned Melissa. "And I was already here."

Stephanie waved a dismissive hand. "Technicalities."

"No. Facts."

Stephanie pouted.

"Seriously, Stephanie. You can't get carried away with this. Jared and I barely know each other."

Stephanie heaved an exaggerated sigh, dropping down onto the couch. "Are you always this much of a downer?"

Melissa took the armchair again. "I'm always this much of a realist."

"Where's the fun in that?"

"It saves a lot of heartache in the long run."

"Disappointment, I can handle. It's never leaving the starting gate that would kill me."

Inwardly, Melissa conceded there was some logic to the argument. "It's only dinner," she said to Stephanie. "And I'm still planning to leave in a couple of days."

"But you're here now," said Stephanie with a sly wink. "What are you going to wear?"

Melissa's cell phone jangled from her bag on the floor.

"I hadn't thought about it," she said, knowing in her heart the call was from Seth. There was no way in the world she could answer it in front of Stephanie.

It rang again.

"Do you want to get that?"

Melissa shook her head. "It can go to voice mail."

"You sure? I don't mind."

Another shrill ring.

"I'm sure. What do you think I should wear?" Truth was, Melissa hadn't seen anyone wear anything but blue jeans and riding clothes since she'd arrived. Her own wardrobe was plain and meager, since she was pretending to be on a bus trip.

The damn phone rang again.

"You sure you don't want to—"

"Completely sure." Melissa reached for the slim phone. A quick glance told her it was, indeed, her boss. She sent the call to voice mail. "There."

Stephanie paused for a moment. Then her expression grew animated once again as she sat forward. "I was thinking, since it's Royce's first night back, we should dress up a little."

Melissa's attention went automatically to the downpour and the rivulets of mud streaking the narrow cottage road. Even if she had brought anything dressy, it was a virtual mud bog between the cottage and Stephanie's house.

"We'll do it up at the house," Stephanie went on. "We're about the same size. You can take a shower up there. We'll play around with your hair. Put on a little makeup, and you can borrow one of my dresses. I have a bunch I've never even worn."

"I'm not Cinderella," Melissa admonished.

"Oh—" Stephanie all but jumped up from the sofa "—that makes me the fairy godmother."

"Did you miss the word *not?*" Melissa struggled to keep a grip on the conversation.

"This is going to be great."

Still in Melissa's hand, the phone rang again. It was Seth. She hit the voice mail button one more time. She was going to have one heck of a lot of explaining to do. Good thing she would have a kick-ass story to offer up.

"Girl talk while we get ready." Stephanie laughed.

Melissa paused.

Girl talk? *Girl talk.*

Why was she trying to get out of this? Girl talk was exactly what she needed for research.

"I'll meet you up there," she agreed. A quick call to Seth, and she'd be ready for all the girl talk in the world.

"Don't be silly." This time Stephanie did jump up. "You'd drown. I'll drive you over in the truck."

Stephanie's house was rustic but undeniably gracious. A large, practical foyer led into a massive great room with polished floors, a high, hewn-beam ceiling, and overstuffed leather furniture decorated with colorful pillows and woven throws. There was a huge stone fireplace at one end of the rectangular room, and a row of glass doors down the side opened onto a deck that overlooked evergreens and snowy mountain peaks. A wide passageway opposite revealed a gourmet kitchen with a long, polished-wood breakfast bar and padded stools and a formal dining room that seated twelve, with a wood-and-brass chandelier and an impressive woven carpet under the cherry table and wine-colored armchairs.

As they made their way up a wide staircase to the second floor, Melissa wished once again for Susan and her camera. Stephanie's bedroom was at the front of the house. It had its own small balcony, a walk-in closet, an en suite bath and a small sitting area set in a bay-window alcove.

"Dresses are way in the back," said Stephanie, flicking on the closet light and gesturing into the long room. "Pick anything you want. I'll hunt through the bathroom and see what I can find for makeup."

"What are you planning to wear?" Melissa gazed through the open door at rows of blazers and blouses, situated above open shelves that held blue jeans and jodhpurs. She stepped over several pairs of polished boots as she made her way across the carpeted floor.

Stephanie hadn't been exaggerating. There were at least two dozen dresses, most with the tags still on. They were black, gold, red, sleeveless, gauzy, and one gorgeous printed silk that shimmered gold and peach, with a jeweled scoop neckline that looked like something off a Paris runway.

"Try that one," came Stephanie's voice from the doorway.

Melissa shook her head. "I couldn't."

"Why not? Royce brought it back from Europe last year. The straps are too narrow for me. It makes me look like I have linebacker shoulders."

"It does not." Melissa laughed. Stephanie had a wonderful figure.

"I'm okay with sleeveless, even strapless, but there's something about those spaghetti straps that don't work. You want to hop in the shower? I put out fresh towels and a robe."

"I feel bad invading your privacy," Melissa said.

"Are you kidding? I can't wait to dress you up and wow my brother."

Melissa placed the dress back on the rack and turned. "I don't want you to get hurt," she told Stephanie honestly. "Jared and I barely know each other."

"You have to start somewhere," Stephanie replied, obviously undaunted by reality.

"The odds against he and I clicking are about a million to one."

"The odds against me winning Spruce Meadows last week were about a million to one."

"But you practiced. You worked hard for years and years to win that competition."

"I'm not expecting you to marry him next weekend."

Melissa took a step closer to Stephanie. "I'm not going to marry him at all. You have to understand that. He's a nice man. And maybe he thinks I'm pretty—"

"He's going to think you're a knockout in that silk dress."

Melissa sighed. "You're killing me here, Stephanie. I need to know *you* know this isn't going anywhere."

Some of the optimism went out of Stephanie's blue eyes. "But you're going to try, right?"

"It doesn't matter whether I try or not, the odds are still stacked way against it." And those odds were a whole lot higher than Melissa could admit.

"I'm not afraid of the odds," said Stephanie, a new equilibrium coming into her eyes. "I'm just leading a horse to water. He drinks or not will be up to him."

"I take it Jared's the horse?"

"And you're the water."

Relief poured through Melissa. Stephanie understood just fine. She wasn't some flighty young girl with impossible dreams. She was simply trying to match up her brother and bring some balance to the family's gender numbers.

The plan didn't have a hope in hell of working with Melissa, but she could respect the effort.

"Robe's on the door hook," said Stephanie. She nodded to the en suite. "Towels are stacked on the counter."

"Okay," Melissa agreed. She could play dress-up and ply Jared with questions. Maybe they'd have wine with dinner. Even better. She'd sip slowly and let his tongue loosen up.

She followed Stephanie's directions, enjoying the marble tub and the luxurious bath products. The towels were big and plush, and Stephanie's hair dryer gave Melissa's straight, blond hair some body and bounce.

She exited the room to find Stephanie sitting in front of her vanity in a white robe, her auburn hair damp around her ears.

Stephanie swiveled on the small stool. "What do you think?"

Melissa blinked at the unexpected sight. Stephanie's delicate features had been all but obliterated by glaringly bright makeup. With spiked lashes, bright blue shadow, dark blush and a fire engine–red lipstick shade, she looked ready for the lead in a 1980s disco flick.

"Uh...I..." Melissa struggled to find words.

Stephanie's face fell. "It's that bad?" She glanced back to the mirror.

Melissa rushed forward, reflexively putting her hands on Stephanie's shoulders. "The look's a little dated. That's all."

Stephanie hardened her jaw, glaring at her features. "Is it me? Do I just not have a feminine face?"

Melissa's jaw dropped open. "Are you kidding me?"

"I can never quite seem to pull it off." She gestured vaguely toward the closet. "It's not that I don't have the ingredients. I've got plenty of clothes, shoes, beauty products. But I can never figure out what to do with them. I bought a makeover magazine once. I ended up looking like a clown."

"You're beautiful." Melissa recovered her voice. "Beyond beautiful. You're stunning."

"I have a little-girl nose, ugly freckles and funny-color eyes." She leaned forward, screwing up her face in the mirror.

"Most women would kill for your nose," said Melissa honestly. "The freckles are pretty, and you just need a new shade of shadow." She turned the stool, looking critically at Stephanie's skin tone and features. "Go wash your face. Let's start over."

Stephanie perked up. "You'll help?"

"You bet I'll help."

Stephanie jumped up and headed for the bathroom, turning on the taps in the sink. "Did you have a mom and sisters and stuff?" she called.

"A mom, yes," said Melissa. "But I have five older brothers."

Stephanie popped her head back into the room. "Five?"

Melissa nodded. "Adam, Ben, Caleb, Dan and Eddy."

"So probably no makeup tips from them."

"Nah. But I can frame up a cabin, change a car's oil and whistle."

Stephanie laughed as she rubbed cleanser over her face. "And I can rope a calf in under thirty seconds."

"You never know when these skills might come in handy."

Stephanie rinsed and dried, walking back into the bedroom, clad in her terry robe. "Where did you learn about makeup?"

"Girlfriends at school, cable TV, demos at the mall." Melissa glanced around the room and realized the wide sill on the bay window was a good height.

"My friends were in the 4H club. And we didn't get many channels out here while I was growing up."

"Can you hop up there?" Melissa gestured. "That way I won't have to bend over."

"Sure." Stephanie held her robe as she got settled, her bare feet dangling.

Melissa selected some lotion and a few cosmetics and piled them on a small table in the alcove. "It's all about subtlety now," she explained, tipping Stephanie's chin toward the light. "Women want to look natural, just a little more beautiful than nature intended. Earth tones will bring out the subtle silver in your eyes, instead of clashing with it."

"Can you cover up my freckles?"

Personally Melissa liked the freckles. "I'll tone them down a bit. They'll be less noticeable. You have amazing skin."

"Fresh air and healthy living."

"It works. I'm in an office all day, air-conditioning and recycled smog."

Stephanie's forehead wrinkled. "You have a job?"

"I used to have a job." Melissa cursed inwardly at her stupidity, struggling to recover from the gaff. "I delivered office mail for a while. Very boring."

"You seem so smart."

"I'm not that smart."

"Jared said you knew about Sierra Benito."

"That was a stroke of luck." Melissa found a thin brush and some powdered, charcoal eyeliner. "I happened to read an article in the newspaper."

"But you remembered it."

"I suppose. Close your eyes."

"You must have a good memory."

"Decent." Memory was a critical attribute for a journalist—names, dates, faces, events. Melissa gently stroked on the liner, chose silver, blue and pale purple for shadow, added a subtle blush and finished off with a neutral lip gloss.

Then she found a comb and piled Stephanie's thick, wavy hair in a loose twist at the top of her head, freeing a few locks to frame her face and trail at the back of her neck.

Melissa stood back. "Go take a look."

Obviously self-conscious and nervous, Stephanie hopped down from the ledge. She gingerly crossed the floor to the mirror, squinted, opened her eyes, then stared in silence.

"Wow," she finally breathed, turning her head from side to side. "I'm gorgeous."

"You certainly are."

Stephanie raised her brows to Melissa, mischief lurking in her silver-blue eyes. "Let's do you."

Seven

It wasn't often Jared saw his little sister dressed to accentuate her femininity. Not that he ever forgot she was feminine, but she'd run around the ranch yard like a tomboy ever since he could remember. So tonight when she waltzed into the great room in an ultra-flirty dress, he was momentarily stunned. It was white on top, with bows at the shoulders and a full black skirt that billowed around her knees. She'd done something with her hair, too. And her face looked—

Melissa appeared from behind Stephanie, and the jolt took his breath away. Where Stephanie was feminine, Melissa was sultry. She wore a shimmering thin silk sheath of a dress that clung to her figure like a second skin. Spaghetti straps adorned her smooth shoulders, while the gold and peach shimmered under the warm light. Her hair was upswept, her face flawless, and her long, tanned legs and spiked heels were going to invade his dreams for at least the next year.

He swallowed.

"Is Royce here yet?" asked Stephanie.

When Jared finally dragged his gaze from Melissa, he saw the twinkle in Stephanie's eyes. He had to hand it to his sister, she knew how to matchmake. Nothing would happen between him and Melissa, but it sure wouldn't be from a lack of desire. Given his own way, he'd drag her off to his bed right now.

"Sunset Hill flooded out," he answered. He'd talked to Royce a few minutes ago, and his brother had decided to wait the storm out at the main house with McQuestin.

Fine with Jared.

He didn't particularly want Royce laying eyes on Melissa, anyway.

Stephanie's lips pursed in a pout. "Why doesn't he ride up?"

"Probably because he'd be soaked to the ass in the first half mile." Jared gave a quick glance at Melissa to see if his coarse language had offended her.

Her little grin was the last thing he saw before the room went black.

Forks of lightning streaked through the thick sky, while thunder cracked and raindrops smashed against the roof and the wooden deck outside.

"Uh-oh," came Stephanie's disembodied voice.

"What happened?" asked Melissa.

"Could have been anything," Jared answered as he made his way toward the mantelpiece. He found a box of matches by feel, struck one and lit a couple of candles. Power outages were common in ranch country, doubly so during storms.

Stephanie crossed to the front window. "I don't see the cookhouse," she said.

"Give it a minute," Jared suggested, flipping open his cell phone. He punched in Royce's number.

Melissa joined Stephanie at the window, and Jared let himself enjoy the view of her back.

"Why would you see the cookhouse?" asked Melissa.

"They have an emergency generator," said Stephanie.

"Hey, bro," came Royce's voice on the phone.

"Lights out down there?" asked Jared.

"Just now."

"Us, too. Any problems?"

"The boys aren't back from the canyon yet," said Royce.

"McQuestin worried?"

"Won't be for a couple more hours."

"Keep me posted?"

Melissa turned, and Jared quickly averted his lecherous gaze.

"Sure," said Royce.

Flickering lights came on in the distance.

"Cookhouse is up," said Jared, and Melissa turned back to the window.

"We're striking up the gas barbecue," said Royce.

"Don't let McQuestin talk you into poker."

Royce laughed as he signed off.

Stephanie had moved into the dining room. She was on her own cell phone, checking to make sure the employees were all accounted for.

Jared tucked his phone in his pocket.

"What now?" asked Melissa.

He checked to make sure Stephanie was out of earshot as he moved toward Melissa and the window. He kept his voice low. "Now I tell you you're gorgeous."

"Stephanie's idea."

"My sister's not stupid."

"Your sister is Machiavellian."

He moved his hand forward and brushed Melissa's fingertips. "Seems a shame to let her down."

"Seems a shame to lead her on."

"Hey, she's the one playing us, remember?"

"Mrs. Belmont left lasagna in the oven," came Stephanie's voice.

Jared reflexively backed off.

"Salad's in the fridge," Stephanie finished.

"I guess we're dining by candlelight," said Melissa.

"Romantic," Stephanie put in, scooping one of the lighted candles and heading for the dining room.

Melissa followed.

Jared allowed himself a lingering glance at Melissa as she walked away. "Better than poker with McQuestin," he said out loud.

They settled at one end of the big table, Jared at the head, flanked by the two women. Lasagna, salad, rolls and a bottle of merlot were spread out in front of them. He'd lit a candelabra for the middle of the table, and kerosene lamps flickered against the rain-streaked windows.

Melissa's soft blond hair shimmered in the yellow light. Her lips were dark. Her eyes sparkled. And the silk shifted softly against her body as she moved her hands.

"Do you have political aspirations?" she asked him.

The question took him by surprise. "Why the heck would you think that?"

"You've got it all," she responded, taking another sip of the merlot, which he couldn't help but note was exactly the same shade as her lips. "Money, success, community standing, charitable work, and now you're palling around with the mayor of Chicago."

"How did you know about the mayor?"

She concentrated on setting down her glass. "One of the cowboys mentioned something about your building and the city."

Jared turned to glare at Stephanie. "How does anybody get any work done around here?" he demanded. "Melissa's been here three days, and she knows every-thing but my birth weight and shoe size."

"Don't be such a bear," said Stephanie.

"You're exaggerating," said Melissa.

"Not by much."

"Eight pounds nine ounces," Stephanie put in with a giggle.

"Ouch," said Melissa.

"Don't let that put you off," Stephanie came back. "It's not necessarily hereditary."

Both Jared and Melissa stared at her, dumb-founded.

"What?" Stephanie glanced back and forth between them. "You guys don't want kids?"

"Several," said Jared, deciding his sister deserved everything she got from here on in.

He took Melissa's hand and raised it to his lips. "How does four sound to you?"

"Are you going to hire me a nanny?" she asked, surprising him by playing along.

"You bet. A nanny, a chauffeur and a housekeeper."

"Okay, then." Melissa gave a nod. "Four it is. But we'd better get started—I'm not getting any younger." She reached for her wineglass. "Better enjoy this while I can. Once I'm pregnant, it's off the alcohol. And this wine is fantastic."

"I know you're messing with me," Stephanie put in. "But I don't care. I have hope, anyway."

"We have a very good wine cellar," said Jared. "It was a hobby of Gramps."

"Why don't you show it to Melissa?" Stephanie quickly suggested.

"You hoping I'll get her pregnant on the tasting table?"

Melissa sputtered and coughed over a drink.

He squeezed her hand by way of apology.

"I think Stephanie's overestimating the power of this dress," she wheezed.

Jared hesitated. Then he stepped into the breach. "No, she's not."

Stephanie clapped her hands together in triumph.

* * *

It was ten o'clock when Stephanie succeeded in getting Jared and Melissa alone together. They were in the truck, and Melissa peered in pitch-darkness and driving rain as they rounded the bend to the row of cottages by the river, the headlights bouncing off the oak trees and the dark porches.

She had to admit, she wouldn't have wanted to walk all the way back. And she wouldn't have asked Stephanie to slog through the mud to get to the truck. And that left Jared.

Then he had insisted on carrying her from the ranch house porch to the truck—which was an experience all on its own.

Now they pulled up to the front of her cottage and he killed the lights and turned off the engine.

"Stay put," he told her as he opened the driver's door and a puff of cool wind burst in. "I'll be right around."

Part of her wanted to insist on walking, but her shoes were impractical, the mud was slick, and she knew the black road would be a patchwork of deep puddles. So she waited, her heart rate increasing, her skin prickling in anticipation and her brain fumbling through sexy projections of being in Jared's arms again.

Her door swung open, and she shifted from the seat into his arms, wrapping her own arms around his neck. She'd put a windbreaker over the dress, but her legs were still bare and his strong hand clasped around the back of her thigh.

"Ready?" he asked, husky voice puffing against her cheek.

"Ready," she confirmed with a nod, and he pulled her against his chest, his body protecting her from the worst of the rain. He kicked the truck door shut and strode over the mud and up the porch stairs, stopping under the tiny roof in front of the door.

He didn't bother putting her down. Instead, he swung the door open and carried her into the warm cottage.

It was completely dark, not a single frame of reference.

He slowly lowered her to the floor. "Don't move."

"Do you have matches?" she asked as he stepped away from her.

"There'll be some on the mantel." Something banged, and he cursed.

"You okay?" she called.

"I'm fine."

Then she heard a crackle, and a small flame appeared across the living room. She could just make out Jared's face as he lit three candles on the stone mantel. There was a mirror on the wall behind, and the light reflected back into the room.

"Thanks," she told him.

He shook out the match and tossed it into the fireplace. "You want a fire?"

"It's not that cold." She hung the damp windbreaker on a wall hook. Then she wiped her face, pulled the clip from her hair and finger-combed out the rainwater.

It was late enough that she planned to snuggle into bed with her laptop and record notes from the evening.

Stephanie had predicted the power would be back on by morning. If not, the staff would gather at the cookhouse for breakfast, and they'd set priorities for animal care.

Jared crumpled up a newspaper, threw it into the fireplace and added a handful of kindling. "It's not that warm, either." He crouched down and struck another match, lighting a corner of the newspaper.

The orange flame quickly grew, reflecting off the planes and angles of his face. There was something about the actions that warmed Melissa's heart. He hadn't exactly saved her life, but he'd shown a tender, caring side that surprised her.

She automatically moved closer to the fire. "I wish I could offer you coffee or something."

He rose to his feet in the flickering light. His short hair was damp, and his cotton shirt was plastered to his chest. Power and masculinity seemed to ooze from every pore.

He eased closer, and she was instantly awash in desire.

"Coffee's not what I want."

She was dying to ask, but she didn't dare. She opened her mouth, then closed it again, warning herself that the slightest encouragement was going to bring his lips crashing down on hers, and they'd be trapped all over again in the tangle of desire.

His lips came down on hers, anyway.

And she might have stretched up slightly to meet him.

Okay, she'd definitely stretched up. And she'd tilted her head to accommodate him. And now she was opening her mouth, meeting his tongue, snaking her arms around his neck and pressing her body tightly against his own.

His clothes were damp, but she didn't care. His hands were roaming, and she loved it. His mouth was sure and strong, but still tender, and oh, so hot.

Passion quickly obliterated reason. She clung tightly as his nimble hands pulled down the zipper of her dress. He eased it over her head and discarded it on a chair. He worked at the buttons of his shirt, alternating between kissing her and staring deeply into her eyes. His were nearly black with passion, while desire pulsed through every fiber of her body.

Her hands went to his jeans, popping the button, sliding the zipper.

He groaned, tossed his shirt and pulled her back into his arms. His kisses roamed her cheeks, her neck and down to where he pushed her bra out of the way. His hot mouth surrounded a nipple, and she threw her head back, her hands grasping his shoulders for support.

He wrapped a strong arm firmly around the small of her back, holding her steady, his mouth sending sparks of desire from her breasts to the base of her belly. He released her bra, dropping it to the floor. Then he scooped her into his arms and carried her to the small bedroom.

The sheets were cool against her bare back. She could barely make out his outline as he discarded the remainder of his clothes. Then his warm, hard, musk-scented body was sliding next to her, and she was enveloped in kisses and caresses that seared heat over every inch of her skin.

She kissed his chest, tasting his salty skin, her hands roaming down his back, over his buttocks, along his strong thighs.

He groaned his approval, kissing her deeply. "You are gorgeous," he breathed. He kissed her again. His fingers found their way into her flimsy panties.

She gasped at his touch, flexing her hips, transmitting an unmistakable invitation.

He peeled off her panties, produced a condom from somewhere, and covered her body with his own. Their bodies were flush together, tight at the apex, and her legs were wrapped around his waist.

He kissed her deeply, sliding his hands to her bottom, adjusting the angle of their bodies as he eased inside. Driving rain splattered against the bedroom window. Lightning chased across the sky while thunder vibrated the cottage walls.

Then the world around Melissa disappeared. Nothing existed beyond Jared, and every sensation was magnified a thousand times, his touch, his scent, the taste of his skin, the sound of his voice as he recited her name, calling her beautiful, urging her on.

Their tempo increased. The hot and cold and electric sensations heightening to unbearable. As thunder crashed around them, her body stiffened. Her toes curled. Her hoarse voice cried out Jared's name as she tumbled from the pinnacle down into the exquisite arms of release.

As she floated to earth, Jared tucked a quilt around

them. He turned slightly to the side, keeping them locked together, but taking his weight from her body.

Their deep breaths rose in unison, both of them sucking the moisture-laden oxygen from the dark room, recovering, reframing, realizing the magnitude of what they'd just done.

"I'm not sure that was such a good idea," she ventured on a gasp.

He didn't let her go. Didn't back off a single inch. "Because you work for me?" he mumbled against her neck.

Because I'm writing an article on you. Because you don't know who I am. Because I lied to you. The reasons were endless, and she couldn't admit to any of them.

"At least for tonight," she ventured, instead, "do you think we could be clear that I work for Stephanie?"

Jared's chuckle rumbled through his frame. "So what's the problem?"

"I'm leaving in a few days."

He smoothed her hair from her forehead. "Just because something's short, doesn't mean it can't be fantastic."

"I suppose." If you took away her deception, a one-night stand certainly wasn't the end of the world. But eventually he was going to find out her true identity.

She couldn't do anything to change the past hour, but she did need to control herself going forward. Not that she'd *ever* divulge any intimate details. Every single thing that happened in the cottage tonight was off the record.

But she did need to back off. She couldn't let their circumstances get even more complicated.

She eased away from his warmth. "Stephanie's probably counting the minutes you've been down here."

"Are you asking me to leave?"

"I think that would be best."

He stilled, and she assumed he was staring at her in the dark.

A lightning bolt lit up the room, and his stark expression of disappointment tugged at her heart.

"I think it would be best," she repeated, wanting nothing more than to burrow down under the covers and sleep in Jared's warm arms for the rest of the night. But she had to be strong.

He rolled from the bed. "Of course." There was a tightness to his voice that bordered on anger.

She closed her ears to it and clung to the passion they'd shared.

His jeans rustled. Then he padded into the living room.

She held her breath while he dressed. Would he come back? Say something more? Kiss her goodbye?

Suddenly his silhouette appeared in the doorway. "Good night," he offered without coming back inside.

"Good night," she echoed, struggling to keep the hollowness from her voice. She'd asked him to leave. She was silly to feel hurt.

He waited a moment more, then turned away, heading out into the storm.

The truck engine rumbled to life. The headlights

flared up. Then the big treaded tires churned their way over the muddy road.

Melissa dragged herself from the bed. She wrapped a robe around her body, retrieved her laptop, powered it up and forced her thoughts back to the discussion at dinner. The fling with Jared might be over, but she still had her job to save.

"Seth Strickland," came the terse answer at the other end of the phone.

It was morning. The rain had stopped, and the lights were back on as Stephanie had predicted. Melissa was dressed in blue jeans and a simple tank top again, trying to push the insanity that had become her life back into perspective.

"Seth?" she said into the phone, thanking her lucky stars that he was in the office on a Saturday. "It's Melissa."

"Where the hell have you been?" he shouted without preamble.

She wasn't ready to answer that question yet. "If I could *guarantee* the Jared Ryder story, can you buy me a little time?"

"No! And what the hell are you talking about? Why didn't you call me back yesterday?"

"I'm in Montana."

"You said you were working from home."

"I'm at the Ryder Ranch. Right now. I had dinner with Jared Ryder last night."

Seth went silent.

"I need a few more days, Seth."

"You had dinner with Ryder?"

"And his sister. And his brother's just arrived."

"How the hell did you—"

"They think I'm a stable hand."

"You're undercover?" There was a note of respect in Seth's voice. "It's an exposé?"

"Yes, I'm undercover."

"What've you got?"

"A bunch of stuff. His family. His childhood. Their charitable foundation."

"Ryder has a charitable foundation?"

"Yes. But I need a few more days. Can you give it to me?"

"You're in a position to guarantee the story?"

"Yes."

There was a long silence. "If I go to Everett and you don't deliver, you know both our asses will be out the door."

"I understand."

"And you can still make the guarantee?"

"I can." She didn't have enough on the construction business yet. But she'd let Stephanie matchmake some more, and she'd find a way to meet Royce. She'd get what Seth needed or die trying.

"I have to have it Wednesday. Five o'clock. And the copy better be bloody clean. We're not going to have time for much editing."

"Five o'clock Wednesday," Melissa confirmed.

"And, Melissa?" Seth's voice was gruff.

"Yes?"

"Lie to me again, and you're fired."

"Yes, sir."

Seth hung up the phone, and she realized she was shaking. The stakes couldn't be higher, and she barely had four days to pull it off.

"Have a good time with Melissa last night?" Stephanie asked as Royce's pickup appeared in the distance on the ranch road.

"It was fine," Jared answered, keeping his voice neutral. He fully expected Melissa to make herself scarce for the rest of the week.

He wasn't sure what had gone wrong at the end of the evening, but he'd obviously made some kind of misstep. A woman didn't go from crying out a man's name to kicking him out of her bed in the space of two minutes if the guy hadn't screwed up somehow.

He started down the stairs to meet Royce at the driveway.

"You going to see her again?" asked Stephanie, keeping pace.

"I expect I will. Since she's living here." Odds were that he'd run into her eventually.

"That's not what I meant. Are you going to ask her out? I noticed you stayed down there for a while."

"I bet you did."

The sound of the truck's engine grew louder. Mud sprayed out from the tires as Royce took a corner far too fast.

"Did you sleep with her?" asked Stephanie.

Jared shot his sister a glare of irritation. "What is the matter with you?"

She shrugged. "You were only gone an hour. Not a lot of time, but then maybe you weren't very—"

"Young lady, you shut your mouth before you get yourself into a world of trouble. Where did you learn to talk like that, anyway?" Maybe he'd stayed away too long. Maybe leaving Stephanie here on her own was a mistake. Or maybe Gramps's death had affected her more than Jared and Royce had realized.

"I'm just asking a question."

"You're out of line, little sister."

Stephanie pursed her lips in a pout. "So are you going to ask her out again?"

Jared frowned.

"That can't be out of line. I'm not asking about sex."

The truck skidded to a halt, and Jared walked forward. "Let's just get through the weekend, all right?"

"I know I have to get through the weekend," Stephanie muttered as they walked down the front pathway. "I was only hoping for something to look forward to at the end of it."

Jared felt a pang of guilt. The whole reason he'd started the charade with Melissa was to keep Stephanie's mind occupied. Sure, it had run way off the rails last night. But that wasn't Stephanie's fault.

He slung an arm around his sister's shoulders, moderating his voice. "Fine. I'll ask her out again. But I can't guarantee she'll say yes."

Stephanie turned in to give him a tight squeeze. "I know she'll say yes. I saw the way she looked at you."

The words caused a sudden tightening in Jared's

chest. How she'd looked at him? What did that mean? He wanted to probe for more information. But Royce appeared across the hood of the truck, and Stephanie broke free to hug her other brother.

"Baby sister!" cried Royce, dragging Stephanie into his arms, lifting her off the ground and twirling her around.

Jared caught a glimpse of Melissa across the yard, and their gazes met. She was shoveling manure again, and for some reason, that made him angry. She was capable of so much more. She was intelligent, full of insightful opinions and thought-provoking questions.

It occurred to him that he could offer her a job in Chicago. She could work for Ryder International or even the Genevieve Fund. There had to be any number of things a woman with her intellect and curiosity could handle.

In a split second he realized what he was doing. He was working out ways to keep her close, ways that he could see her again, maybe sleep with her again. Though, judging by the expression on her face, the latter was unlikely. But what did it say about him? Was he buying into Stephanie's fantasy?

He could almost feel a debate going on inside Melissa's brain. She'd seen him, and she knew he knew. Did she duck her head and go back to work? Did she avoid him, or get the first, awkward moment over with?

While he waited, she squared her shoulders, leaned the manure fork against the fence and determinedly marched toward him. Good for her. He couldn't help a surge of admiration, and he moved to meet her in the driveway.

"Melissa!" Stephanie's voice surprised him. "Come and meet Royce." Hand in Royce's, Stephanie tugged him to intersect Melissa's pathway. The four of them met up off the hood of the truck.

"Royce, this is Melissa," said Stephanie. "She's dating Jared."

Melissa's eyes widened slightly, but she held her composure.

Royce turned to stare at Jared.

Jared gave his brother an almost imperceptible shake, and Royce immediately held out his hand to Melissa. "Great to meet you. I'm the black sheep of the family."

Stephanie laughed, while Melissa accepted Royce's handshake. "Melissa Webster. I'm the black sheep in mine."

"She has five older brothers," Stephanie put in.

"Worse off than you," Royce teased, arching a brow at his sister.

"I'd better get back to work," said Melissa. Her gaze darted to Jared just long enough to let him know she wished they'd been able to talk. Well, so did he. He felt like he owed her an apology of some kind. At the very least, he wanted to make sure things were okay between them.

"Can you come and help me with Rosie-Jo?" Stephanie asked Melissa.

Since Rosie-Jo had half a dozen grooms, Jared recognized the ruse for what it was. Stephanie wanted to pump Melissa for information. But from what he'd seen of Melissa so far, she'd be up to the task of sidestepping anything too personal.

"Dating?" Royce asked as the two women walked away.

"More like flirting," said Jared. "But I didn't have the heart to disillusion Stephanie this weekend."

"Are you going to disillusion poor Melissa?"

Jared shook his head. "She knows the score. She's leaving in a few days, anyway."

Royce reached into the back of the pickup truck and retrieved his duffel bag. "How's Stephanie holding up?"

"Too cheerful," said Jared. "You just know she's going to crack."

"Maybe going up to the cemetery isn't such a good idea this year. Gramps's grave is awfully fresh."

"Go ahead and suggest we skip," said Jared as the two men headed for the house. Quite frankly, Jared would rather avoid the cemetery. He wanted to pay tribute to his grandfather, but the anger at his parents hadn't abated one bit. His whole life, he'd admired and respected them both, never doubting their morals and integrity. But he couldn't have been more wrong. He wanted to yell at them, not lay flowers beside their headstones.

But he couldn't let on. Bad enough that he knew the truth. He couldn't drag Royce, and certainly not Stephanie, into the nightmare. At the moment, he wished his grandfather had taken the knowledge to his grave.

"She'd never go for it," said Royce, yanking Jared back to the present.

"Of course not," Jared agreed as they crossed the porch. Stephanie considered herself tough. She'd never admit how much visiting the cemetery hurt her.

"I hear there's a debate over Sierra Benito." Royce tossed his duffel on a low bench in Stephanie's foyer.

"There is. You're the deciding vote."

"You going to try talking me out of the project?"

"I am. I don't want another death on my conscience." An image of Jared's father sprang to his mind. There was no excuse. No excuse in the world for what his father had done.

Royce paused and peered at his brother. "*Another* death?"

"Slip of the tongue," said Jared, turning away to move into the great room. "I don't want anyone to die on a Ryder project."

He also didn't want to keep lying to his brother, about his parents, about Melissa, about *anything*.

Eight

Under the small light above the cottage's kitchen table, Melissa typed furiously on her laptop. She'd composed and discarded at least five openings to her article. She knew if she could get the beginning right, the rest would flow. It was always that way.

But she needed to capture Jared's essence. No small feat. Every time she thought she had him pegged he'd show her another side of himself, and she'd have to rethink the package.

Maybe it would be easier if they hadn't made love. Maybe if she hadn't seen him naked, or gazed into the depths of his eyes, or felt the strength and tenderness of his caress.

She drew a frustrated sigh as the words on the screen blurred in front of her. Unless she wanted to sell the article to a tabloid, she was going to have to nix that train of thought.

Someone tapped lightly on her front door.

The sigh turned into a frown. It was Sunday night, and the two young women staying next door had invited her over for drinks. The two had seemed very friendly, but Melissa had begged off. Between her ranch chores and allowing for time to fly back to Chicago, she only had two more evenings to pull the article together. There wasn't any time for socializing.

The knock came again.

With the light on, there was no sense in pretending she was asleep. Besides, they would have seen her through the window on their way up the stairs.

She pushed back from the table and crossed to the door.

"I'm sorry," she began as she tugged it open. "But I really can't—"

"Sorry to bother you," came Jared's voice.

His broad shoulders filled the doorway. His head was bare, and he still wore his business suit from the cemetery visit earlier. He wore a crisp, white shirt and a dark, red-striped tie. There was a frown on his face and worry in his eyes.

"Jared."

"I was out walking and I saw your light," he apologized.

Even if she had been inclined to give up a chance to get more information, his expression would have melted the hardest heart. She knew he'd been up to the cemetery with his sister and brother this afternoon, and it had obviously been tough.

"How did it go?" she asked, stepping back to invite him in.

He shrugged as he walked inside. "About how I'd expected." His voice was hollow. "We all miss Gramps."

Melissa nodded, closing the door behind him. "This is probably the worst year," she ventured.

"I suppose." His gaze focused on something, and she realized he was staring at her laptop. "You travel with a computer?"

Panic spurred her forward. She closed the lid, hoping she'd saved recently. "It's compact," she answered. "Very light."

"I guess. Did I interrupt—" he paused "—work?"

"I'm writing a letter," she quickly improvised. "Can I offer you something? Coffee?" She gestured to the small living-room grouping, taking his attention away from the table and her computer. "Or there's a bottle of wine…"

"I'm fine." He eased down into the worn armchair.

Melissa curled into one corner of the sofa, sitting at right angles to him. "How's Stephanie doing?"

"She's asleep now."

Melissa nodded. She was starting to feel close to Stephanie. The woman was fun-loving and generous. She wasn't exactly worldly wise, but she was perfectly intelligent and worked harder than anyone Melissa had ever met.

"I wish there was something I could do to help."

Jared gazed at her without speaking, an indefinable expression on his face. It was guarded, yet intimate, aloof, yet intense.

"Tell me what you were writing," he finally said.

Melissa could feel the blood drain from her face. The air suddenly left the room, and an oppressive heat wafted over her entire body.

"A letter," she rasped.

"To who?" he asked.

"My brother," she improvised, dreading what Jared must know, hoping against hope for a miracle.

"Which one?"

She waited for his eyes to flare with anger, but they stayed frighteningly calm.

"Adam." She swallowed. "I promised…I promised him…that I'd, uh, be careful."

Jared nodded. "And have you? Been careful."

"Yes."

He raked both hands through his short hair. "Oh, God, Melissa. I don't want to do this."

She jumped up from her chair, too nervous to sit still, sweat popping out of her pores. "Do what?"

"It's so unfair to you."

What was he talking about? What was he planning to do to her? She found herself inching toward the door, wondering if the women next door were still awake. Would they hear her if she screamed?

"I didn't know where else to go." His voice was suddenly thick with emotion.

The tone made Melissa pause. "What do you mean?"

Was he going to yell at her? Toss her out of the cottage? Throw her off the property?

She was starting to wish he'd just get it over with. Should she try to grab the laptop?

He shook his head. "Never mind."

Never mind?

He came to his feet, and she struggled not to shrink away.

"Did you say something about wine?" he asked.

She gave herself a mental shake, struggling to clear her brain.

"Melissa?"

"Are you angry with me?"

"Why would I be angry with you? I'm the one invading your privacy." A beat went by. "And attempting to drink your wine."

She forced herself to move. "Right. It's on the counter." What had she missed? What had just happened?

She heard him moving behind her as she opened a wooden drawer. "I think I saw a corkscrew in here."

"It's a screw top."

"Oh." Classy. She was willing to bet he didn't often drink wine from a screw-top bottle. "One of the cowboys picked it up in town," she explained.

"Did you have to flirt with him?"

"For screw-top wine? Please."

Jared grinned. "I forgot. I'm talking to the master."

"I gave him ten bucks and told him to do the best he could." She hunted through the cupboard, but gave up on wineglasses. "These do?" At least they weren't plastic.

"You sure you should be spending your hard-earned money on wine?" he asked. He poured while she held the glasses.

"You tripled my wages, remember?"

"Did we agree on that?"

"We sure did."

He set down the bottle, taking one of the short water glasses from her hand. "Get it in writing?"

"Didn't have to." She gave him a mock toast. "I know your secret."

"No, you don't," he responded dryly, downing a good measure of the wine.

She watched his stark expression with a whole lot of curiosity. Jared had a secret? Something other than playacting for his sister?

Okay, it couldn't be as big as Melissa's secret. But it might be interesting. And it could be exactly the hook she was looking for to get the story started.

Jared hadn't meant his words to sound like a challenge. But he realized they did. And if the expression on Melissa's face was anything to go by, she'd reacted the same way.

"So?" She sidled up to him, green eyes dancing with mischief.

"None of your business."

"Then why'd you bring it up?"

Fair question. Better question, why was he even here? It had been one roller coaster of an emotional day. He'd been half blind with anger at the cemetery, holding on to his temper by a thread, knowing he couldn't let Stephanie or Royce catch on.

He could tell Royce was suspicious. So when Stephanie went upstairs to bed, Jared had escaped from the house. Then he'd seen Melissa's light, and his feet had carried him to her door.

He thought he knew why. He needed to spend time with someone completely separate from his family. Melissa didn't know any of the players in their little drama. She knew nothing about his family but what he'd told her. She might annoy him or argue with him or frustrate the hell out of him with her approach to life, but she wouldn't threaten his composure.

She grazed her knuckles along his biceps. "You said you had a secret?" she prompted.

Here was another reason to darken her doorway. Her musical voice soothed him. Her scent enticed him. And when he gazed at her lips, all he could think about was capturing them with his own, tasting her all over again and letting the softness of her body pull him, once more, into oblivion.

And maybe it was as simple as that. He'd come to her because he needed to forget for a while.

He captured her hand, holding it tight against his sleeve, the warmth of her palm seeping through to his skin.

"I want you," he told her honestly.

Her voice went husky, stoking his desire. "That's not exactly a secret."

He smiled at her open acceptance of his declaration.

He liked it that she wasn't coy. She was confident and feisty. She flouted convention, ignored advice. There was something to be said for a woman who marched to her own drummer.

"I was expecting something more interesting," she said.

"Like what?"

"I don't know. A secret takeover of a multinational corporation. News that Ryder International was sending a manned mission to Mars. Maybe that you were really a CIA agent masquerading as a businessman."

Jared couldn't help but laugh at the last one. The knot of tension in his gut broke free. "The CIA?"

"Didn't you read the article?"

"What article?"

"In the *Chicago Daily*. Two years ago. Well, they outed you as a spy in the lifestyle section. Though, I suppose if they'd had any real evidence, it would have made the front page."

"You remember what you read in the *Chicago Daily* two years ago, yet you can't remember how to tie a quick-release knot?"

"Are we still talking about sex?"

"You're amazing." He'd never met anyone remotely like Melissa. She was smart, sassy and stunningly gorgeous. How had the men of Gary, Indiana, let her get away?

"So you're not in the CIA?" she pressed with a pretty pout.

He slipped an arm around her waist, settling her close and letting the balm of her company soothe him.

A breeze wafted in over the river, fluttering the plaid curtains above the small sink. The lights were low, the evening cool, the woman beautiful.

"You caught me," he said, setting his glass on the countertop and sliding hers from her fingers. "Ever slept with a spy?"

"You'd lie to get me into bed?"

"Is it working?"

"I'm not that impressed by a spy. I'd rather you were an astronaut going to Mars."

He settled his other arm around her waist, squaring her in front of him. "I can be anything you want."

He kissed her, gently, savoring her essence, forcing himself to keep it short. It was a struggle. If he let his hormones have their way, he'd be scooping her into his arms and tossing her on the bed all over again. But he pulled back.

"Is this why you came here?" Her cheeks were flushed, her lips parted and soft, but her eyes were slightly wary.

He felt like a heel. "No pressure," he quickly told her.

"Is it because I'm leaving?"

"Yes," he answered honestly. Then he realized how that sounded. "No. That's not it." He cursed himself for stumbling. "Well, it's partly…"

What was the matter with him? "I like that you don't know me, don't know my family." He wrapped his hand around the back of a kitchen chair, giving it a squeeze. "It's been a rough day."

She moved forward. "I understand."

She didn't, but it didn't matter. What mattered was that the wariness was out of her eyes. What mattered was that she was touching him, drawing forward, stretching up to kiss his lips.

There was something unfair about the situation, something unbalanced, unequal, but he couldn't put his finger on it. A split second later, he didn't even want to try.

His arms went firmly around her. He wanted to pull her inside him, keep her there, cradle her while the world moved on without them.

Her arms snaked around his neck. She tipped her head, and he deepened the kiss. Her tongue was sweet nectar, the inside of her mouth hot and decadent. She smelled like wildflowers and tasted like honey.

His hands slipped down, cupping the softness of her bottom, kneading and pressing her against his driving arousal.

She moaned his name, and he felt her breasts burning into his chest, like a brand that would mark him forever.

He lifted her, shoving the chair out of the way, perching her on the table, tugging the curtain shut behind her, before his hands went to the buttons on her shirt.

She reciprocated, her breath coming fast, head down to concentrate as she worked on his long row of buttons.

He freed her shirt, slipping it off her shoulders, kissing the velvet softness, letting his tongue explore the taste and texture of her skin. He snapped open her bra, and it fell to the floor, revealing firm, pert breasts, capped with pink nipples.

She pushed his shirt down his arms, and they were skin to skin. She was impossibly soft, impossibly warm, silken and sweet and everything a man could possibly dream.

Their lips came together, open, full on. He led her through a tumultuous kiss that left them both panting and needy for more. He kissed her again while he slid his palm up her rib cage to cover her breast, testing the hardened nipple, drawing a gasp from the back of her throat.

He caressed her body, leisurely, thoroughly; while her own hands splayed on his back, her lips found his flat nipples, and her silken hair teased his skin with an erotic brush. He scooted her forward, forcing her thighs farther apart. His fingers went to her blue jeans, releasing the button, sliding down the zipper. His knuckles grazed her silken panties, and his mind fixated on the treasures beneath.

A gust of wind cooled his back. The crisp scent of the river and the sweet aroma of the fields swirled through the room. The moon rode high above the mountains, while layers of stars twinkled across the endless sky. Horses whinnied in the distance, while leaves rustled in the oak and aspen trees.

There was perfection in the world tonight. He was home and she was in his arms, and nothing else mattered for the moment. Tomorrow would have to take care of itself.

He tugged off her jeans, then slipped off her panties,

drawing her exquisite, naked body against him for a long lingering kiss.

He finally drew back, gazing down at her ivory skin, unblemished against the scarred wood of the kitchen table.

"You are stunning," he whispered with reverence.

"You're overdressed," she said back, her hand going to his waistband.

He closed his eyes, tipped his head back and let his body drink in the erotic sensations as she slowly dragged down his zipper, her smooth warm hands removing his pants, releasing his body, highjacking every molecule of his senses.

"You're stunning, too," she whispered, body wriggling, hand moving, sliding, squeezing.

He sucked in a tight breath, holding on to his control as he feathered his hand along her thighs. He stared into her bottomless eyes. She stared back as his fingertips climbed higher, and her hands roamed further, each of them daring the other to crack.

Her beautiful mouth parted. Her eyes glazed. Her hand convulsed, and he pulled her to him, slipping slowly, surely, solidly inside.

She gripped his shoulders and leaned in for his kiss. He melded his mouth to hers, slipped his hands beneath her and settled the angle, settled the rhythm, let the roar in his ears and the pounding in his brain obliterate everything but the incredible sensation of Melissa.

He wanted it to go on forever. He was determined to make it last. She finally cried out, body pulsating before going limp. But he kept on kissing her, muttering words of need and affection.

And then she was with him. All over again, building toward a second crescendo. And he held back until the very last second before allowing himself to tumble over the cliff with her, his body drenched with sweat, his mind filled with amazement.

He carried her spent body to the bed, climbing in beside her, settling the quilt around them as he drew her into the cradle of his arms.

"You okay?" he whispered as his head found the indent on her pillow.

She drew two deep breaths while he kissed her hairline, then her temple, then her ear. He burrowed into the crook of her neck, inhaling deeply. How could a woman possibly smell so good?

"Define okay," she whispered back.

"Still breathing?"

She nodded.

"Nothing strained or broken?"

"Nothing."

"Want to do it again?"

An hour later Melissa could barely lift a finger. But she could see why Jared was the fantasy of half the women in Chicago. Word had obviously gotten around.

She was lying on her back, eyes closed. The covers were a tangle at their feet, and a cool breeze relieved her heated skin. Jared was beside her, propped up on one elbow, his fingertips feathering a small zigzag pattern over her stomach. She was amazed he could move anything.

"You still breathing?" he rumbled.

"Barely."

He chuckled at that.

"I don't think I've ever been this exhausted," she said.

"Never?" There was a hint of pride in his voice.

"Well, maybe once," she couldn't help teasing. "The day my brothers decided to build a tree fort. I was eight and insisted on helping. They nearly killed me."

"You're saying I'm a close second to your brothers?" The pride was gone.

She opened her eyes and managed a grin.

"Still feisty," he said.

"Even when I'm beat."

"Tell me about these burly construction-worker brothers of yours."

"What do you want to know?"

"If they'll have my name on a hit list when I get back to Chicago."

"If I was eighteen you might be in trouble."

"If you were eighteen, I wouldn't be in this bed."

She chuckled. "But they've mellowed over the years. Caleb wouldn't hurt a fly. Eddy's head over heels for a kindergarten teacher right now. He doesn't even call anymore. Adam, Ben and Dan are married with little kids and more important things to worry about than their sister's virtue."

"It's strange to hear all that," said Jared. "I keep picturing you as an orphan. How does such a big family let you wander off on the bus system without money? It doesn't make sense."

"It's my pride. I don't talk to them about money."

"Still, if it was Stephanie—"

"What about you?" Naked in Jared's arms, Melissa really wasn't in the mood to have to lie to him. "Extended family? Niece and nephew prospects?"

"No niece and nephew prospects. Stephanie's too young, and Royce...well, you haven't had a lot of time to spend with Royce. It's hard to picture him with a wife and a white picket fence."

"And you? Do you really want four kids?"

"I like kids," said Jared. "But I wonder..."

"It's not like you can't afford them," she put in. And he'd certainly have his pick of women. She could give him a list right now if he was interested.

His hand stilled on her stomach. "Money isn't everything."

"Said like a man who has plenty."

"There's love, affection, fidelity."

"Fidelity?" she questioned.

He didn't respond.

"Aren't you getting a little ahead of yourself?" she asked. He might want to marry the lucky woman before he planned the divorce.

Jared shifted. "It's not a given."

She tipped her head so that she was looking at his face. "Maybe. But you don't go into something planning for failure, either."

He was gazing through the open window at the near-full moon. "You can love each other, or appear to love each other, and your marriage can still crumble."

"You're a cynic."

"I'm a realist."

A sudden unease came over her. "Jared? Have you been divorced?"

He shook his head. "No."

But she could tell there was more. She waited as long minutes ticked by.

"What's wrong?" she finally asked.

Tension radiated in waves from his body.

"Jared?"

"My mother was unfaithful."

The admission hit Melissa with the subtlety of a brick wall. She was too shocked to speak.

"The old cabin," Jared rasped. "That bedroom." His hand raked through his messy hair. "Until I saw it, I'd hoped Gramps's memory had somehow…"

Melissa's stomach clenched around nothing. "Oh, Jared."

He met her gaze, his irises dark with the depth of his pain. "My whole life, I thought their deaths were an accident."

"They weren't?" Melissa struggled to understand what he was saying.

"My grandfather told me. Before he died. I guess he thought…" Jared drew a ragged breath. "I don't know what he thought. I wish he hadn't told me at all."

"Somebody killed your parents?"

"My mother's affair started a chain reaction, and three people ended up dead."

"Three?" Melissa squeaked.

Jared's tone turned warning. "Stephanie and Royce don't know. I have to pretend everything is normal."

Melissa nodded her understanding. "You went to the graveyard to keep the secret."

"Yes."

And he'd come to her afterward. She had no idea how she should feel about that.

He suddenly pulled her close, his face getting lost in the length of her hair, his arms and legs imprisoning her against his body.

"It's stupid," he told her. "I barely know you. But when I think of another man…" Jared drew another breath. "For a second tonight, I understood why my father shot him."

Melissa reflexively stiffened. "Your father shot your mother's lover?"

"Yes."

She swallowed a sickening feeling. "And the man died?"

"Yes. And that same night my parents' truck went off the cliff. But my grandfather didn't know that. So he threw the gun in the river. Two accidental deaths and a homicide with no clues. Nobody ever made the connection. *I* never made the connection."

Melissa's heart went out to Jared. What an incredible burden. And he was bearing it all alone.

"You should tell Stephanie and Royce," she advised.

Jared scoffed out a cold laugh. "Why?"

"They could help you cope."

"I'll be fine." His voice grew stronger. "Today was the worst. It'll get easier now." He gave a sharp nod. "I'll be fine."

Melissa wasn't so sure. "Do you think maybe they deserve to know?"

"Nobody deserves to know this."

She wasn't going to argue further. She barely knew the family. Who was she to give them advice?

"I wish I could stay here," he said.

"Me, too." She'd like nothing better than to sleep in Jared's arms. The morning might be awkward, but at the moment she was willing to risk it.

His hug loosened. "I leave for Chicago tomorrow afternoon."

"Oh." She thought he was talking about staying the night. But he meant he was leaving the ranch. She backed off, slightly embarrassed by her presumption. She forcibly lightened her tone. "Of course. I know you have a big company to run."

"Come with me."

"Huh?"

"Come to Chicago. I have a Genevieve Fund event Tuesday night. We could go together. Spend a couple of nights in the city. Afterward, I'll buy you a plane ticket to Seattle. You'll be right back on schedule with your trip, and you won't have to worry about the bus."

Nine

There were a dozen reasons Melissa should have said no. Not the least of which was Stephanie's resultant excitement and Royce's knowing grin. There was also Melissa's deception and the article and, though she hated to admit it, the very real possibility she was falling for Jared.

She glanced at his profile across the aisle in the compact private jet. Royce was in the pilot's seat, while the two cream-colored, leather seats facing Melissa and Jared were empty. Four others behind them remained empty, as well.

Jared had offered her a drink and snacks after takeoff, but her stomach was too jumpy for either. Was she crazy? What if there were press at the charitable event? What if somebody recognized her?

As the jet began its descent, Jared reached across the aisle for her hand. "The ball's at the Ritz-Carlton, so I booked us a suite. Royce is staying in my apartment."

Melissa nodded. She'd have loved to see Jared's apartment, but she understood he wanted them to be alone. And so did she. She wanted a night with him to herself—no Stephanie up the hill, no ranch hands next door and definitely no Royce in the neighboring bedroom.

Maybe heartache would hit her afterward. And she might be weeks recovering. But she knew a stolen fling with Jared would be worth it.

"You have a spa appointment tomorrow," he continued. "And we can wander down North Michigan Avenue and find you a dress."

"You do know how to spoil a girl." She had several perfectly acceptable dresses at home, but she couldn't admit that to Jared.

She felt another twinge of guilt over the deception. But it would end soon. And Jared might never read the article. Even if he did, he'd have to be pleased with it, she told herself. She intended to show him in a very good light.

His gaze was warm. "I'll spoil you for as long as you want."

"You don't need to spoil me at all." She brought his broad hand to her lips. "What I want from you is free."

"I'd rather give it to you at the Ritz-Carlton."

She affected a deep sassy drawl. "You can give it to me anywhere you like, cowboy."

He pursed his lips and hissed a drawn-out exclamation. "I sure hope Royce plans to entertain himself after we land."

"What are you doing now?" Stephanie's voice came through Jared's cell phone while he sat in a comfortable armchair by the window in St. Jacques boutique overlooking the lake.

"Watching Melissa try on dresses." He'd made three overseas calls and consulted with his finance department while Melissa had paraded past in about a dozen dresses. She looked great in them all.

"I bet she looks gorgeous."

"She does."

Melissa walked out of the changing room in a short gold sheath with spaghetti straps and a diaphanous scarf. He wasn't crazy about the scarf, but he liked the dress.

He held up four fingers. He'd been giving rankings out of five, since he'd been holding his PDA to his ear through the entire fashion show.

Melissa leaned forward and pointed to a looped gold-and-diamond necklace the salesclerk had fastened around her neck. He simply gave a thumbs-up to that.

"Did you have fun last night?" Stephanie asked.

"None of your business."

"It's quiet here. I miss you and Royce."

"We miss you, too. Come to the party. Royce will pick you up."

"I can't." She sighed. "We've got our first junior elite

rider starting tomorrow. He's been blowing them away on the young rider circuit."

"That's a good thing, right?"

"It's a great thing."

"Then quit your whining."

Melissa pranced back into the changing room, and he wished he'd thought to comment on the shoes. Black, sleek and high, with flashing rhinestones around the ankles. He definitely wanted her to keep the shoes.

"Is this tough love?" Stephanie asked.

"Absolutely."

"What's going on with Melissa?"

"She's going to blow them away tonight."

"Will she blow you away?"

"Don't get your hopes up, Steph."

"You have to fall in love sometime."

"Not necessarily."

But then Melissa appeared again. This time she was wearing an emerald-green strapless party dress. The bodice was tight satin, stretched snugly over her breasts, while the skirt puffed out around her thighs, showing off her toned calves and sexy ankles. It was perfect for a late-night club. It was also dress number thirteen, and he realized he wanted to take her out in all of them.

"Gotta go," he said to Stephanie, needing to end the conversation.

"Keep an open mind," she called into the phone.

"Don't worry." No point in Stephanie worrying. Jared was the one who needed to worry.

He was starting to think about jobs for Melissa again, jobs at Ryder International. Or better still, jobs at affiliated companies in the city, so she wouldn't work directly for him. But she'd still be around to date him.

He was starting to think about her skill set and who owed him favors. They had one more night together, then maybe half of tomorrow. But he knew that wasn't going to do it for him. And that was a very worrisome development.

"She's a knockout," came Royce's voice as he dropped into the armchair beside Jared.

"No kidding."

Melissa gave Royce a welcoming smile and a little wave.

Royce's long lecherous look at her legs irritated Jared, worrying him all over again. Just how deep had he let himself fall?

"You serious about her?" Royce asked.

"Why?" Jared demanded, wondering what might have given him away.

Royce gave a smug grin. "Guess that answers my question."

"She leaves for Seattle tomorrow." And that was the disappointing truth. He'd suggested she stay longer, but she'd insisted she had to get back on her trip. Whatever feelings might be building inside Jared, this was the time to shut them down.

"You want me to fly her out?"

"No." Jared did *not*. He might not be pursuing anything with Melissa himself, but that didn't mean the field was open to his brother.

Royce's grin widened. "This is fun."

"Back off."

"Not a chance."

Melissa floated out in a calf-length ivory gown. It had snug, three-quarter-length, flat lace sleeves and a sweetheart neckline gathered with a line of jewels at mid-bust. There was a wide ribbon waist band and a two-layered, flowing skirt that flirted with her legs. She grinned and gave a twirl. Her diamond earrings twinkled under the bright lights.

Jared felt a tightening in his chest. A small bouquet of flowers, and she'd be the perfect bride. Her open smile told him she was oblivious to the image, but he wasn't, and he drank in the sight for several long minutes.

He gave the dress a five, and she turned to walk away.

"Do I need to say it?" asked Royce.

"No." Jared kept his focus on Melissa until she disappeared again.

"So how're you going to keep her here?"

Jared gave up lying both to himself and to Royce. "I haven't decided yet."

They'd chosen a black silk dress with spaghetti straps and a metallic gold thread that made it shimmer under the ballroom lights. The skirt of the dress was full enough to make Melissa feel like a princess as she whirled around the dance floor in Jared's arms to the music of a five-piece string band. Her rhinestone sandals were light on her feet. Her hair was upswept, and Jared had insisted on buying her the looped gold necklace and a set of matching earrings.

He looked roguishly sexy in his tuxedo. Having seen

him in blue jeans, chaps and dust, she realized the formal clothes barely disguised the rugged man inside.

Champagne flowed, and the crystal chandeliers glittered around them as they moved past marble pillars, magnificent floral arrangements and the kaleidoscope of designer gowns. At one point, the mayor paused to chat. And everyone in the room knew and obviously respected Jared.

Though Melissa had promised herself the night was off the record, she'd decided to use a few of her impressions in the article. Jared was an intelligent, insightful man, with an amazing grasp of local issues and Chicago economic trends. There was no way she could leave that side of him out of the article.

Though she'd spent the first hour with an eagle eye out for press and anybody else who might recognize her, it turned out to be a private party. No press, and Jared's social circle was far from hers. While she might recognize the notable figures from their pictures and television appearances, she knew they'd never recognize her.

She felt like Cinderella when they finally made their way out of the ballroom and into the promenade. Her arm was linked with Jared's, and Royce was by their side.

"Barry left them at the front desk," Royce was saying, thumbing a button on his PDA before he tucked it back into his breast pocket.

"I don't want to work tonight," said Jared, and he raised Melissa's hand to his lips, giving her knuckles a tender kiss.

Royce sent Melissa a mock frown. "See what you've done? *I'm* usually the irresponsible brother."

"Not tonight," said Jared.

"Apparently not," Royce growled.

"Is it important?" asked Melissa. She was anxious to get Jared alone in their suite, but his conversations at the ball had taught her his time was valuable. His business interests were even more significant and far-reaching than she'd realized.

"Yes," said Royce.

"No," Jared put in over top of his brother.

"Do you want to get up early, instead?" asked Royce.

"No," Melissa quickly put in. She'd have to pretend to get on a plane to Seattle sometime tomorrow, but she'd been entertaining a glorious vision. One that featured a leisurely breakfast in bed with Jared, maybe a dip in their whirlpool tub and a long goodbye before they went their separate ways at, say, noon.

"Just sign them," said Royce. "I'll go over them with Barry before I countersign."

"Who's Barry?" asked Melissa.

"Ryder's financial VP," said Jared, and she could feel his hesitation.

"I don't mind waiting," she quickly put in as they stepped into an open elevator.

Royce quirked his brows at Jared, and Jared gave a nod. He pressed the button for the lobby. The door closed, and the car *whooshed* smoothly down twelve floors.

"I won't be long," Jared assured her, hand resting

lightly on the small of her back as they stepped into the opulent lobby.

She gestured toward the far side of the huge room. "I'll check out the paintings while I wait."

He nodded, and left with Royce for the front desk.

It wasn't much of a hardship to wander through the lobby. Marble walkways, elegant, French-provincial furnishings, magnificent sculpture and glorious flowers combined with the soft lighting to create a serene ambiance. It wasn't the kind of hotel where Melissa normally stayed. Then again, this wasn't exactly the kind of week she usually experienced, either.

Her heels clicked as she rounded the fountain, moving toward the main glass doors. There were a couple of furniture groupings that looked inviting. Her new shoes were comfortable, but the heels were high, and her calves were beginning to tighten up. A gold armchair beckoned. It would give her a nice view of the front desk. She could people-watch, while keeping an eye out for Jared.

But then she spotted a man on the sidewalk and halted in her tracks. He was in profile, smoking a cigarette in the muted light outside, but it was definitely Brandon Langard.

Melissa gasped, then whirled around before he could spot her. The rest of a lobby blurred in front of her panicked eyes.

"Melissa?" Her coworker Susan Alaric suddenly appeared in front of her. "*Melissa?* Oh, my God. You're back. How'd it go?"

Melissa opened her mouth to speak, but only a squeak emerged.

Susan's face nearly split with an excited grin. "Seth said you got on the ranch. Did you get the interview? Did Ryder figure out who you were?" She tipped her head back in glee. "Oh, man, Brandon is going to have a cow."

Melissa grasped Susan's arm. "Susan..." she rasped, but then her gaze caught Jared's face over Susan's shoulder, and her stomach roiled.

"The *Bizz* is going to have the scoop of the year," Susan finished.

"The *Bizz?*" Jared's voice and eyes both darkened to thunder.

Susan heard his voice and took in Melissa's stricken expression. She twisted around to look at Jared. Then she swallowed. She opened her mouth, but gave up before she could find any words.

Royce appeared, taking in the trio. He noted Susan's camera, then paused on his brother's expression. "What the hell?"

"Jared..." Melissa began, mind scrambling with panic.

She'd explain it was a good article. It would focus on the most complimentary things. He was successful, hardworking and kind. And his family was wonderful. It wasn't like they had any skeletons in their closets.

Okay, so there *was* the thing with his grandfather, but that wasn't relevant, and she sure wasn't going to write about that. And everything that had happened between them was way off the record. This wasn't a tabloid tell-all. It was a serious journalistic piece.

But before she could pull her thoughts together, his hand closed over her arm and he pulled her away from Susan and Royce.

"You *lied* to me." His graveled voice was harsh in her ear.

She didn't answer.

"You're a reporter?" he demanded.

She closed her eyes, but then forced herself to nod the admission.

"And *I'm* your subject."

"Yes, but—"

"You are going to walk out that door." He stopped, jerking her to face him. His words were measured, but she was subjected to the full glare of his anger. "You are going to walk out that door. You are going to do it quickly and quietly, and I *never* want to see you again."

"But—"

"Do you understand me?"

"I'm not going—"

"Do you understand me?"

She closed her mouth and nodded, chest tight, throat closing in. She told herself he'd read the article. Eventually he'd know she hadn't betrayed him.

"Good." He flicked his hand from her arm, his eyes filled with contempt.

She had to try one more time. "Jared, please let me explain."

"You already have. I know who you are. And I know what you've got."

"I'm not going to—"

"Know this," he cut her off, leaning in, lowering his voice to steel. "If you do *anything* to harm my family, I will destroy you."

Then he turned away, sharply and with an absolute finality to his posture.

Before she could get another word out, he was past the fountain and heading for the elevators.

"Melissa?" Susan's voice was hushed as she pressed against her shoulder.

"That was Jared Ryder." Melissa's voice was hollow. Her body was hollow. Her life was hollow.

"No kidding."

Melissa knew it didn't matter what she wrote in the article, what secrets she kept or what she revealed, Jared was never going to forgive her. She'd never see him again, never be held in those strong arms, hear his voice, smell his skin, taste his passionate kisses. She realized now how very much she'd been counting on their last night together.

"You okay?" asked Susan.

Melissa forced herself to nod. Her eyes were burning, but she blinked the sting away.

"Wow," Susan continued. "I hope your research was finished."

Melissa didn't know whether to laugh or cry. Just then, she couldn't have cared less about the article. "It is," she told Susan.

"What are you doing here?" Susan glanced around

the hotel lobby. "Brandon and I were hoping to catch the mayor."

Melissa coughed a hollow laugh. "I chatted with the mayor upstairs."

"Really?" Susan took in the dress. "You were at the Genevieve Memorial Fund ball?"

"Jared and, uh, his brother invited me along." The last thing in the world she wanted to do was invite questions about her relationship with Jared.

"Wow," said Susan, gaze going to the elevator where the two men had disappeared. "I am in awe."

Where Melissa was exhausted, both emotionally and physically. It had been a week of hard work and long nights. She'd labored over the article every spare minute. Well, every spare minute that she hadn't been falling—

She froze for a second, drew a stunned breath and closed her eyes.

Every spare minute that she hadn't been *falling in love with Jared*.

Her hands curled into fists, and she fought against the knowledge that had just exploded in her brain.

"Your article is going to kick butt," Susan was saying.

How could Melissa have been so stupid? Why hadn't she seen it coming? She should have done something to stop it. But no, she'd hung around him like an eager little puppy dog, throwing herself into his arms, into his bed, pretending she somehow belonged in his life.

Susan squeezed Melissa's shoulder. "You are *so* going to get that promotion. Seth might even smile." She paused. "Hey, Brandon's outside. You think we should go tell him?"

"No." The word jumped out with more force than she'd intended. But Melissa didn't want to talk to Brandon or anyone else. She wanted to go home and hole up alone in her apartment. Some way, somehow, she had to get over Jared and get words on the page in the next twenty-four hours.

"You slept with a reporter?" Royce confirmed the obvious as the hotel-suite door swung shut behind them.

The fact that Jared had slept with Melissa was the least of his worries. Sure, maybe she could write about seeing him naked or detail his kisses and pillow talk. But it wasn't like he was into handcuffs or women in French-maid outfits.

"You didn't suspect?" Royce went straight for the bar, snagging a bottle of single malt from the mirrored top shelf.

He flipped two crystal glasses over, ignored the ice bucket and filled the tumblers to halfway.

"Yeah," said Jared. "I suspected. But I figured, what the hell? She's got a great ass. Why not sleep with somebody who'll splash it all over the front page?"

Royce rounded the bar again. "Sarcasm's not going to help."

"Neither are stupid questions." Jared took one of the glasses and downed a hefty swallow.

"Nothing gave her away?"

Jared dropped into an armchair. "She was a stable

hand. We have dozens of them. Yeah, she didn't know much about horses. And maybe her background was vague. And maybe she seemed too smart for a drifter. Which was what attracted me in the first place. She was…"

Royce cocked his head meaningfully.

"Son of a bitch," said Jared and polished off the scotch.

He'd let his sex drive override his logic. It was a clichéd, blatant, pathetic scenario. And he'd bought it hook, line and sinker. "She slept with me to get a story."

"That surprises you?"

Yes. It surprised him. He knew there were women in the world who used sex as a bargaining chip. He met them all the time. But Melissa sure hadn't struck him as one of those. She was down-to-earth, honest, classy.

"She told me she had brothers." Jared coughed out a flat chuckle. "I was afraid they might come after me."

"For defiling their sister?"

"I think about Stephanie sometimes…"

Royce stood and picked up the empty glasses. "Someday, some guy's going to sleep with Stephanie."

"He better be in love with her."

"He'd better be married to her." Royce poured a refill for each of them. This time, he added ice, then he wandered back to the opposite armchair.

"So what does she know?" he asked.

Jared slouched back, loosening his tie and flicking his top shirt button open. "The ranch, Stephanie's jumping, you, Anthony, the Genevieve Fund."

"What you look like naked," Royce put in.

Jared waved a dismissive hand. "It's not like we took pictures."

"Good to know."

Jared gazed out the wide window, letting his vision go soft on the city lights. He'd expected the night to turn out very differently. Even now, even knowing Melissa was a traitor, on some level he wished she was lying in the king-size bed, sexy, naked, waiting for him to join her.

"What's she got?" Royce asked quietly.

Jared blinked his attention back to his brother.

He had to tell him. There was no way around it.

He'd been colossally stupid to share it with a perfect stranger.

"Gramps," he said. Then he tugged off his tie, tossing it on the table.

Royce's eyes narrowed.

"He told me something. Right before he died." Jared drew a breath. "He told me Dad killed Frank Stanton."

The room went completely silent.

Jared dared to flick a glance at Royce.

His brother was still, eyes unblinking, hands loose on the padded arms of the chair. "I know."

Jared drew back. "What?"

Royce took a sip of his drink. "I've always known."

Jared took a second to process the information. Royce knew? He'd kept silent all these years?

"I don't understand," said Jared.

Royce came to his feet, then carried his drink across

the room, turning when he came to the window. "The day it happened. The day they died. I found a letter Mom had written to Dad. It was half-finished. It said she loved Frank. It said she was leaving Dad. She was leaving us." He took another sip.

"You didn't *tell* me?"

His brother was silent for a long moment. "You know, sometimes, when you *have* to keep a secret? The only person who can know is you. The second—" he snapped his fingers "—the second you let that knowledge out of your brain, you put it at risk. I knew that. Even at thirteen years old."

Jared couldn't believe his brother hadn't trusted him. "I would never have—"

"Our father was a murderer. Our mother was unfaithful. And Stephanie was two years old."

"You should have—"

"No. I shouldn't have. I didn't. And I was right." Royce paused. "I didn't know Gramps knew."

"He threw the gun in the river," said Jared.

Royce gave a half smile. "Good for him."

"He got rid of the gun before they found Mom and Dad. He thought Dad would go on trial for murder."

"Yeah." Royce returned to his chair. "Well, what do you do? He protected his son. Who are we to decide how far a man goes?"

"Do you kill your wife's lover?" The question had been nagging at Jared for weeks now. He couldn't help picturing Melissa. And he couldn't stop the cold rage that boiled up inside him at the thought of another man.

"I don't have a wife," said Royce. "I don't have to make that decision."

Jared nodded. "Simpler that way."

"It is," Royce agreed. He sat back down. "Do we tell Stephanie?"

Jared hated the thought of hurting his sister. But if the story came out in the article, she needed to be prepared. He hoped it wouldn't come to that, but he feared it might.

"Not yet," he answered Royce.

The *Bizz* was a monthly magazine. He'd have at least a few days to think about solutions.

So far, all he'd come up with was a plan to kidnap Melissa and lock her up in a tower in Tasmania or Madagascar with no telephone or Internet. Unfortunately his mind kept putting himself in the tower with her, in a big bed, where they'd make love until he tired of her. Which, if his wayward imagination was anything to go by, would take a very, very long time.

Ten

From the moment Melissa clicked the send button, she feared she'd made a mistake. While she certainly had the legal right to file her story on Jared, she wasn't so sure she had the moral right to do it.

Then she'd tossed and turned all night long, imagining his anger, his reaction, Stephanie's thoughts and feelings when she found out Melissa had been a fraud. Melissa was going to get a promotion out of this, no doubt about it. Seth was nearly beside himself with glee. Brandon was surly and sulking. And Everett himself had sent her an e-mail congratulating her on the coup.

Susan had guessed she was feeling guilty. But in her usual pragmatic style, she'd advised Melissa to put it behind her and focus on her future. Jared was a big boy, and he'd get over the inroad on his precious privacy.

It was a positive article. The quotes Melissa had used were accurate. She hadn't made anybody look foolish or mean-spirited. She'd mentioned Stephanie's jumping trophies, Jared's hardworking ancestors, his move from cattle ranching to construction to save the family's land. And she'd made Royce look like a fun-loving maverick. He'd probably get a dozen marriage proposals out of the coverage.

She hadn't used a single thing she'd learned from sleeping with Jared. Still, she couldn't shake the feeling she was wrong.

It lasted through her morning shower, through the breakfast she couldn't bring herself to eat, during the train ride to the office in the morning, up the elevator to her floor and then all the way to her desk.

Jared was an intensely private man. She'd invaded his privacy on false pretenses. And even though she hadn't used their pillow talk in her article, she'd crossed a line. She'd befriended him. She'd gained his trust. She'd let him think he could let his guard down, and he had.

Plus, and here was the crux of the matter, she'd fallen in love with him. And you didn't betray the person you loved. You were loyal, no matter what the circumstances, no matter what was to be gained or lost. You were loyal.

That was why Jared's grandfather hid the gun. An extreme example, perhaps. But his loyalty was to his son, and he'd risked his freedom to protect him. Melissa wouldn't even give up a promotion.

She dropped her purse on her desk, her gaze going to Seth's office. His head was bent over his desk—no doubt he was working his way through her article. It would go upstairs by lunchtime, be typeset by the end of the day and move along the pipe to the printing press.

At that point, nothing could stop it from hitting the streets. She had one chance and one chance only to make things right. Jared might not love her, and he might never speak to her again. But she loved him, and she had to live with herself after today.

She crossed the floor to Seth's office, opening the door without knocking.

He jerked his head up. "What?"

"I've changed my mind," she said without preamble, striding to his desk.

His mouth dropped open in confusion.

"The article," she clarified. "You can't run it."

Seth's mouth worked for a second before it warmed up to actual words. "Is this a joke? It's not funny. Now get the hell out of my office. I have work to do."

"I'm not joking."

"Neither am I. Get out."

"Jared Ryder does not want us to print it."

"Jared Ryder can stuff it. We need the numbers."

Melissa began to panic. "You can't run it."

"Yes, I can."

She scrambled for a solution. "I lied, Seth," she lied baldly. "I made it up. The quotes are bogus, and I was never on the Ryder Ranch."

Seth's complexion went ruddy, and a vein popped out in his forehead. "Have you gone insane?"

"I'll swear to it, Seth. I'll tell the whole world I made up the story."

"And I'll fire your ass."

"I don't care!" she shouted. She had to stop him. She couldn't let her work see the light of day.

Seth's gaze shifted to a point over her left shoulder and his eyes went wide.

Fear churned in her stomach, but she carried on, anyway. It was her last chance to make things right. "If you run it, I'll swear I made the whole piece up. The *Bizz* will get sued, and *you'll* lose *your* job."

Seth's mouth worked, but no sound came out.

"Don't test me on this, Seth," she vowed. "Pull the article. I'll quit. I'll go away quietly. You can make up whatever you want to tell Everett."

"Noble of you," came a voice behind her.

Everett. The publisher had heard her threats.

Not that she'd expected to keep her job, anyway, but it was humiliating to have an additional witness. She clamped her jaw, squared her shoulders and headed for the door.

Her stomach instantly turned to a block of ice.

In the doorway next to Everett stood Jared. They both stared at her, faces devoid of expression.

Neither of them said a word as she forced one foot in front of the other. She prayed they'd step aside and give her room to get out the door.

They did, but inches before freedom, Jared put a hand on her arm. Neither of them looked at the other, and his voice was gruff. "Why'd you pull the story?"

She struggled with the cascade of conflicting emotions that swamped her body. She was proud of herself.

She was brokenhearted. She was frightened and unemployed and exhausted.

She decided she owed him her honesty. So she glanced up and forced the words out. "The same reason your grandfather did what he did."

Love. Plain and simple. When you loved someone, you protected them, even at a risk to yourself.

Then she jerked away, grabbed her purse from her desk and kept right on going to the elevator.

Jared's first impression of Seth Strickland was hardly positive, so he didn't much care now that the man looked like he was going to wet his pants. Seth had shouted at Melissa. And while he was shouting, it was all Jared could do not to wring his pudgy little neck.

Jared might be angry with her, but that didn't give anyone else license to hurt her. Sure, she'd betrayed him. But she was fundamentally a decent person. Even now, he was battling the urge to chase after her. Not that he knew what he'd say. Not that he even understood what had just happened.

She'd behaved in a completely incomprehensible manner. Of course, she'd baffled him from the moment they met.

While Jared struggled to put her in context, Everett stepped into the office, moved to one side, then gestured for Jared to enter.

Everett shut the door firmly behind them and focused on the sweating Seth Strickland. "Mr. Ryder, this is Seth Strickland, *Windy City Bizz*'s managing editor. For now.

Seth, this is Mr. Jared Ryder, the new owner of *Windy City Bizz.*"

Seth's jaw dropped a notch further.

Jared didn't bother with pleasantries. It seemed a little ridiculous after what they'd just witnessed.

"Is this a copy of the article?" He advanced on Seth's desk and pointed to the papers piled in front of him.

Seth nodded.

"We won't be running it," said Jared, lifting the pages from under Seth's nose.

He gave Everett a polite smile. "Thank you for your time. One of Ryder International's vice presidents will be in touch next week."

Then he turned and exited the office. He couldn't care less if Everett fired Seth or kept him on. Melissa wasn't fired, that was for sure. And she could write for Seth or for anyone else in the company.

He took the elevator to the first floor, crossed the lobby, trotted down the outside stairs and slid into the Aston Martin idling at the curb.

"How'd it go?" asked Royce, pushing the car into gear and flipping on his signal.

"It's taken care of," said Jared.

"Good." Royce gave a nod. Hard rock was blaring on the stereo, while the air conditioner battled the heat from the sunshine.

"Did you see Melissa come out the door?"

Royce zipped into the steady stream of traffic. "You saw Melissa?"

"She was inside." Jared shoved his sunglasses onto the bridge of his nose.

"And?"

"And." Jared drummed his fingers on the dashboard. "She was trying to get her editor to kill the article."

Royce glanced at him for a split second before turning his attention to the busy intersection. "What? Why?"

"Beats the hell out of me. The guy fired her."

"She lost her job?"

"No. Of course she didn't lose her job. She works for us now, remember?"

"And you don't think *we* should fire her?"

Jared killed the clanging music. He needed to think.

"Jared?" Royce prompted.

"Why would she kill the article?" Her cryptic remark about his grandfather didn't make sense.

"Maybe she's afraid of getting sued."

Jared glanced down at the papers in his hand. He scanned one page, then another, then another. The story was innocuous. It was lightweight to the point of being boring.

"Anything about Gramps?" asked Royce as they turned to parallel the lakeshore. Skyscrapers loomed to one side, blocking the sun.

"Nothing. It's crap."

"She's a bad writer?"

"No. She's a fine writer. But she held back. She had a ton of stuff on me." He flipped through the pages again. "She didn't use any of it."

"Then why did she try to pull it?"

"I asked her," Jared admitted, flashing back to that moment, remembering her expression, remembering the emotional body slam of seeing her again, his desire to attack Seth and to chase after Melissa.

"Bro?" Royce prompted.

Jared cleared his throat. "She said it was the same reason Gramps did what he did."

Royce's hand came down on the steering wheel. "All this, and the woman's talking in riddles?"

Jared rolled it over in his mind. "Why did Gramps do what he did?"

"To protect Dad."

"Why?"

"Because he was his son."

"And…"

The brothers looked at each other, sharing an instant of comprehension. Gramps had protected Jared's father because he loved him.

"Holy crap," said Royce.

"*Not* what I needed to know," said Jared.

"Do you care?" Royce pressed.

Jared swore out loud. "She lied to me. She duped me. She invaded the hell out of my privacy." He slammed the pages onto his lap.

"Yet you love her, anyway," Royce guessed.

Jared clamped his jaw shut. Did he love Melissa? How could he love an illusion? He didn't even know which parts were her and which were the lie.

"And she loves you," Royce continued. He slowed for a stoplight, gearing the car down.

"I need a drink."

The woman was a damn fine illusion. If even half

of what he'd seen of her was real, it might be enough. Hell, it would be enough.

"What are you going to do?"

"Drink," said Jared.

Royce laughed. "Since you're not denying it and since you're even *considering* her, I'd say you absolutely need a drink. You've got it very bad, big brother."

"Why *her?*"

"It doesn't matter why her. It's done."

"Nothing's done." Jared certainly hadn't made any decisions. He was barely wrapping his head around falling for Melissa.

"You forget, I watched you watch her," said Royce. "You were never letting her go to Seattle."

"She never *was* going to Seattle. It was all a lie."

Royce shook his head and laughed. He glanced in the rearview mirror. Then he spun the steering wheel, yanked the hand brake and pivoted the car in a sharp u-turn.

"What are you doing?" Jared stabilized himself with the armrest.

"You *do* need a drink." Royce screeched to a stop in front of the Hilliard House tavern's valet parking. "If only to come to terms with the rest of your life."

Melissa should have realized her brother Caleb would call in reinforcements. She'd found herself at his house Saturday morning, looking for emotional support. Caleb was the most sympathetic of her brothers, and she'd really needed a shoulder to cry on.

Within an hour, Ben and Sheila had arrived, their

baby and two-year-old in tow. Then Eddy showed up, without the new girlfriend, demonstrating how seriously he was taking the situation. He was quick to envelop Melissa in a protective hug, and she had to battle a fresh round of tears.

Soon all her siblings and her nieces and nephews filled Caleb's big house with love and support. The jumble of their conversations and chaos of the children provided a buffer between Melissa and her raw emotions.

She'd told herself she couldn't be in love with Jared. Maybe it was infatuation. Maybe it was lust. She hadn't known him long enough for it to be real love.

But then she'd remember his voice, his smile, his jokes, his passion and the way she'd felt in his arms. What if it *was* real love? How was she going to get over it?

She swallowed, smiling as one of her nephews handed her a sticky wooden block, forcing her thoughts to the present.

The doors and windows of Caleb's house were wide open to the afternoon breeze. Some of her brothers were shooting hoops in the driveway while Adam cranked up the grill on the back deck and distributed bottles of imported beer. His wife, Renee, was calling out orders from the kitchen.

Melissa and her sister-in-law Sheila were corralling toddlers on the living-room floor, amid a jumble of blocks, action figures and miniature cars.

"Mellie?" Caleb's voice interrupted the game.

Melissa glanced up.

Her brother's brow was furrowed with concern, and she quickly saw the reason why.

Jared stood in the foyer, his suit and tie contrasting with the casual T-shirt and jeans Caleb wore.

She scrambled to her feet, drinking in his appearance, wishing she wasn't so pathetically glad to see him as she crammed her messy hair behind her ears. She hoped her eyes weren't red. She hoped he couldn't read how lonely she'd been the past few days. She'd fallen asleep each night with his image in her mind, longing to feel his strong arms wrapped around her.

She'd second-guessed herself a million times. What if she'd come clean right off? What if she'd told him who she was? Maybe he'd have thrown her off the ranch. But maybe he'd have given her an interview. And maybe, just maybe, they'd have had a chance to get to know each other without a lie between them.

She'd tried not to love him. She really had. But it was a hopeless proposition. And seeing him again told her that she'd be weeks, months, maybe even years getting over her feelings.

She heard a rustle from the kitchen and turned to see the rest of her brothers file in. They moved behind her, and Caleb joined them. As if it was choreographed, their muscular arms crossed over their chests and they pinned their gazes on Jared.

To his credit, Jared looked levelly back. "I see you didn't lie about your brothers."

The five Warner men straightened their spines and squared their shoulders. The toddlers' coos and burbles were at odds with the tension in the room.

"How did you find me?" Melissa managed to ask, searching Jared's expression, trying to figure out what reason he could possibly have for tracking her down. Had he somehow read an advance copy of the article? Had he hated it? Did he want her to change it?

"Your personnel file," Jared surprised her by answering. "Caleb is your emergency contact."

"How did you—"

"You're not fired, Melissa." He took a step forward. "I want you to know that up front."

She felt her brothers close ranks behind her.

"Oh, yes, I am," she responded, struggling to keep her voice from shaking. Seth had been crystal clear on that point.

Jared shook his head. "Ryder International bought *Windy City Bizz*. Nobody is firing you for anything."

Melissa peered at him, trying to make sense of his words.

"It was the best way I could think of to kill the story," he explained.

The babies played on in the background, while Renee and Sheila moved in beside their husbands.

Melissa subconsciously moved closer to Jared. "You bought the *Bizz?*"

"Yes."

That was insane.

"You paid, what? Thousands? Hundreds of thousands of dollars to keep my story out of the press?"

"I hadn't read the story when I bought the magazine." He offered a wry half smile. "Had I known it was so innocuous…"

"I did try to tell you," she pointed out.

"I know." His expression softened, and he moved closer still. "But you knew…" He glanced around at her family members, then peered at her to make sure she understood his code. "You know?"

She did, and she nodded. "I never would have used it."

"You lied. And I couldn't tell—"

"I am so sorry." She wished she could start over. If there was one minute in her life she could do over, it would be the first time they met. She'd tell Jared she was a reporter up front and let him do whatever he would do.

"Mellie." Caleb's arm went around her. "You don't have to apologize again."

"Agreed," said Jared, meeting Caleb's eyes, squaring his own shoulders. "It's my turn to apologize. I lied to her, too."

Caleb tensed, but Jared stepped forward, anyway, clasping his hands over Melissa's. His hands were warm and strong, sending sensory memories tingling along her spine.

His expression softened again, and his voice went lower. "I lied to you when I said I never wanted to see you again."

Melissa felt a faint flicker of hope. But she instantly squelched it. She was going down a dangerous road, erasing any gains she'd made since that horrible night at the Ritz-Carlton.

"I do want to see you again," Jared continued, and

she was forced to redouble her effort at dampening her hope. "All the time. Every day from here on in."

Melissa wanted to run. She wanted to hide. Her brain couldn't comprehend that he might be serious.

"Excuse me?" Sheila popped out from behind the men. "What are you saying to Melissa?"

Jared flicked an annoyed glance at Sheila, and Melissa could feel her brother Ben bristle.

"I'm saying," said Jared, a thread of steel coming into his voice, "I can propose to her here under, well, rather stressful circumstances."

His gaze went back to Melissa while her heart thudded powerfully in her chest. "Or we can go somewhere private, where I can do it properly."

Her mind scrambled in a freefall.

"I have a limo out front," Jared continued. "A table on the deck at the Bayside, a florist and photographer on standby, also—" he tapped the breast of his suit "—a ring. I also have a ring."

"Can we see it?" chirped Sheila.

Jared's attention never left Melissa. "Only if she says yes."

Melissa couldn't do anything but blink. Emotions that had been close to the surface for days threatened to erupt. This couldn't be happening. It must be some fevered hallucination.

She looked back at her family.

They were watching expectantly.

Could this be happening? Could it be real? If she'd had a free hand, she'd have pinched himself.

"Melissa?" Jared prompted.

"I think—" she nodded "—the restaurant is a good idea."

"Yeah?" A grin split his face.

"And the photographer." She assured herself it was all real. Jared had found her. And he wanted to be with her. "I have a feeling Stephanie will expect pictures."

Jared's grin widened.

Sheila spoke out. "But can we see the—"

Ben clapped a hand over her mouth.

It took her all of three seconds to escape. "Good grief. It's obvious she's going to say yes. They can reenact it later for the photographer."

Everyone stared openmouthed at Sheila.

"What?" she asked. "Come on, Renee. Back me up. We want to see the ring."

Adam's wife stepped forward. "I have to say, I'm with Sheila on this."

Melissa started to laugh. "Go ahead," she told Jared. She *was* planning to say yes.

"In a minute," he told her, stepping back to pull Melissa into the foyer, around the corner, beyond the view of her family.

He held her hand firmly, staring into her eyes. "I love you."

The world disappeared around them, and Melissa's chest filled with a warm shimmering glow. The worries lifted off her shoulders and the vestiges of pain evaporated from inside her.

"I love you, too," she breathed, touching his face, letting his essence seep through her fingertips and into her soul.

Jared sobered as he leaned in for a kiss. His lips touched hers and magic seem to saturate the atmosphere around them. It was a very long minute before he pulled back.

"We can reenact this part later for the camera," he whispered, reaching to his inside jacket pocket. "But will you marry me?" He flipped open the jewel case to reveal a stunning solitaire.

Melissa nodded. "Yes. Oh, yes." She couldn't imagine a more amazing future than one with Jared.

He slipped the ring onto her finger. Then he kissed her hand and whispered, "Go ahead and show it off."

Though her family was waiting, Jared was her world. She went up on tiptoe, hugging him tight, and he lifted her off the floor to spin her around.

Sheila squealed in the background, and suddenly the entire family was pouring into the foyer, admiring Melissa's engagement ring and welcoming Jared into the family.

2 in 1
GREAT
VALUE

DANTE'S ULTIMATE GAMBLE by Day Leclaire

Forced to play babysitter to heiress Téa de Luca, Luc felt the heat of the Dante Inferno and undeniable passion propelled them into bed. It was supposed to be for just six weeks…

IN BED WITH THE WRANGLER by Barbara Dunlop

Amber had no intention of diving into the cowboy's bed— falling for a man like Royce was just asking for trouble.

SAVED BY THE SHEIKH! by Tessa Radley

Practically penniless, Tiffany Smith had nowhere to turn except to the gorgeous billionaire, dashing banker Rafiq Al Dhahara, who offered his help.

MILLION-DOLLAR MARRIAGE MERGER by Charlene Sands

She had married Tony only for the safety his name—and money—would give her, her winery…and her unborn child. But what about the desire she felt for her new husband?

HIS BLACK SHEEP BRIDE by Anna DePalo

Sawyer Langsford never let anyone stand in the way of building his media empire. If he had to marry Tamara Kincaid to close a merger with her father, so be it. But a child…

THE BILLIONAIRE BABY BOMBSHELL by Paula Roe

Billionaire businessman Alex Rush had no clue the woman he'd once loved was now a mother. But if so, who was the dad?

On sale from 20th May 2011
Don't miss out!

Available at WHSmith, Tesco, ASDA, Eason and all good bookshops

www.millsandboon.co.uk

0511/

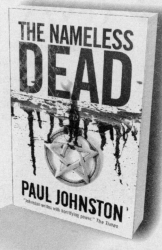

M212_TND

ONE WOMAN'S PRIVATE WAR…

1940, and Vivienne de la Mare waits nervously.
The island trembles to the sound of bombs on the
French mainland. It will be Guernsey next. And
everyone knows that the Nazis are monsters…

Except Captain Lehmann is different…and the
reality of war cannot touch the world they have
built together. Until Vivienne witnesses the casual,
brutal murder of a slave-worker in a Guernsey
prison camp… And her choice to help will
have terrifying consequences.

Available 20th May 2011

www.mirabooks.co.uk

Kaylee has one addiction: her boyfriend, Nash.

A banshee like Kaylee, Nash understands her like no one else. Nothing can come between them. Until something does.

Demon breath—a super-addictive paranormal drug that can kill. Kaylee and Nash need to cut off the source and protect their human friends—one of whom is already hooked.

But then Kaylee uncovers another demon breath addict. *Nash.*

Book three in the unmissable Soul Screamers *series.*

www.miraink.co.uk

Join us at facebook.com/miraink

Love and betrayal.
A Faery world gone mad.

Deserted by the Winter prince she thought loved her, half-Summer faery princess, half-human Meghan is prisoner to the Winter faery queen. But the real danger comes from the Iron fey— ironbound faeries only she and her absent prince have seen.

With Meghan's fey powers cut off, she's stuck in Faery with only her wits for help. And trusting a seeming traitor could be deadly.

www.miraink.co.uk

"To say that I met Nicholas Brisbane over my husband's dead body is not entirely accurate. Edward, it should be noted, was still twitching upon the floor…"

London, 1886

For Lady Julia Grey, her husband's sudden death at a dinner party is extremely inconvenient. However, things worsen when inscrutable private investigator Nicholas Brisbane reveals that the death was not due to natural causes.

Drawn away from her comfortable, conventional life, Julia is exposed to threatening notes, secret societies and gypsy curses, not to mention Nicholas's charismatic unpredictability.

www.mirabooks.co.uk

England's Most Ruthless Queen

The story of Eleanor of Aquitaine is vividly brought to life by Anne O'Brien

Praise for Anne O'Brien

"Better than Philippa Gregory"
—*The Bookseller* on *Virgin Widow*

"With this winning book, Anne O'Brien has joined the exclusive club of excellent historical novelists"
—*The Sunday Express* on *Virgin Widow*

www.mirabooks.co.uk

What would you do if your son was accused of murder?

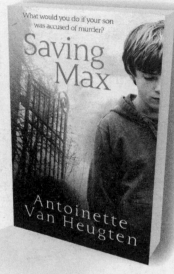

High-powered lawyer Danielle's sixteen-year-old autistic son Max has always been a handful. And when he's discovered, unconscious and bloody, beside a fellow psychiatric patient who's been brutally stabbed to death, it's hard not to question his innocence.

But Danielle swears to save her son from being destroyed by a system that's all too eager to convict him—no matter what the consequences.

On sale 18th February 2011

www.mirabooks.co.uk

Her only hope of survival was her worst enemy

Private security agent Lucie Evans jumps at the offer of escape to South America to become a billionaire heiress's bodyguard. Then her nightmare begins.

With Lucie's life at stake, her ex-boss Sawyer has to ignore their rocky past and forget his contempt for her before it's too late. Lucie's captor will not rest until she is silenced…once and for all.

www.mirabooks.co.uk

FREE BOOK
AND A SURPRISE GIFT

We would like to take this opportunity to thank you for reading this Mills & Boon® book by offering you the chance to take a specially selected book from the Desire™ 2-in-1 series absolutely FREE! We're also making this offer to introduce you to the benefits of the Mills & Boon® Book Club™—

- **FREE home delivery**
- **FREE gifts and competitions**
- **FREE monthly Newsletter**
- **Exclusive Mills & Boon Book Club offers**
- **Books available before they're in the shops**

Accepting this FREE book and gift places you under no obligation to buy, you may cancel at any time, even after receiving your free book. Simply complete your details below and return the entire page to the address below. You don't even need a stamp!

YES Please send me a free Desire 2-in-1 book and a surprise gift. I understand that unless you hear from me, I will receive 2 superb new 2-in-1 books every month for just £5.30 each, postage and packing free. I am under no obligation to purchase any books and may cancel my subscription at any time. The free book and gift will be mine to keep in any case.

Ms/Mrs/Miss/Mr _____ Initials _____

_____

Surname _____

Address _____

_____

_____ Postcode _____

E-mail_____

Send this whole page to: Mills & Boon Book Club, Free Book Offer, FREEPOST NAT 10298, Richmond, TW9 1BR